My Christmas Wish

Jeannie Moon

My Christmas Wish

A Compass Cove Romance

Jeannie Moon

TULE
PUBLISHING

Dedication

Immediate and extended, near and far,
my family is the compass that guides me.
I love you all. This is for you.

Compass Cove, Long Island, New York
f. 1667

In the year 1750, on the north shore of Long Island, a young woman named Lucy Velsor mourned her beloved husband, who had been lost at sea. Not long after his death, his shipmates, hoping to comfort the young widow, brought her his compass—a finely crafted instrument made by the local compasssmith whose family had settled the town of Compass Cove generations before. Lucy cherished the memento, taking care to kiss its face every day. One day, two years after her husband's death, the compass needle began to quiver and spin, unable to find true north.

Desperate to have it fixed, Lucy brought it to the compasssmith's shop hoping he could help. The proprietor, Caleb Jennings, had loved Lucy from afar, never knowing if he should pay a call on the beautiful widow. But when Lucy set the compass in Caleb's hand, it stopped spinning and the needle pointed at him, stunning them both. Tired of waiting for his perfect moment, Caleb put aside his fears and took the compass's strange behavior as a sign. He began to court Lucy. It didn't take long for the couple to fall in love, and marry. They spent many wonderful years together, making a home and family, living into their eighties, and dying just a few days apart. Before he left this world, Caleb credited the ghost of Lucy's first husband for setting the compass spinning and helping them find their way to each other.

To this day, Jennings Fine Compasses and Watches still

resides on Main Street and is owned by one of Caleb's and Lucy's descendants. Many families in Compass Cove keep a compass in their home as a symbol of selfless love and as a reminder that hearts meant to love will always find each other.

Prologue

NATALIE MILLER DIDN'T run away from challenges. Not recently, anyway. But what was a girl to do after clocking an aristocrat in the nose with a semi-valuable piece of art? It had been a month since what had been dubbed "the incident" came to pass, and after her most recent conversation, there was no returning to her life in the city she called home.

It certainly wasn't how she expected her time in London to end. Normally, Natalie handled the inappropriate advances at the gallery without too much trouble. A smile and a step away, or a flick of her hand almost always worked like a charm. This time, however, it wasn't about only her; it was about the terrified college student who had been cornered by a group of drunk, entitled men who were at the gallery for a private lunch. The aggressiveness of one client in particular crossed every line of decency. It was one thing when he put his hands on Nat, but the other woman was young and terrified. Natalie would not allow it. Absolutely not.

It was the beginning of the end.

What was the saying? *No good deed goes unpunished.* A cliché, to be sure. But sometimes things were clichés for a reason.

The threats that had been leveled regarding her future left her with few options. It was time to go. She wouldn't be a fugitive; there wouldn't be criminal charges…as long as she left the country permanently.

She'd gone home to her family in New York right after it happened, spending time at the beach and with her future sister-in-law preparing for the upcoming family wedding. It had been a good cooling-off period for her, and she hoped it would all blow over, but the letter that arrived from the earl's solicitor limited her options.

Maybe it was all for the best.

Two months ago, Natalie was happy. Better, she was content. She was settled in a place she loved, had a guy whom she deeply cared for, and a job that gave her satisfaction. She'd been running from herself for so long, she thought she'd finally be able to stop. To settle down and make a life, but fate had other plans for her.

Natalie shuffled over to the curio that held her collection of antique glass. Reaching in, she picked up an elegant giraffe and let him catch the sunbeam streaming through the window. The light reflected the colors in wavy patterns on the wall. Gold, and yellow and amber…if she tilted the animal, she could guide the light up the wall to the decorative ceiling. The shards of light flickering around like daytime fireflies.

It was a gorgeous late summer day, and she was packing one final box to take home with her. There wasn't anything left to do once her menagerie was packed. She'd hired a moving company to ship the rest of the boxes, and the furniture would stay with the apartment. She'd lease it out for now, but she expected she'd sell it sometime down the road. When she was ready.

This wasn't her place anymore. Maybe it never was.

Isn't that what the earl had said? She didn't belong. She wasn't wanted here.

Maybe she was in over her head. The drama that was her life was always going to end with a crash. What happened at the gallery was the final act.

A gentle rap on the door startled her. "Natalie, are you in there?"

Damn. The deep voice, with its clipped boarding school English set every nerve ending on fire. But the last thing she wanted to do was have an actual conversation with him.

"Aren't you supposed to be at school?" How did he know she was in town? She'd kept her text messages short and sweet…and noncommittal.

"I need to talk to you, Nat. Open the door."

"I can't right now." Her voice cracked on the last word. Dammit, she couldn't cry. A deep breath helped her get a grip. "Go to your apartment. I'll call you later." No, she wouldn't.

She tried to ignore him, but he rattled the doorknob so thoroughly she thought it might snap and fall out. He knocked again. "Bloody hell, Nat. Don't be so bullheaded. You've been blowing me off for weeks. Is this still about the gallery?"

She was certain he'd heard some of the story. Whether there was a grain of truth in it was another matter altogether. His stepdad—the Earl of Rutherford—had likely given him the part that painted Natalie as a complete loon.

"Natalie! I can't help if you won't talk to me."

"James, please go away." No doubt he wanted to be her knight. Her savior. Didn't he know the only one who Natalie needed saving from was herself?

"Let me in or I'll shout so loud they'll hear me clear to Westminster."

God, he was stubborn. Determined. And it was one of the things she loved most about him. Whether he was fighting for a cause or a person, he never gave up. Right now, he was fighting for her.

But he shouldn't. Natalie was back in her old territory of feeling like a disaster magnet. Problems had a way of following her, and that's the last thing James needed in his life. Natalie had brought enough trouble to her family at home, embarrassing and worrying them. She wasn't going to add somebody on a new continent to her list.

"Natalie, open the door." Now James sounded pissed. While she always wanted a man to be desperate for her, this wasn't what she had in mind.

Still, her heart fluttered and flipped. Thinking about him always did that to her, but she didn't want to see him—couldn't see him.

He was pounding the door now. "Natalie!"

Certain that every single person on her block in Belgravia could hear him shouting, Natalie came to the conclusion he wasn't going away, finally flicking the dead bolt and yanking the door open.

"You are out of control," she snapped. "Have you no sense?"

That got his attention. His eyebrows shot up and two stormy green-gray eyes narrowed as he considered her. "Me? I think you're the one who's run out of sense. What's going on? Why didn't you tell me you were back in England? I've been calling you every hour since yesterday."

"Have you? My phone must be off."

"Well, that's brilliant. Is this still about my stepfather and the problem at the gallery? He keeps waving me off, saying it was some sort of disagreement."

"Disagreement. I see. That's what he's calling it?" This was exactly the kind of psychological manipulation she was dreading. It left Nat with few options. The earl would keep his mouth shut about her assaulting him if she kept hers shut about the way he had harassed both herself and the other woman in the gallery. It didn't matter who saw what he did, discretion was expected when the titled and privileged were involved. However, Natalie was at peace with her behavior. He'd put his hand on the woman. It was a vile power play and Nat had been angrier than she'd ever been in her life.

London was a modern, vibrant city—and she loved living here—but it still had a bit of a class problem. Of course, the old Lord Rutherford didn't think it was a problem. Assaulting a woman in a public place for kicks and giggles was just *de rigueur* for someone like him. That was more a function of his age and entitlement than any inherited status. The problem rested with Natalie standing up to him. It was, in his eyes, altogether unacceptable.

The questions leveled at her by the detectives when it all went down were downright insulting, but even they could see it was best to let it drop. The police didn't want to be in the middle of a scandal with a member of the old guard. Natalie was warned, sternly, to keep her head down. The earl was more direct. He recommended an extended visit with her family.

James was looking down at her, a lock of his thick auburn hair was falling across his forehead and his face—with those high cheekbones and straight nose—showed a determination often found in those who had to fight for what they wanted.

Natalie might be in love with James, she was almost sure of it, but her feelings didn't change anything. She had to go home. Permanently. "I have to leave. I just need to…"

"You just got back and you didn't even tell me you were

here. What the hell happened? This makes no sense."

What was she going to tell him? That his scheming and pompous stepfather propositioned and manhandled a random woman at a small exclusive gallery event? That every one of the people with him laughed and patted the old chap on the back? Or maybe she'd tell James that his stepfather had to go to hospital to get stitched up after she plunked him with the phallic statue he'd wanted to buy. No, he already knew that part. That was the only thing he did know.

"I don't want to get into it. But after being home for a while, I realized it was time to make a change."

"A change?"

"Yes. I—I need some time to think about what I want to do since I no longer have a job. My brother is getting married, the holidays will follow not long after, so it's a good time to head back."

Not that there wouldn't be questions. Her family and friends were already wondering if there was something wrong. Three weeks ago she blew into town for no reason. No one expected Natalie until right before the wedding. An extended visit would definitely raise eyebrows. She wasn't known for her stability.

James was stable though. He had been the most dependable thing in her life. Brilliant, steady...and oh, so handsome. She had to get out before she wrecked that, too. Better to walk away now than screw it up and break her own heart.

Taking a few steps to the window, she folded her arms across her belly. She loved the view from her flat on Eaton Square. The garden across the street was still in full summer bloom. The colors—pinks, yellows and purples surrounded by green—gave the impression that the world was excited and happy.

Her body warmed when James slid his hands over her shoulders. She leaned into him when he wrapped his arms around her. Loving the safety and security, she rested her cheek on his right hand.

"Do you have a plan?" His gaze was trained on the large, half-filled suitcase lying across her sofa.

Natalie didn't know how to answer him. Originally, her only plan was to put some distance between herself and this place. It wasn't that moving home was the wrong decision, but now her heart hurt when she thought about the person she was leaving behind. She should have told him first. Running away wasn't fair. They may not have a future, but they had a past, and she owed him that.

Turning in his arms she looked up. God, how she would miss this face. "No. Not really. I'm going home, like I told you."

He nodded. "I understand. It will be good for you to take some time away. A visit—"

She cut him off. "I don't know how long I'll be there. I'm putting my apartment up for let."

"I'm not following." He held her at arm's length and

blinked a few times as if trying to process what she said. "Natalie…"

"We've only been together a few months; I think it's better if we move on."

"A few? It's more like six months and I'm bloody crazy about you."

"The length of time doesn't matter. This isn't going to work."

"Why would you say that?" He took her face in his hands, those wide, somber eyes blinking to focus on her face, to make sense of what she said. "Nat? Why?"

Why? There were a multitude of reasons. Did she want to tell him that his mother had said as much when she'd taken Natalie to tea at The Savoy two weeks ago? Or that his stepfather said so straight out when confronting her at the gallery?

She was "unsuitable."

The snobbishness was ironic when she thought about it. His lordship made a crack that Natalie was "no Vanderbilt," referring to one of the New York Gilded Age socialites who wed a British nobleman and secured herself a title. If only they knew the silly American girl they so disapproved of could have given Lord Rutherford's bank account a bit of competition.

But it wasn't about money. It was about her. It made sense when she thought about it. If she was too much for her own family, she couldn't expect James's family to accept her.

No, she couldn't tell James anything. He was close to his mum, and Natalie had no intention of mucking that up for him. There wasn't a place for her in his life, and it was better that she end it now before she got in any deeper.

His lips came down on hers…gently, sweetly…as if the kiss would prove his commitment and convince her to stay. His fingers threaded through her hair, her body responding eagerly to his touch. He pulled her closer, but Natalie stepped back before she drowned in him, taking his hands in hers. She loved his hands. Weathered and strong from working in his garden, they knew exactly how to touch her. "Let's go to bed," she whispered, pressing a finger to his lips before he had a chance to question her.

There were probably a thousand things wrong with the idea, the biggest being that it would give him false hope, but she wanted him. She wanted this one last moment of intimacy and closeness between them because saying goodbye to James would be the hardest thing she ever had to do.

Chapter One

Autumn

J AMES PHILLIPS STARED out the window of his office watching the soupy fog drop over the River Cam. It was very much like his mood on this unusually cold October day. It had been almost two months since he watched Natalie walk into Terminal 3 at Heathrow, and he hadn't heard a word from her since. Not a call back, not a text…nothing.

What was it his students called it? Ghosting?

It was an apt term. Why his mind was on her today, he didn't know. His relationship with her had vanished like a vapor. He thought giving her space was the right thing to do, but it appeared that wasn't the case.

He knew only cursory details of what happened at the gallery, that she had been dismissed, but she hadn't told him what had precipitated the trouble. All he knew was that his stepfather had been involved, that his nose had been broken, but nothing more.

If he was honest with himself, James wasn't surprised. The last time they were together something in his heart told him she was bolting, that she wasn't coming back. There was desperation in her kisses, fear in her touch. He should've paid more attention. Natalie loved with abandon; everything about her was free of pretense or inhibition. That time it felt like…it felt like a goodbye.

He should have confronted her about her plans instead of just accepting her reasons for going home at face value. The woman had more nerve than anyone he'd ever met, so what made her run?

His back was to the door, so he started when he heard his name echoing down the long corridor. Harry Stern, a fellow in North American history, was beloved by his students and his colleagues for his no-nonsense New York attitude. A Brooklynite, he possessed an intellect that was as sharp as a well-honed sword, and a personality that was as big and open as the country from which he came.

Harry was more than six feet tall and rail thin. His mother would have called the man a bean pole. His dark hair was coarse and smattered with gray, and even though he was several years younger than James, he looked older. It was his humor that drew people to him. Warm and funny, he had a way of connecting with people that was almost superhuman.

Harry said his ability to make people laugh is how he managed to woo his wife. Esme was an artist, and so beautiful, she could have been a model for all the masters.

"My friend," he said, his New York accent subtly affecting his speech. "You've been looking out your window for weeks. Don't you have someplace to be?"

Technically, James was on sabbatical all year. He was planning to stay in London to finish researching his book this term, but the place had no appeal since Nat left.

"Not really, no." His response was as flat as he felt. He should be digging into the emigration records from the 1600s at the National Archives, but he had no motivation to do it. So much for his stiff upper lip.

"Good," Harry stated matter-of-factly. "I got a…a proposition for you."

"A proposition?" The way he said it, James felt like he was being recruited by a mob boss. Still, he was intrigued. "Go on."

"A friend of mine from Harvard is the Dean of Humanities at a small liberal arts college in New York. They need someone to come in as acting chair of their history department while they conduct a search for a permanent replacement. It would be a bit of administrative work and you'd take on the undergraduate researchers. You'd be expected to serve until the end of spring semester."

"Acting chair? Why don't they just pick someone in house?" Bringing in someone from the outside seemed unnecessary. There had to be someone on their side of the pond who was qualified to take on the job.

"Because the faculty members who are qualified are interviewing for the position. Besides, she wants some new blood, some fresh perspective."

James scratched his head. Was Harry serious? Should he

just pack up and head to the States? "It's October. The term's started, hasn't it? I'd need a place to live, a visa…"

"The semester started, yes, but everything you mentioned can be handled by the college. As far as a place to live, one of the perks of the job is a house." He waved his hand in front of him as if he were presenting the newest model Jaguar. "You will have a waterfront cottage for as long as you are in residence."

Waterfront? That sounded nice. Maybe it was on a river, or perhaps a mountain lake. Now he was curious. "What's the name of the institution?"

"Jennings College. It's on Long Island. The area is gorgeous—used to be called the Gold Coast—and the school has a stellar reputation."

The mention of Long Island positively laid him out. Natalie was from Long Island and suddenly it felt like the universe was being cruel. Right when he was ready to accept the fact that she'd left and wasn't coming back, an opportunity to go to New York dropped in his lap.

That he was even considering it was madness.

He should say no, just stop Harry's pitch and move on. The proposal wasn't just daft with the term having started and a move to the States; it was problematic. He didn't want it to look like he was following her. *Stalking her.* The woman had a right to walk away from him even if it left him bloody miserable.

However, James was intrigued by the job. A small American college wasn't familiar ground for him, but that alone shouldn't eliminate it from his consideration. This experience would broaden his horizons. He'd never stepped out of his comfort zone. First it was the Royal Marines, then uni. After finishing his doctoral studies at Cambridge, he was offered a teaching position straightaway. Staying in Cambridgeshire, with his family house a stone's throw down the road, was comfortable. If he wanted a change he could go to the townhouse in London. His existence was safe and predictable, especially now that Natalie was gone. It wouldn't be a bad idea to embrace change, would it? This would give him some time to think. The time away from his family, from London, from his colleagues—from everything—would allow him to focus on his writing. James never put much stock in the idea of fate, but it did seem like the universe was presenting him with exactly what he needed.

"Get me the details. I'll consider it."

"Excellent. I'll have my friend ring you. Just be aware, they want to move on this quickly. You might not have a lot of time to think it over."

"Understandable."

Harry leaned in and patted him on the back. "You won't regret it."

James wasn't so sure about that. He surmised there was a good chance he could end up with a lot more than a belly full of regret. Which why he was probably going to stay exactly where he was.

TWO NIGHTS LATER James nursed a neat scotch by the fireplace in his study, immersed in stories of seventeenth- and eighteenth-century emigration. Some people left for religious reasons, of course, but others…others wanted adventure, a better life. Some had no choice. Reading the diaries and personal histories made him think about his own family. They were so settled. James fancied himself as curious, but was he?

He'd traveled abroad, spending time in countries close by, and halfway around the world. He'd been to Asia, South America, and he'd gone above the Arctic Circle in winter. Yet when he read history, he felt like he'd done nothing of consequence—much like his inordinately comfortable English ancestors. The colonists went into the unknown when they went across the ocean, he checked into a hotel.

He heard the front door open and close, and the breeze whipped through the old house carrying with it the scent of falling leaves and colder temperatures. His brother had left a message that he would be coming to stay for a couple of days.

It was James's house, but really it was part of the family estate, so his brother would come and go, sometimes with his wife and children, other times not. James wondered if he used the excuse of business in the area for a bit of downtime. Edward and his wife Phoebe had brought five children into the world in seven years. Three girls and a set of twin boys who had just turned two.

He could understand why his brother would need a break, but he imagined someday Phoebe might strike him dead in his tracks if he tried to leave without her. Theirs was not an easy life. His brother, the second son, was quite well set and didn't have the burden of the blasted title. But at the rate James was going, one of his brother's sons was going to inherit.

"By the fire, Edward," he called. "What brings you—"

He trailed off when he saw his brother's face.

"What's wrong?" James asked wondering if someone had died. Edward nodded in greeting, dropped his coat and fetched his own scotch, taking a healthy swallow before he leaned in.

"What do you know about why Natalie left you?"

The question, blunt and unexpected left James speechless. "I beg your pardon? I know what I told you. Something happened in the gallery, Rutherford's nose was broken, and she was dismissed. Ultimately, she moved back to New York."

Edward took another swallow before dropping in the chair facing him. "Hmm."

"Hmm?" James repeated, annoyed with his brother's cryptic response. "That's it?"

Edward exhaled. "In my position at the bank, I hear things. Some of it is confidential, but some isn't. And when it has to do with my family, I pay close attention."

His brother was a good man. He and Edward were never particularly close, but they were both loyal to each other, and the family. If there was anything that might taint the reputation of the Phillips name, the two of them would combine their forces to set things right. "What do you know?"

"It seems Natalie was set up by our dear stepdad."

Set up? The revelation hit him like a club to the gut. But once the shock wore off, again, he wasn't surprised. *The fucking bastard.* "How do you know?"

"One of my biggest clients is an art collector. He's a complete prick, but he knows everyone, including your Miss Miller and Rutherford." Edward stood, his mouth drawn tight. He circled the room, picking up a fire iron before poking at the dying logs in the hearth. He was thinking, which meant there was more. His brother's expression told James he wasn't going to like it.

"What else?"

Edward continued to poke at the fire, taking a deep breath before turning to him. "You know Natalie broke Rutherford's nose, but she was provoked. And he set out to do it with the intent of driving her back to her own people."

James had suspected as much, although this was the first time he'd had his suspicion confirmed. There were times he would have liked to soundly pop his stepfather, so hearing he'd provoked Natalie at least gave some context to the accusations his mother and the earl had been leveling at her.

"So, he made sure she had to leave? Gave her no choice?"

"It certainly appears so."

The anger churned inside him. James didn't react emotionally. He was a researcher, a scholar. He thought things through. But this time, he didn't give himself a chance to rationalize his way out of what he was going to do. Phone in hand, he acted. With a few flicks on his screen he made his call.

His brother looked puzzled.

"Harry?"

"Buddy, this better be good. I need my beauty sleep." Harry's voice was gravelly. James hoped he didn't wake Esme, as well.

"Yes, sorry. I know it's late. Tell your friend I'll take the job."

"What?" he responded. "You decided?"

"I'll be on a flight the day after tomorrow. Tell the dean we can talk when I get there."

Finishing up with Harry, who was completely confused, he turned to his brother.

"I was offered a job in New York," he said matter-of-factly.

"Were you? That's convenient." Edward wasn't easily amused, but this seemed to do the trick.

"Isn't it though." James had risen from his chair so he could top off his scotch.

Edward grinned, obviously pleased at the turn of events.

"Whatever should I tell Mum?"

He sipped thoughtfully. "Tell her that I've run away from home."

NATALIE MILLER WAS addicted to the sunrise. No matter what the previous day had been like, no matter how horrible or confusing, the sunrise represented a fresh start. So, as long as the weather allowed, Natalie came out to the beach at her family's estate, spread out her yoga mat, and let the sun dictate her mood. Her yoga practice centered her, even when it felt like her life was crashing down around her.

Today felt different, like there was a change coming. For the life of her she couldn't put her finger on it. Her family didn't understand her intuition, her *woo-woo*, as her brother Jack had named it, but they'd stop doubting it. It was a Natalie thing: different, odd...crazy.

Normally, she settled herself facing north—true north—for the clarity the symbolic direction represented. However, this morning she made an adjustment, facing northeast toward the ocean.

Toward the regrets she'd left behind.

The new light bathed her, its rosy tendrils circling around her like the morning mist that was so common in London. She missed her adopted city today, missed the energy, the beauty, the vibe of the people. She missed her quirky gallery, her apartment, and her favorite coffee shop.

And she still missed James.

It had been almost three months since she'd first come home. Summer had slipped into fall, the days grew shorter, and Natalie tried to feel grateful for the small comforts that were back in her life now that she was on her own turf again. The beach was one such gift, and breakfast at Rinaldi's was a delight not replicated anywhere in the world.

She was also grateful for the people. Beyond her family she had Jordan and Lilly, her very best friends from childhood, as well as her new friend Maddy. While part of her viewed being back in Compass Cove as an indictment of her choices, she couldn't help but feel wrapped in the warmth of the place.

Her heart didn't hurt as much. The pain was fading. She had adjusted to not being in London, and she had a sense she could put her life back together. She was happy to have had the time to help her brother Adam and Mia get ready for their wedding. Her new nephew, Ben, was funny and smart. She'd loved spending more time with her grandmother, and since her brother and her nieces had moved in while Doug weathered a nasty divorce, she had endless fun being the crazy auntie. Her family was the perfect distraction. Even though she was at loose ends, no one sensed how lost and isolated she felt. If living in England had taught her one thing, it was how to master the cool exterior.

Anxiety? What anxiety?

It was why she came out here every morning, weather permitting, to meditate. The water, the air, the seagrass that waved with every puff of wind settled her. And the sunrise represented hope—hope that things would get better, and that she'd weather this storm just like all the others. Her personal meditation might not have been understood by her knucklehead brothers—sometimes she didn't understand it, but it gave her peace.

It was going to be a mild day for early November. She could feel the temperature climbing even at this early hour. When Natalie opened her eyes, she marveled at how pristine the air felt in her lungs. She could see clear across to Cove Landing, a small piece of land that jutted out into the bay. It was nature's reminder to boaters to slow down or end up grounded. There used to be a lighthouse sitting on the bluff, but now there were just a few small cottages looking out at one of her favorite views in the world.

She'd have to go up there to paint. There was a lovely overlook that had been constructed several years ago and there was plenty of room to set up an easel and explore the view. She imagined a canvas filled with the colors of dawn, or better, at twilight as shades of pink and blue gave way to the winking stars.

Since she had been home, Natalie's desire to make art had reappeared. It was the damnedest thing. For so long she'd forgotten what it was like to create. Managing the gallery, flying all over the world, being part of the scene wherever she was, took her away from herself and the things that had once mattered. Initially, she hadn't majored in art history or archives, Natalie had been a fine arts major. She'd done deep dives into different mediums allowing whatever story was playing in her head to come out on paper or canvas or in clay. Maybe it was the upheaval in her life, the broken heart, her family and their endless questions… Whatever it was she was happy to have that spark back. It had been gone a long time. Maybe the angst in her life allowed her to reach that part of herself again. The connection was good. It was the only good thing.

"Good morning, dear!"

Natalie turned at the familiar voice. Grandma? What was she doing out here this early in the morning? The woman was almost eighty years old, but nothing much stopped Anna Miller—even a rugged trail early in the morning. She came toward Natalie and sat on an old wooden garden bench that was nearby.

"What brings you out here so early, Gram?" Her grandmother was a notorious early riser, but usually she was just finishing her second cup of tea at this point of the morning. "Something on your mind?"

"I just wanted to see what brings you out here every morning. It's quite beautiful. I'd forgotten how the morning looks from the bluff."

"It's a spectacular way to start the day," Natalie agreed. "It gives me hope."

Grandma nodded, seeming to understand. "When your father died, I lost track of the time I spent looking out at the water. I stood in this very spot for so many hours your grandfather installed this bench for me." She smiled at the mention of her husband who had been gone for seven years. "I felt like John was with me. I still do. Maybe that's what brings you out here, too."

Natalie barely remembered her father. He died when she was very young, and her family had been swept into absolute chaos. Fortunately, her grandparents were there for her mother to lean on. When Nat was about ten, she'd started to wander down here to the bluff above the beach to draw. It felt like a safe space—comfortable. Maybe her dad was here.

"Anything is possible." Natalie eyed her grandmother. "Is that the only reason you're here?"

The grin that spread across Grandma's face was classic. Mischief shone in her beautiful blue eyes. Curious, Natalie rose from her mat and sat on the bench next to her. "What's up, Grandma?"

"Nothing really, I'm just worried about you. It's been a few months since you came home, and it still feels like you're looking for something."

"I was away a long time. I think I've earned some time off." She wasn't really "off." She had a part-time job at Rinaldi's Café. She waited tables three times a week to keep from becoming a hermit. And her tips kept her in art supplies and her favorite English tea.

"You practice your yoga up here?" The small talk was a tell that her grandmother was leading up to something. Natalie had a feeling the big question was coming. "Do you think I could do it?"

"If you really want to try, I could modify some moves for you because of your hip. It's actually great exercise for people of a certain age. I won't be able to stay outside much longer, so if you want to meet me in the ballroom, we can set up in there."

Yes, her family home had a ballroom. She and her friends used to pretend they were Olympic figure skaters sliding around the polished wood floor in their socks.

"A certain age, indeed." Gram giggled, a delightful sound that was like a bell ringing. "You can say the word *old*, you know. I'm not offended by it. Growing old is a privilege denied to many."

"True enough." She wanted her grandmother's wisdom, which Nat knew was grounded in years of experience, growth, and a healthy dose of self-awareness. Granny was an amazing woman. "Chair yoga is another option. You never have to get on the floor."

This brought a nod of approval. "That sounds like a good idea since getting on the floor means I'd have to get *off* the floor, and I don't do that particularly well these days."

They sat in companionable silence. With the way life buzzed around her, Natalie was grateful for the quiet she found in her little slice of home.

"What are your plans today, Grandma?"

"I'd like to go into town today. Would you join me?"

"Of course. I'd love to." A trip into Compass Cove was always a nice way to spend the day, especially since lately she'd only been heading downtown for her shifts at the café.

"Good. We'll go to lunch and do a little shopping—it's time to get the holidays started, don't you think? I also have to pick up a necklace that Liam repaired for me."

"Wonderful, I always look forward to the opportunity to tease Liam."

"Ever since you were a little girl. Did you know he bought a house? Right up there." Grandma pointed her long, still-elegant finger at the Cove Landing bluff.

"Really? That lucky stiff. I've been keeping my eyes open for a house up there, but there are only a handful, and most are owned by the college."

"He bought the old lighthouse keeper's residence. It needed a lot of work, but I hear it's coming along."

Natalie would have to see if he'd let her set up in his yard to paint. The house had spectacular, unobstructed views. In fact, the dwelling itself would make for an interesting study.

Grandma pushed off the bench and stood straight as an arrow, her impeccable posture a sign of her patrician up-bringing and equally strong will. "I will see you at ten thirty. I'm looking forward to it."

"I'll walk you back—" Natalie stood, but Grandma waved her off.

"No need. I'll see you later. Thank you for sharing your sunrise with me."

Natalie watched as her grandmother retreated down the path toward the big house. If nothing else, coming home allowed her to indulge in little moments just like this one. Being more present with her family was her priority.

There were so many regrets. She wasn't about to add her family to the list.

Chapter Two

ONE THING NATALIE loved about Compass Cove was that no one rushed the holidays. Never was a Christmas decoration seen before Halloween, which was a very big deal on its own, but now that the spooks and witches had packed it in for the year, twinkling lights, ribbon and garlands adorned every lamppost and storefront. All bets were off, and she could see the holiday magic coming to life.

It wouldn't be the grand displays she'd become used to in the different London neighborhoods, but was more reminiscent of the small towns and villages that dotted the landscape outside the city. The charm, the warmth exuded in small markets and shops, sparked Natalie's anticipation.

Natalie didn't know why her mind was on Christmas. Usually, she was shopping the day before and was up half the night wrapping presents, as procrastination was one of her most notable traits. Maybe it was being in the family hub. With all the activity of the last couple of months surrounding the wedding, she'd gotten used to the togetherness.

That didn't mean she didn't need a little space once in a while, but for the most part she was content leaning into the familiar. Feeling like she'd won the lottery when she spotted a parking spot on Main Street, Natalie maneuvered the car into the space right in front of Jennings Compass Shop.

A mainstay in the town since its founding in the 1600s, the Jennings family crafted precision compasses and watches for generations of Long Islanders. Sailors who manned ships docked in New York Harbor or Brooklyn sometimes traveled out to Compass Cove to purchase one of the finest compasses to sail the seas.

The shop, which was in the same location just a block from the waterfront, still produced custom compasses, but most of the instruments were designed as sentimental keepsakes for families to commemorate special occasions. The tradition, rooted in an old love story, still charmed her.

"You know," Grandma said, "your grandfather bought my engagement ring and wedding band at this shop. Liam's grandfather was an artist. He would say he was just a watchmaker, but we all knew otherwise."

"Liam is following in his footsteps. His jewelry is stunning." Natalie coveted a few of the pieces she'd seen in the shop window. One day she'd have to take the plunge and treat herself.

"It is. But you should see the glass."

"Glass?" Glass was her obsession. Natalie pulled open the door to the shop and followed her grandmother inside.

The shop, with its wide plank floors and warm wood-paneled walls was elegant and inviting, but the furnishings weren't what had caught her attention. At the center of the store was a large display case that was home to the most exquisite blown glass she'd ever seen. "Oh, wow."

The glass work literally took her breath away.

The last five years of Natalie's life had been spent being unimpressed by artists in general. Many people had talent and drive, but few had a gift. Apparently, her friend Liam had a wonderful gift.

Reminiscent of Chihuly, but more accessible because the pieces weren't grand and all consuming, Liam's sense of shape and flow was magical. She felt drawn into the different pieces. Embraced by the color and curious about the way light played with the designs.

The man needed a show.

"I told you," Granny whispered.

Natalie felt her head bob slowly up and down. "Yes, you did."

"Hey there!" Liam came out from the workroom behind the counter, his smile wide in his handsome, boyish face. "How are you lovely ladies today?"

Her grandmother tilted her face toward him and was rewarded with a sweet peck on the cheek. "It's lovely to see you, Liam. I came to pick up my necklace."

"Of course! But you didn't have to make the trip to town. I would have brought it to you."

Gram patted his hand. "You are very sweet to offer, my dear, but it was a wonderful excuse to take my granddaughter to lunch."

With a wink at Natalie, he smiled. "Then let me get your necklace."

Liam was a sweet man. For the life of her she couldn't figure out why he wasn't married with a passel of kids.

When he returned with Gram's necklace, he made his way to where she was standing. One piece stood out for her. It was an orb, beautiful in its structure, flawless in every way. The blue color went from dark ocean blue at the base, and wound through the glass like it was actually water.

"I'd appreciate hearing what you think." He was asking for her opinion. She was flattered.

"Oh, Liam…" Natalie leaned in and examined another piece of glass. This one looked like it could be hung in the sky. A deep midnight color, it went off in numerous points, the ends tipped with gold and silver. It sparkled. "I am without words."

"That bad?"

It took her a second to process what he said. *Bad?* "What? Oh, God no! Everything is lovely…perfect. I'm amazed. You are a singular talent. I haven't seen fine glass-work like this…well…I don't think ever. It is stunning. Every piece is stunning."

She could hear him audibly exhale. "Wow. From you that's a rave. Thank you."

"Is this the only place you're selling your work? You need an agent. I mean, I know it's a leap, but…"

"An agent? I don't think anyone would want to rep me, Nat. I have no track record."

She had to admit he was probably right. "A show then. You need a show. Do you have a portfolio?"

He shook his head. "Nothing official."

"That's your first step. I can help with that. God, Liam, I had no idea. Where do you work?" A glass house was no little thing. He needed space.

"I work on the farm." He shrugged.

The farm had been in the Jennings family since they moved to Compass Cove in the late 1600s. Passed down from generation to generation it had been a working dairy farm until just after World War II. There were a number of buildings on the property, including two residences. About fifty years ago, Liam's grandpa donated most of the former farm to the town to use as a learning center and nature preserve.

"Seriously? I need details! Also, I heard you moved up to Cove's Landing, and I'm going to need to see the house."

"Wow, you have lots of questions. You should come around more."

The dig was subtle, but effective. "Ouch."

"Sorry." He nodded his head in apology, but Natalie deserved the dig. This was the longest stretch she'd been at home in years.

"So, the glass house kind of just evolved," he continued. "There's a long stone building on the eastern edge of the property. It used to be a smokehouse. It was an easy conversion. Relatively." He smiled in a way that let her know it wasn't easy, but he was modest, that Liam. "As far as the house, come up anytime. If I'm home, you're welcome."

"How about if you aren't home?" She heard her grandmother chuckle at the blunt question.

"Ah, okay...I guess."

"Not to raid your fridge, but to borrow your view. To paint."

"Oh! Yes. Sure. Absolutely. There's a new deck right on the edge of the bluff where you can get a view of all three sides of the peninsula. You're painting again?"

Natalie was dabbling; she didn't know if she was all in just yet. "That sounds perfect. And I mean what I said. I'll help you put together a portfolio. People need to see this glass."

"I appreciate your confidence." His response was formal and she half expected him to bow the way one of his ancestors might have when acknowledging a lady. That was Liam, very old-school.

"I'm going to take Grandma to lunch. We will talk soon."

There was something deep and smoldering in Liam's gray eyes. It wasn't a sexy smolder, but a passion, a drive she'd never seen in him before.

"Liam." Gram reached out a hand and touched his forearm. "Would you like to join us?"

"Thank you, Mrs. Miller, but I have two appointments this afternoon. Both are coming in for engagement rings. It's that time of year!"

Natalie wandered away while the two of them were chit-chatting and her eyes fell on the wooden case that housed Lucy Velsor's compass. The compass was legend in town and even Natalie, who made it a point to keep her sentimentality in check, was charmed by the centuries-old love story. The compass itself was gorgeous, with intricate engraving and a tiny sundial that folded in the case, but it was the story, the core belief that hearts meant to love would find each other, that affected people. Next to the compass were letters Lucy and Caleb, who were married into their eighties, wrote to each other and a small portrait of the couple when they married.

Pulling out her phone, she snapped a picture of the display, including a close-up of the compass. It was a vital piece of art, as well as an artifact.

"It was designed by Caleb's uncle," Liam said as he moved behind her. He was close enough that she could hear the fabric of his button-down shirt rustle when he moved. "Edmund Jennings was the most talented of the brothers, bringing a real artistic, old-world flair to the pieces he designed. Compasses, watches, sextants—everything was functional and beautiful."

"I never noticed how intricate the engravings are. There's an entire scene on the inside of the cover." How had she not noticed? She'd been in this shop a hundred times, and she'd never picked up on the tiny details. Why now? What was different about it today?

It was like the damn compass was speaking to her.

"I have more of his pieces in the safe. He painted, you know. A few are on loan to the Maritime Museum."

"Seriously? You've piqued my interest. Let's have a drink one night and you can tell me all about him."

"You're on." Liam smiled. "Do you want me to take the compass out so you can hold it?"

Natalie's back stiffened, a tingling flicking through her limbs. "Hold it? Ah, no. No, I don't want to hold it." She absolutely wanted to hold it, but didn't dare.

"It doesn't bite, Nat."

Maybe it didn't, but there was enough turmoil inside her already—she didn't need an antique compass with a mind of its own to broadcast it to the world.

"Thanks, Liam. We'd better go before there are no seats left at the café. Your work is beautiful." Natalie stepped away from the display case but felt the pull. It was eerie, and time for her to get out of there. "I'll see you soon."

After fumbling with the door handle, Natalie rushed on-to the sidewalk. She could feel her heart slamming into her chest. A chill crested unexpectedly.

The anxiety she'd tamped down for so long came roaring back. Lucy's compass knew something, and Natalie was not in the mood to listen.

Chapter Three

GRANDMA SLIPPED HER hand through Nat's elbow as they left the compass shop and headed toward Rinaldi's for lunch. She looked over her shoulder back at the shop's front window, and she thought she saw Liam watching them, but she shook it off. What the devil went on back there?

"I'm so glad you got to see Liam's glass. It's really very special."

"Special is an understatement. It's breathtaking." It was like nothing she'd ever seen, and Natalie felt the familiar clicking in her brain. Her mental checklists ticking off on one side, and insecurity crowding the other. "I might have pushed him a little too hard, though. Do you know what his plans are?"

"Don't you worry about that. He needs a push. Filled with self-doubt, that one. His father told me he's working on Christmas decorations right now. His studio is filled with ornaments and tree toppers."

Ah, yes. The crushing self-doubt that often paired with a creative heart was something Natalie knew well. She could help him. She had the contacts. Maybe she could find a place for him to have a showing that focused on his ornaments and tree toppers. It was short notice, but it was possible. Wasn't it?

Natalie had known Liam her whole life, and their families had known each other for centuries. Literally, centuries. It made her chuckle a little because in some ways she wasn't so different from the people she left behind in England. The peerage…that collection of old, titled families had been connected to each other by land or blood for hundreds of years. The Millers, the Jennings family, the Velsors, and the Andersons were very much the same. They were well established, well respected and privileged. There was something very special about being one of the founding families. It wasn't about being better than anyone, it was about the connections. It was something she was only really learning to appreciate.

She'd have to see more of his art, and make sure other people saw it as well. Passing the bridal shop, Natalie stopped short in front of a pretty clapboard building that used to house a small educational toy store. The place was empty.

"The toy store closed?" It had only been in town a few years, but Natalie really liked the owner. When Nat came to town for the holidays, it was a relief to be able to buy her nieces' gifts someplace local.

"Yes, it's a shame. It was a lovely shop, but Brianna

wasn't from here and she missed her family. She went back to the Midwest. I hope someone else takes a chance and opens something lovely."

Natalie cupped her hands around her eyes and leaned into the glass. It was good space. Open and airy, it had polished wood floors and white walls. She saw stairs along the back wall, and that made her curious. Stepping back, she went to the front corner of the building to check out the roof. Skylights. There was a second floor, and at least part of it was well lit.

Natalie's mind started spinning with ideas. Racing.

Maybe it was time for her to stop curating collections for others and do it herself.

The building had possibilities. Taking out her phone, she snapped a picture of the poster that identified the Realtor managing the property.

"Are you interested in the building, dear?" Her grandmother tried to sound innocent, but Nat had the distinct impression Grandma had ideas of her own.

"I might be. But I have a feeling you knew that."

Gram smiled, and her eyes twinkled in that way that made all Natalie's worries go away. "I know you're looking for direction. Sometimes, a little inspiration is all that's needed. I saw that the toy store left when I met the ladies for breakfast last week."

"I see. And you maneuvered me down here for a shopping trip hoping for what?"

Gram steadied herself on the flowered cane she used for extra support. She reached out and patted Natalie's cheek. "I was hoping you would look past your worries and see the possibilities."

"God, Gran. I don't know." They walked again, and while Nat had some ideas, she wasn't sure she had the nerve to follow through. "I mean...am I ready?"

"Only you can answer that for sure, but I think so. I talked to Elena, the Realtor, and she said in addition to the retail space, the upstairs is large and open with wonderful natural light. It sounds perfect for a studio." Her granny had thought of everything.

This was why she hiked out to the bluff and invited her to lunch. Not to tell her what to do, but to show support. Her grandmother believed in her. "Thank you, Gram."

Ideas flooded her head, and it made her discovery about Liam's glass all the more prescient. She could host his first show. A holiday show where he could showcase the tree toppers, ornaments and sculptures that would be acquired by savvy collectors.

She knew what to do, and she still had connections, especially in New York. That was something the people in London couldn't take away. Her education in the city, her work in museums and galleries, had helped her cultivate an extensive network. A network her former employers would no longer have access to.

Entering Rinaldi's Café had a calming effect, even

though it was one of the busiest places in town. It didn't matter how many times she walked through the door, the familiarity settled her. The café was the heart of Compass Cove serving an amazing menu of comfort foods and offering the best baked goods—well—anywhere. Lina Rinaldi, who owned the café, was a master who could compete with the best pastry chefs in the world. Additionally, she could tell you all the town gossip and how to improve your life while laminating her puff pastry.

The café was actually two establishments. The original bakery where you could get donuts, pies and sweet treats to go with your morning coffee, and the café, which offered breakfast and lunch every day, and dinner on Thursday and Friday nights.

The restaurant was beautiful in the classic sense, with black and white floors, white wainscoting, soft yellow walls, and booths with checkered seat cushions. A U-shaped, marble-topped counter with a dozen stools was the centerpiece of the shop and when she wasn't making magic in the kitchen, Lina took her post behind the counter to argue with one of the regulars, catch up on the news of the day or refill coffee cups. She was a fierce, headstrong businesswoman who loved her family, her friends, and this town with abandon.

The café was slowly being decked out for Christmas. Festive garlands were strung over the doorways and windows, and a small gift section in the corner near the register was filled with ornaments, cookbooks and kitchen utensils. Lina would wait until December to go full out with a tree and all the sparkly bling she'd built up over the years.

The one thing Natalie knew had been gearing up for a few weeks was the chocolate-making operation. Twice a year, Lina fired up the chocolate melter in the bakery's basement and set out to craft a myriad of holiday confections. She had already started making solid and hollow snowmen, Santas, dreidels and chocolate lollipops. She started taking orders in October, and this year her chocolate charcuterie board was a bestseller.

The work was meticulous, and the hours were long. But Natalie loved the process and helped Lina whenever she was in town. Being that she'd moved home, she'd already spent a lot of hours down there.

Gram slipped into her usual booth and was already looking at the menu when Natalie sat down. "Oh, good. Lina made her chicken soup today. I think I'll have that with half a sandwich. What do you think you might like, dear?"

Natalie ate there at least a couple times a week and she had her favorite go-to salads and sandwiches, but today she felt like a burger. A big, juicy, calorie-laden specialty burger. It wasn't her usual fare, but she was starving and nothing else looked good. "I'm going to have the burger with the fries. If I get a basket of onion rings, will you share with me?"

"I never turn down Lina's onion rings."

Nat felt herself smile. There wasn't a person in town who would say Lina's onion rings were anything less than orgasmic. Okay, maybe her grandmother wouldn't use that word exactly, but the onion rings were kind of magical.

"I think we should plan on dessert, you know...*to celebrate*," Natalie said before she picked an olive off the relish tray the server had left on the table.

"Oh?" Gram inquired, her smile growing wide. "What are we celebrating?"

"Compass Cove's new gallery." Natalie couldn't believe she'd said that aloud.

Grandma's hand reached across the table and gave Nat's a gentle squeeze. The approval was unspoken, and very welcome. "Then we'd better make it chocolate."

"I heard the word *celebrate*." Lina shooed Natalie over so she could slide into the booth. "What are we celebrating?"

"Nothing," Natalie said. "I was just thinking..."

"Thinking? About what? About doing something with your fancy education other than waiting tables and making candy?"

Nat knew Lina loved her, but that was a little too blunt. "Don't be a snob, Lina. Work is work. It's better than sitting around on my privileged behind."

"I know, but you're not meant for this. I love you, Natalie, but you gotta get out of your own head and get your life together."

Ah, if only it were that easy.

"I'm doing my best. It's been a bit of an adjustment..."

"Pffft. Who was he?" Lina's tone was unconvinced.

Okay. That was just creepy—the woman read minds. "I beg your pardon," she said in a barely there British accent. "I don't recall mentioning anyone—him or otherwise."

Her grandmother gave her what she and her brothers called "the look." There was no avoiding *the look.* "Natalie, I never pressed but it's fairly obvious that your heart is broken. You don't have to tell me anything, but you never let a relationship with a man define you. Broken hearts are terrible but—"

"But what?"

"You need to get on with your life!" Lina waved her hands like she was singing an aria. "Rent the old toy store. Open—"

Natalie cut her off. The plot was becoming clear. "Good grief! Really? The two of you are incorrigible." What a setup. All of it—lunch, Liam's art, the idea of a gallery—God, these women were such sneaks.

"Just because we gave you a nudge, doesn't mean it's a bad idea. Don't be stubborn." Again, Lina minced no words.

Stubborn was Natalie's middle name, but it wasn't relevant. The gallery *wasn't* a bad idea. The truth was that for the first time in a while she was excited about the possibility of something that was hers. She'd been treading water the last few months and it was now obvious that her cheerful façade hadn't fooled anyone.

Maybe she had to stop trying to fool herself. That would at least be a start.

JAMES STOOD BEFORE Sailors Hall with the dean of humanities and had to admit, he'd never seen such a beautiful college. It was small, especially when compared with Cambridge, but the campus, set right on the Long Island Sound, was picture-perfect.

He could see himself here. Maybe not permanently, but a semester or two would be a welcome change in routine. The grounds, which were meticulously landscaped, were dotted with old-growth trees. Oaks and maples with leaves that had started to turn various shades of red and gold stood in contrast to the cool colors of the verdant lawns and the dark blue water.

The buildings, designed mostly in the academic Gothic style, were well proportioned to the campus and were made all the more impressive by the large windows, attached outdoor patios and gardens for students and faculty to appreciate. He'd never seen an institution so subtly attuned to the population's well-being.

"Your office is in this building. I think you have a view." The dean clasped her hands together, obviously taking great pride in her academic home. Denise Holcomb was a lovely woman with curly ginger hair and catlike green eyes that made clear her Irish roots. She was tall, only a few inches shorter than he was, and every movement was with purpose.

"Another view? I've been told the cottage has a view as

well. Originally, I was thinking a brook or a pond—apparently it's much grander than that."

James remembered Natalie talking about her hometown. She once said the place was "lousy with views." She was right.

"After this, I'll take you to the library. It has a wonderful history collection, and the librarians are magicians. Even the most obscure bit of information is no match for their skills."

A good library was always an advantage, but a skilled librarian was gold. He was going to enjoy his time here.

"Have you ever visited Long Island?" she asked.

"No, but I have an acquaintance who is from a town nearby, I believe. Compass Cove?"

"Downtown Compass Cove is about ten minutes east. Your house is in one of the small hamlets connected to the town proper. Cove Landing."

His house. The drastic nature of the move was starting to sink in. He'd said repeatedly that the change of scenery was good for him, as was the chance to refocus on his work, but he knew Natalie was at the core of his decision and it was so out of character all he could do was shake his head.

"Is something wrong, James?" Dean Holcomb must have seen his expression change.

"No. Not in the slightest. I'm marveling at the weather. Sunshine and a cool breeze. It's just beautiful."

"It is. Don't be fooled, though. We do get some bad storms now and again. Nor'easters. Blizzards. Hurricanes.

November is windy, and the spring can bring days of drenching rain. But we handle it. Come on. Let's meet your colleagues."

There was a short set of stairs before they entered the building through a pair of antique doors with a bronze relief of a sextant embedded in each one. Normally, he would have found the embellishment unnecessary, but not here. It suited and tied the building to the nautical history of the area.

"These doors came off the boathouse that was part of the original estate. The structure was damaged in a storm, but the doors were saved. You'll find a lot of mementos from the seafaring history of the town. The founding families are still very involved." They made their way to a grand staircase and she continued talking as they started up. The woman was a consummate storyteller, the mark of a true historian.

"The Jennings family bequeathed over one hundred and fifty acres of their original farm to the college as a nature preserve and science center. The Andersons donated heavily to the athletic facilities and support the equestrian center. And the library was completely renovated and expanded five or six years ago. That was the Miller family's contribution."

James stopped. Her words froze him in his place. Surely it was a different family... Miller was a common name. "Miller?"

"Yes. Why?"

"Oh, nothing in particular. The names have English roots."

"Some. The history of the area is quite interesting. I'm sure we'll get you up to speed."

They turned left at the top of the stairs and approached an arched doorway as grand as anything he'd ever seen at home. At the top of the arch was a gold-leafed sign that said, "Department of History."

His new home. At least temporarily. "This is impressive."

"We are very proud of the facilities we provide for our students—they are the priority—but the buildings are only special because of what we do inside. You're part of that now. Part of the legacy."

He thought about this very small school with a history of a little over two hundred years, and how it humbled him to be here. James taught at one of the most prestigious universities in the world, but it was possible his time at Jennings would give him the chance to see what kind of teacher he could be. To step out of his comfort zone.

He felt the change in energy as soon as he walked in. The department common area was an active space with desks occupied by assistants and secretaries, several couches and a round wood table—scarred and almost fossilized—where a small group of students were engaged in a discussion. There was a large conference room to the left with the requisite table and a wall lined with over-stuffed bookshelves. Faculty offices encircled the perimeter, while the sea-green walls were covered with local maps from various eras.

By the time he had taken in his surroundings, all eyes

were on him. Professors stood in the doors of their offices, curious he supposed, students looked up from their work, and the secretaries, all of whom looked to be in their fifties, appeared delighted to see him. Not a bad start.

Dean Holcomb smiled at the assembled group and brought her hands out in front of her. "I'm glad you're all here. I'd like to introduce the acting chair of the history department, Dr. James Phillips. As you know, he comes to us from Cambridge, and I have no doubt you will enjoy working with him. James, welcome."

There was a muffled greeting from the group coupled with a smattering of applause. He supposed he should say something. Three women, five men most of whom were around his age, but two of the men were easily in their sixties. All of them looked pleasant and approachable. He smiled as he stepped to the center of the room, hoping he didn't muck it up. "Hello and thank you for being here to welcome me. I'm looking forward to getting to know everyone." There was a collection of voices from the hall behind him, causing the group to turn their eyes in the direction of the hallway. The savory smells that came along with the voices let him know his plan had gone off without a hitch. "To facilitate that, I thought a little lunch would be a good idea. I was tipped off that Rinaldi's Café has smashingly good fare, so I placed an order for us." When the delivery people walked in, James directed them to the conference room.

The surprised expressions morphed into approval. That was a good first step.

"Why don't you get started, and once I've deposited my coat and papers, I'll join you."

Turning to the dean, he saw she was smiling. "You are very good, James. That was a masterstroke."

"A meal is the best icebreaker, my old dad always said. It's the least I can do. I feel like an interloper."

"You aren't. I think you're exactly what we need. Your office is down that short hallway, through the double doors. Go get settled and then join your department for lunch."

"Thank you, Denise. You'll stay?"

"I think I'll head out, but I can pop back in an hour if you still want the library tour."

He shook his head. "I can find it myself. It will be good to explore a little on my own."

"Very good," she said on her way out, giving James leave to find his office. He followed her directions, admiring the intricate woodwork and art in the abbreviated corridor. The moment he stepped through the doors, he stopped in his tracks. In front of him was the water. His office was substantial and beautifully furnished with a large mahogany desk, a credenza, bookshelves and a comfortable seating area, but the crowning glory was the wall of windows behind the desk that faced Long Island Sound. It was breathtaking. Walking closer, he dropped his satchel on the leather chair behind the desk and took in the whole scene.

The lawn rolled off behind the building down to a cobblestone terrace and accompanying wall that traveled off in both directions. The area was a hive of activity with students playing Frisbee, reading or talking in small groups. "Wow. No wonder they all want the job," he murmured out loud.

"That's not too far off," said a feminine voice from behind him. When he turned, he saw one of the secretaries from the front office. She was a handsome woman in her fifties, he gathered; slender, with her dark hair in a neat bob that reached her shoulders. She was dressed in a tailored skirt and blouse, with a pair of leather riding-style boots. She was professional and, he was certain, exceptionally good at her job. "I wanted to introduce myself, Professor. I'm Emma Deem, your executive assistant. Welcome to Jennings." She extended a neatly manicured hand.

Taking her hand, he bowed his head reflexively. "Thank you. It's a pleasure to meet you. Please call me James. I look forward to working together."

"Likewise. Please let me know if there's anything you need right away. Otherwise, I thought it would be a good idea for you to meet with the administrative staff so we can fill you in on general procedures and get a sense of how you would like things to run."

"That would be excellent. Do you have a time in mind?" He knew she did. The woman was more efficient than ten of the best people he knew.

"Tomorrow at eight? Does that work?"

"I'll write it down."

"I'll also enter it into your calendar."

"My calendar?"

"Yes, I keep your digital calendar."

"I see." He was starting to feel like a stodgy old prof. "That sounds very efficient."

"It is. As a matter of fact, you have an appointment today at four o'clock." Her sly smile let him know he was going to be expertly managed.

"I do?"

"The tech department will be sending someone to get you online and up to speed with our systems, specifically your email, digital calendar, budget and accounting program, and access to your student files."

"Ah. Very good." He was just about to thank her again, when he felt a pressure winding around his ankles. To his surprise when he looked down he saw a rather large white and orange cat. The beastie was more white than orange, and its coat was long and regal. Somehow James sensed he was being sized up.

"Well, hello there. Come for lunch, did you?"

Emma's eyes widened. "I didn't expect to see you today, ma'am." She crouched down and lifted the cat into her arms. She purred and bumped Emma under the chin. "This is Eleanor. She's, well...she's the department cat."

"Is that so?" James reached out and scratched the fuzzy creature under her chin. "It's a pleasure to meet you, Eleanor."

"She's named for Eleanor Roosevelt and has the run of the place. There are beds in most of the offices, but she tends to settle herself wherever she wants."

James looked around. "I don't see one in here…"

"Oh, no…she likes your couch the best."

"Good to know. I'll make sure to keep valuables off my desk, as well."

Emma nodded her agreement.

"Now, why don't you enjoy some lunch," James said. "I'll be out in a moment. I'm going to soak up the scenery every moment I can."

With the cat in tow, Emma left the room. Leaving James with his thoughts and too many questions. He walked to the center window and flipped a small latch that allowed him to push it open. The sound of gulls circling overhead, coupled with the breeze from the water was heady. It also brought some necessary clarity.

The sky and sun, the water and the land—this place felt like Natalie. Kinetic, powerful…*beautiful.*

She was all the elements, combined with magic and stardust, the pixie and water sprite he'd read about in the old legends, and at that moment James realized he'd never fully understood her.

This place was more than a hometown; it was Natalie's refuge, her touchstone. When trouble found her, she made her way back. Looking at the scene, he understood. It was no wonder she'd come back here. Maybe he could fix things between them, maybe not. But he had a feeling if it didn't work out between them, at least he would know why.

Turning back to the desk, James spied a six-point, cherrywood box. The view had so distracted him, he hadn't noticed it when he first walked in the office.

Moving the small hook to the side, he lifted the lid to find a compass. Ornately engraved and elegant, it was three-sided, all brass, with a sundial, and a curved bar to set the latitude. Instruments such as this were used in the eighteenth century to help sailors establish time, location and direction.

The maker's mark was engraved on the lower edge of the compass and indicated it had been made by Jennings Fine Compasses and Watches, Long Island, New York.

When he picked it up, he saw a small card in the felt-lined box.

Dr. Phillips,
Welcome to Compass Cove. We hope this compass helps
guide you on your journey.
Best wishes,
The Faculty of the School of Arts and Sciences,
Jennings College

A journey, James thought. A fitting description indeed.

Chapter Four

L UNCH WAS A success, and James patted himself on the back for a marvelous icebreaker with the department. He was only there temporarily, but there was no need to create an adversarial environment. Since he had no ties to the institution, and no plans to stay, he could advocate for the professors—and their pet projects—and have no worry about repercussions. As long as he had time to work on his book, he'd make a general pest of himself.

He liked the faculty. Every one of them was brilliant and considered an authority in his or her respective areas, with deep and diverse educational pedigrees and credentials. He discovered the college had deep pockets and was intent on attracting some of the top scholars in the various disciplines.

One such scholar was William Harris, a professor of American History who specialized in the old west. James walked away from their luncheon conversation with a completely new understanding of the American cowboy, especially as he existed in the mountain states, like Montana and Idaho. As his students said, James had no idea this was "a thing."

He'd just finished his meeting with the computer tech and while he'd knew he'd have some questions, he was signed into all his accounts. When he opened his calendar, he could see Emma was not just efficient, she was thorough. He only had a few meetings set up so far, but each category was color coded, while each meeting entry had pertinent details attached.

He decided this was a good time to explore the campus. The sun was hanging low in the sky but there was still some good light left in the day. It cooled down considerably, so James turned up the collar of his coat and headed in the direction of the library.

As he walked along the cobbled path, he again marveled at the old trees that lined all the walks and dotted the landscape. Cambridge had clusters of trees and his home at Kings College was as grand as any institution, with imposing buildings, a library with rare works and the river as a definitive part of the landscape. However, that's what it was...grand, imposing, heavy with history and tradition. It wasn't bad; he'd miss the town, his favorite coffee shop where he'd grade papers and write lessons, and he'd miss market square with its colorful tents and delicious variety of food, but being here at Jennings showed him the English way wasn't the only way. It was good he'd gotten out of his...what did one of his new colleagues call it? His *bubble*.

He hadn't been familiar with the term until today, but it was an apt description.

He saw the sign for the library not far up the path, and he was happy to find that it was so close to his office. It was also blessed with the same view. He stopped short at the bottom of the entrance of the building.

The James A. Miller Memorial Library.

Bloody hell. If this was a member of Natalie's family, there had to be some story for him to have a building named after him.

The doors of the library slid open, revealing a towering open space. A central desk was surrounded by comfortable furniture, high-top tables and displays. The second level looked to be a combination of offices and stacks, and the third level held books for as far as he could see. The crowning glory was the ceiling, which was dominated by a stained-glass dome. As he moved into the room, he noticed signs for special collections, the stack rooms, and conferencing space.

"It's amazing, isn't it?" James shook off his stupor and looked down to see a rather attractive young woman with a college ID hanging around her neck.

"Uh, yes. It's stunning. Are you the welcoming committee?"

"Nope, just walking by. I do enjoy watching newcomers swallow their tongues when they look up for the first time, though."

He chuckled. He was going to like it here. Like his friend Harry, and Natalie, he found Americans refreshing. He loved their lack of filter.

"I'm Mia DeAngelis, one of the librarians. You must be Dr. Phillips. Denise said you'd be coming by."

The woman extended her hand, and James felt immediately welcome. "Please call me James. It's wonderful to be here."

"I can give you the nickel tour if you're interested, or you could just wander around on your own."

"I can wander about myself. If I have any questions, I know who to ask."

"I'm here to help. There's also a librarian dedicated to history and classics. Melissa isn't here today, but I'll tell her you stopped in. I'm sure she will reach out."

"That would be wonderful. I'm doing a book on British emigration and I would love to learn more about the area and the settlers. I think it will be so much more interesting if I can tap into personal stories."

Mia's eyes narrowed. "Hmmm. Come with me." She turned with a purpose and strode off toward the special collections. He didn't know what else to do, so he followed.

"You're going to want to see this."

She walked through an arch opposite the entrance, then made a quick left. The room was painted a rich navy and unlike most of the spaces on campus, this one only had narrow windows bordering the ceiling. The light was filtered, muted almost. Display cases and cabinets with glass doors housed old texts and artifacts.

"This is the local history collection. It's been curated for generations. It includes historical documents, records from businesses, diaries, and family archives. There are a large number of artifacts, as well. Only a few are on display. You should be able to get quite a bit of information for your research."

James turned in a circle. This would do very nicely. When he'd just about completed his survey of the room his eyes landed on a very large photo of an older man, standing on a beach, smiling. He looked happy, comfortable. The water was at his back and his hands were in his pockets. There was something in his eyes that told James he'd enjoy sharing a pint with the gentleman.

Mia came up beside him and followed his gaze. "That's James Miller, the library's main benefactor. My husband's grandfather."

"Your husband?"

"Yes, I was married last month, I still use my maiden name out of habit."

"Well then, congratulations." He was certain she had been an exquisite bride.

"Thank you. Adam adored his grandpa. Everyone did. I wish I'd met him."

On hearing her husband's name, everything started clicking. Adam was the name of one of Natalie's siblings. Her older brother. "Your husband, he's a footballer. An American footballer?"

"Yes! He doesn't play anymore. He's the coach of the

Jennings team. That's how we met."

Unexpectedly he found himself in a nest of Millers. What should he do now?

"Hey!" Mia exclaimed. "You should come to the game on Saturday. It's always fun, and it's supposed to be a gorgeous day. What better way to get initiated into the Jennings family!"

"That sounds intriguing. I'm afraid I'm a little soft on American football rules."

Mia waved him off. "Please, I'm married to the coach, and I don't get most of what's going on. You'll probably follow it better than I do."

"That does sound like fun. I'll make a point of it."

"Excellent. I'll see you there. We're usually seated right around the fifty-yard line, about ten rows back. I'll save you a seat."

"Thank you, Mia. For the welcome and for showing me this treasure. I can't wait to dive in."

"One other thing," Mia began, her large eyes twinkling. "Make sure you stop in at the compass shop on Main Street. There's a lot to be discovered there, especially if you're looking for stories."

"Is that so?"

"Probably the best story in town."

Jennings was proving to be a wonder at every turn. James thought he knew everything about academia, but he was finding that wasn't the case. He realized the small American institution was going to give him an education like he had never had before. His prestigious background, his title, his education didn't compare with the warmth he was finding in this close-knit small town and this gem of a school where teaching and research went hand in hand. Nothing about it was typical, and the people were proving to be the greatest surprise of all.

"Is there anything else I can help you with?" Mia asked.

"As a matter of fact, yes. I need directions to Cove Landing."

JAMES WAS GLAD he asked Mia about directions because the address he had been given wasn't showing up in any navigation app on his phone. She was able to print out directions and in addition she gave him some landmarks to look for so he wouldn't end up driving into the bay. He made a point to motor through town, and it was as charming as he'd been told, but the ride up the bluff was positively awe-inspiring. There was a small shoulder where he pulled off and snapped a few photos. He'd send them to his family, and a few colleagues, but mostly he wanted them for himself. This was proving to be a memorable trip already.

Coming around the bend, he approached what looked like rebuilt sections of a stone wall with a sign that said *Lighthouse Lane, Cove Landing.* As he proceeded into the small cul-de-sac, with its eclectic collection of houses and cottages, James finally understood what home felt like.

Number six Lighthouse Lane was a fairly good-sized, gray-shingled house that had a porch and what appeared to be an ample garden. The front steps of the house were adorned with pots of yellow, white, and red chrysanthemums. Not to be outdone, an old oak was ablaze with color, its leaves red and orange.

With the car in the drive, he fished the key from his pocket and made his way to what would be his home for the next eight months. He could hear the rumble of the waves and smell the salt of the water; the breeze blowing around the house was distinctly coastal, rustling the leaves, the grass and plants surrounding the house. Once inside, he was again struck by the light, open feel of the place. There was a well-equipped kitchen, a living room and dining room. The furniture looked comfortable, and his own belongings, still in boxes, were stacked neatly in one corner. A small water closet and a wardrobe were in the front hall, and the main bedroom was on the first floor right off the living room.

Like his office, there was a wall of windows facing the sea. The view was everything he'd been told, and more. He'd thought he'd be able to get a lot of work done while he was here, but now he wondered if he'd be too distracted.

He was about to step outside when a familiar movement caught his eye. Looking left his heart clenched. There, on the edge of the bluff, with her easel, palette, and brush, was

Natalie. How was she here? Lithe and beautiful, her short dark hair fluttered around in the breeze while she dabbed at the canvas on the easel. Wearing jeans and a Cambridge hoodie that he remembered her taking from his bureau one cold morning, she turned briefly allowing him to see the delicate features of her face. She looked relaxed. Content.

Happy.

He'd wanted to fix things for her. To find out what his family did to drive her away, but James had a sinking feeling that coming to the States, inserting himself in her life again, could be a colossal mistake. When he saw a man walk toward her from the house and hand her a white porcelain mug, he felt like a child whose balloon had burst.

"YOU ARE AN exceptional host, Liam. Thank you." Natalie lifted the mug to her lips and sipped the hot amber liquid. The tea was delicious, but she was intrigued by the wine in Liam's glass. "When the light hits the glass, the wine positively glows. Your vintage?"

"We had a good harvest two years ago, and Dad experimented with a blend. Would you like me to pour...?"

She waved him off, fascinated at the way the Jennings family kept their roots while still moving forward. Compass Winery was becoming quite a presence on Long Island's North Fork, about ninety minutes east of Compass Cove.

Liam's father was spending more and more time at their vineyard perfecting his pinot noirs and merlots, leaving Liam to continue the shop's legacy in town. "How's the painting? Feeling inspired?"

"I'm loving it. Thank you for letting me work here. It's a perfect spot."

He considered her work, and Natalie wondered what he thought. Liam was a talented artist with a critical eye. "Well?"

"I like your use of color, and there's great movement in this part of the water." He motioned with his glass over the area.

"But?"

He leaned his hip into the nearby deck rail. "I don't think it tells the whole story."

"What is that supposed to mean?" The painting was raw; she didn't know what the story was yet.

"I'm not talking about the painting, not really. I'm talking about you. You're not being honest about why you came home. I've known you a long time, Natalie, and there's a lot more to the story than you're telling."

Nat froze, the mug brushing her lips, while uneasiness wound its way through her belly. "I have no idea what you're talking about. There was an *incident*. I was fired. I came home."

Liam took a sip of wine and looked out at the sound. He didn't say a word, he just sipped. Looked. Sipped again. His silence was grating.

"Good Lord. What?" she snapped.

"You were one of the premier gallery curators in the world. You had a stellar reputation. You could have landed a position at another London gallery in a heartbeat. What happened?"

The question stung her like the spray off the ocean. Natalie hung on to her mug with both hands and sook a long sip, mulling over her response. How did one tell a friend that she'd torpedoed her dreams? That she walked away from the man who was quite possibly the love of her life? Simple—she would lie because that was easy, and it wouldn't require her to dive back into the pain.

"There's no story beyond what I told you. The fallout from my poor judgment was too much. I was better off coming home and taking stock."

"So, you're going to paint, do yoga and wait tables at Rinaldi's?"

"You know, I'm really tired of being scolded for doing honest work. Don't be a snob."

"Cut the crap, Natalie. I'm not a snob and you know it. What's the deal?"

"It's what everyone expects of me, isn't it?"

The intention was to come across as flip, like she didn't care, but instead Nat sounded like she felt: angry and hurt. She was defensive, and Liam's relaxed posture showed he wasn't affected by her outburst. She was just about to tell him her plan, when he started up again.

"You're going to chuck it all, then. Play the Bohemian. The poor little rich girl."

His attempt at pressing her buttons was succeeding. Nat was getting pretty pissed off.

"What exactly are you trying to do here, Liam? Because I don't understand. You're doing the same thing as everyone else. Making assumptions. Maybe you don't know everything."

Yeah, best she didn't tell him anything.

She turned and walked away from him, hoping she could contain the combination of rage and sadness that was churning in her belly. He wasn't saying anything new. Natalie was seen as that poor little rich girl, wasn't she? Why not embrace her?

She could travel, paint, buy and sell art for wealthy clients…Natalie had options. But when Liam pointed this out, it pissed her off. Why?

Because that was never who she was, now especially. Nat liked work and if the new gallery became a reality, she'd have more than just a job, she'd have a purpose. She still had some money in her trust, even though she'd seriously depleted it paying for the statue she broke during the scuffle with the earl. A piece of cast metal, the stupid thing had snapped when it hit the polished concrete floor almost as easily as the earl's nose broke when her fist connected.

She was more than a spoiled debutante with a bagful of

family money. She always had been, but unlike her brothers who wore uniforms of one kind or another, Natalie went into what was considered a glam profession. Designer clothes, galas and private jets were not foreign to her. It didn't matter to anyone that she worked damn hard in a cutthroat business. Craving independence—and distance—she'd left New York.

Going to London had allowed her to be herself, to be who she was without the labels that had been applied her whole life. Now that she was back, she'd been shoved back into her box. And no one realized they'd done it.

Oh, Natalie. It was her mother's favorite refrain. A not-so-subtle dismissal of whatever she did or said. Mom didn't know it stung and the one time she mentioned how much it hurt, Adam told her not to be so sensitive.

Sensitive was Natalie's middle name. She'd just learned to hide it well.

Yep, she was one big pressure cooker of feelings. The only one who had begun to crack through her veneer was James. And see where that got her.

She startled when Liam's hand dropped on her shoulder. He was the brother Natalie always wished she had. She loved Doug, Adam, and Jack—they were good men. But Liam understood her. The artist in him could see the abstract world in which Natalie lived.

"Natalie, stop. I've known you too long to believe for one second that you're going to settle into that kind of life.

You left Compass Cove so you could live life on your terms."

"I did. And it was great. Until it wasn't."

He turned her to face him. "What happened?"

"I couldn't stay. There was someone…and…" Natalie sucked in a breath. She couldn't cry. Not today. "It wasn't going to work. I had to leave."

"People break up all the time. What about this pushed you out of the country?"

There were a million tiny details that drove her decision, but most of it was grounded in the day in the gallery when the old man and his entourage harassed a woman Nat believed was a university art student who had come in to look at a local artist's exhibit. The young woman was, maybe, twenty-two.

It was the inflection point, but even before that Natalie knew she had been deemed unacceptable. Although she and James had only been together for less than a year, it was obvious to anyone paying attention that their relationship was becoming very serious.

His mother, the Countess Rutherford, had come to that conclusion as well. And she was not pleased.

It all came to a head that day in the gallery. In an impossible situation, she fell right into the trap that had been set for her. Natalie lost control, lashing out like a warrior protecting an innocent.

Yes, she was extremely well educated. She came from an excellent family. She knew how to read a table setting and the value of a hand-written note. Natalie had been raised well. She had also been raised in New York, and it was her New Yorker that came roaring to the surface and took that malicious fool to the ground with one pop.

Lord Rutherford promised humiliation would rain down on her, and on James. He would be disgraced and could lose his position at the university for associating with her. His mother would be crushed.

"I made the decision to leave so I wouldn't hurt someone I deeply cared about. I wasn't good for him. It was just…" She swallowed hard to staunch the flow of tears. "It was just better for him if I left."

As soon as the final words left her mouth, her heart broke all over again. Natalie couldn't hold back anymore, and the tears broke free. The pain, raw and burning, was as fresh as the day that she walked into the terminal at Heathrow three months ago. She could still hear his voice, still feel his arms around her, warm and safe, imploring her to tell him what was wrong. The hoodie she was wearing, his hoodie, still held the faintest trace of his cologne. She missed him so much, and she hadn't told anyone about him until now. Not her friends, or her family. No one knew that Natalie's heart had been smashed into a million pieces.

"You've been suffering in silence, haven't you? You haven't told anyone." His words, kind and understanding, brought more tears.

She nodded, sucking in air fighting against the spasms

that came involuntarily as the sobs shook her. "You're...th-the first person I've told. No one knows about him, I mean, it's better that way, b-but, I miss...I miss him."

Liam took the mug of tea from her hand and Natalie went willingly when he pulled her into his chest and held on. It was permission for her to cry as long and as hard as she wanted.

She did. Holding on to her friend as if her life depended on it. For the first time since she came home, Natalie didn't feel so alone.

"Tell me everything. You know I'm a vault."

That was true. Liam had been the keeper of many secrets over the years, as had the Jennings family members before him. They treated every confidence as if it were a valuable antique that needed to be locked away. She could trust him.

"He's a professor at Cambridge," she sniffled. "He's brilliant and compassionate. I could talk to him for days and never tire of it. He's interested in people, in the world. He's a gentle man and has the biggest heart."

"He sounds a lot like you. What happened?"

"The incident with the client? It was his stepfather. The Earl of Rutherford. The earl and James's mother, the countess, decided we weren't a good match, and I was warned off. They said they would ruin my life and make my family's life—and James's life—a living hell if I didn't step back. There was also an assault charge they wouldn't press as long as I got out of the way."

"Wait a second, wasn't that self-defense? Didn't he touch you?"

"He did, but I was really defending another woman, or so I thought. It turns out, she was an actress, and I was set up. She claimed nothing happened to either of us. That the earl was a perfect gentleman, and I just went off."

Liam stiffened and leaned back. His eyes met hers, and she could see the anger bubbling up. "Are you shittin' me?"

"I wish I were. There was no gallery to hire me. It was a very thorough hit job. Like right out of the movies."

"People do that? It's insane."

"Some do. Lying, hurting people…it depends on what's at stake. In this case it's an antiquated concept of power, but there is money. Lots of money. The countess didn't want her son with me. You know, the gold-digging American with dreams of castles and crowns." The whole idea was laughable. Natalie didn't need James's money. Feeling more in control, Natalie stepped back and sat cross-legged on the ground, tucking her knees up inside the sweatshirt.

"Okay…is your boyfriend royal?"

"No. He's not part of the ruling family, but he is a member of the nobility. He's a viscount."

"A viscount? What is that?"

How did she explain it? There was an abstract quality to the idea of titles in the United States. That's what happened when you threw out the ruling class. "In the ranks of the peerage he's just below an earl, but above a baron. He inherited his title, which comes with land and homes, he could be elected to the House of Lords, and he is entitled to seek an audience with the queen."

"So, he's a rich dude." Liam wasn't impressed. "Does he have a crown? Because that would seal the deal for me."

"He's more than that. You're being a snob again. Like I said, he's a professor. He also works with several committees in the area, most dealing with farming and conservation."

"But he let you take the hit for this mess with his family?"

"Of course not," she said.

Because Natalie hadn't told him.

Liam's eyes narrowed. "No? Then I fail to see the problem?"

Natalie rubbed her chest trying to ease the ache that had settled there.

"He doesn't know. You didn't tell him." Liam was too intuitive for his own good. It was like the compass woo-woo had rubbed off on him.

"No, I couldn't. I was warned that the earl would sic the media on us. James is well-known. He's young, handsome… He could lose his position at the university. I would be hounded relentlessly. My family could be targeted. What they tried to do to Adam after his car accident would look like child's play."

Her brother had been a fast-living professional athlete. One of the best quarterbacks to play the game until he took his car into a tree and wrecked it all. He'd been a magnet for the paparazzi when he was at the top of his game, but nothing was more appealing than watching the powerful fall. They were unmerciful.

"Shouldn't that be his decision?"

"It's complicated." The situation was no-win, and she didn't need James's approval, or Liam's, to walk away. The damage that could be done to her reputation, to her family, and to him was not worth the risk, no matter how much she loved him.

"You made everyone believe that what happened at the gallery was nothing. That you handled it. For God's sake, you cracked jokes about it. You let everyone believe you screwed up."

"It was easier that way. No questions."

Natalie sniffled and rubbed her eyes with the sleeves of the sweatshirt. She remembered the morning she took it from his dresser. Little moments, just like that one, would be the ones she would hold on to forever.

"I'm sorry you're hurting, Nat." Liam crouched down, taking her hand in his. He was a good man, and a good friend. She was glad she'd told him. "But I never took you for a coward."

Ouch. That stung.

Normally, the words would make her angry, or at least defensive. But she was a coward. That was the truth—not only didn't she want to face her problems, she'd also run away from a life, and a person, she loved.

"I never thought so either, Liam," she conceded. "But I guess there's a first time for everything."

Chapter Five

AMERICAN FOOTBALL WAS a mystery. It wasn't that James had never seen a game—he had—but he was truthful when he told Mia he was soft on the rules. While he understood the basics, some of the intricacies of the game escaped him. It was similar to rugby, but not, and it didn't resemble a proper football match in any way. Still, this wasn't about the actual match, it was about the camaraderie. About being part of the team.

He could have said no. His job here was only until the end of the spring term, and as long as he did his best work with his students and colleagues, the rest didn't really matter.

Or did it?

James genuinely liked the department faculty. Each one had a different quirk, a different focus, but each point of view added to their collective depth. The department was completely devoid of the professional jealousy he'd seen rampant in academia. The students were the absolute priority, and the department functioned with them in mind. To be called a teacher was not an insult.

He could be happy here. Work was a pleasure, and the

cottage at Cove Landing provided a wonderful respite after a long day. He hadn't seen Natalie again since the day he arrived, but he couldn't deny the fact that she looked spent when she left. He shouldn't have been watching her exchange with his neighbor, whom he had yet to meet, but it didn't look very pleasant.

At one point it was clear Natalie was crying.

It took all the strength he could muster, but he didn't interject himself into the exchange. He wanted to, desperately, but he held back. When he saw her sink to the ground, his heart dropped with her, and James felt every bit of sadness flood through him. It hit him hard and fast, cutting off his air. It was inexplicable. James was forty years old, and he'd been in a number of failed relationships, but he'd never had the pain of loss linger like this.

Logically, he should be getting over her. In reality, his feelings had only grown more intense. He was at a loss as to what to do about it.

The walk to the stadium from his office was about a mile, but it was another beautiful autumn day, so it wasn't a hardship to make his way on foot. He'd been walking to different parts of the campus the last few days and each time he'd discovered something that made him like the place even better.

With a full stable of horses right on site, he'd be able to get a ride in now and then. He'd left his card with the stable manager in the event any of the horses needed exercise.

Yesterday he'd discovered the original gardener's cottage, which was now a horticultural center. It hosted local gardeners for workshops and helped troubleshoot issues they might be having before a problem went out of control.

He'd met the librarian who specialized in history and classics, and she'd given James a complete overview of the collection, the archives and a list of experts in the area who might be able to augment his own research. Overall, he was quite pleased with his move.

However, as the sport park came into sight, his mind went back to Nat. He had no idea if she would be attending—he hadn't asked—but he surmised there was an excellent chance. He expected she'd be there with her family. How would she react to him?

Then there was the question of the big bloke who was comforting her. Would he be there with her? Relationship or not, he gathered Natalie would be none too pleased to see him. She would likely be ripping pissed off.

He started to wonder if it was too early in the day for a pint.

As he rounded the corner toward the entrance, he saw a full-blown party taking place in the car park, complete with barbeque grills and tables full of food. Music was blaring as students moved from group to group. There were a number a food vans that looked tempting and when his stomach growled he realized he hadn't eaten anything in hours.

"Professor Phillips!" James heard his name and turned to

see one of the department student aides coming toward him.

"Hello, Tyler. How are you this fine day?"

"Good, good getting ready for the game." Tyler was an affable young man, a senior who was already accepted to a graduate program in California. James had liked him immediately. He was sharp and insightful. At this moment, he was also completely legless.

"What is all this?" James asked, eyeing the festivities.

Tyler smiled and waved his hand presenting the scene. "This is a tailgate. A sacred American football tradition."

He'd heard about football being a kind of religious experience at universities in the States, but he didn't think he'd see this kind of devotion at a small school like Jennings. "Sacred? Sounds quite serious."

Tyler grinned, then shrugged. "It's just an excuse to drink early. You want a beer?" The young man was moving back to his friends.

"I'll pass, thank you." James waved and started moving again. "Maybe you should take a pass on the next one, too."

Ever good-natured, the young man laughed. "Probably a good idea, but what fun is that? See ya around, Professor. Enjoy the game."

James smiled and proceeded to the stands, which were set into the sloping ground like a bowl. He took the stairs, looking left and right until he spotted Mia at the same time she saw him. She waved enthusiastically and he made his way to where she was standing.

"You made it!" she exclaimed.

"Yes, I had no idea it was such an event." The stands were awash in deep blue and gold, the school colors.

"This game is a big deal. We're playing our longtime rivals and Jennings hasn't won a game in five seasons."

"Ah. A grudge match. That explains the energy, and the alcohol, in the car park…I mean the parking lot."

Mia nodded and took a swig from a water bottle. "I wish I could drink. I'm as anxious as Adam about the game. Maybe more. If we lose…" She sighed. "I don't want to think about it."

Laughing, he appreciated her frank admission, as well as her concern for her husband.

"Let me introduce you to some people." She went down the row introducing him to another one of the librarians, her brothers-in-law Jack and Doug Miller, and her friend Lilly Vasquez who—apparently—was engaged to Jack.

As the pleasantries ensued, an unnerving sense of familiarity washed over him. James already knew them. Devoted to the people she loved, even if they were an ocean away, Natalie had spoken about each and every one of them, often, and it felt disingenuous to pretend he didn't know who they were.

There was a commotion behind him on the stone steps and a cadre of young voices raised in excitement were getting closer. Except for one. One voice was clearly adult, lilting and musical. Hearing it again was like a gentle kiss.

"Okay, the girls and I have returned. I have more hot dogs than people, so I hope everyone is hun—" She dropped the word, her face going white. "*Crap.*"

Instinctively, James had turned when he heard her voice and as soon as their gazes met, Natalie froze. Her mouth agape, eyes wide, the expression on her face was a combination of shock, fear and anger. He on the other hand was so happy to see her he couldn't speak.

"I have to go." Putting down the trays of food, Natalie spun and took off up the stairs. She was fast and he knew he couldn't make any excuses if he wanted to catch her.

He took a quick glance at Mia before following Natalie. "I'm sorry."

Usually, James planned out difficult conversations, but this time he had no idea what he was going to say. He didn't know if Nat would even speak to him, if being on her side of the Atlantic was a complete overstep, if not letting her know immediately that he was going to be here at Jennings pushed him into stalker territory... There was no handbook for this.

His goal now was to catch up with her. That was all. He'd figure out the rest later.

"NATALIE!" HE WAS getting closer. Damn those long legs of his. She slowed down on the path right near the library and wondered if she should go up the hill toward the art studios or down along the path next to the water. Or she could just face him and find out what the hell he was doing there.

With Liam's words about her being a coward echoing in her head, Natalie stopped running, fighting against her flight reflex, which seemed to be working overtime. She'd run away so fast it was hard to catch a breath. But deciding passing out wouldn't be a good look, she bent at the waist, put her hands on her knees and dropped her head trying to stave off the stitch that was forming in her side. *Keep breathing, Nat*, she thought to herself. *Deep breaths.*

He reached her quickly enough, leaving Natalie without any sense of what she should say or do. Part of her was angry, and she wasn't sure why. But the other part? That part was so happy to see him it actually hurt.

"Natalie, I—" His voice—that beautiful, deep baritone—flowed over her like water. But she couldn't let it affect her. Nope. Her resolve had to be stronger than the warmth spreading in her belly.

"What are you doing here?" Straightening, her instinct was to look at his face, go deep in the steely depths of his eyes, but she thought better of it. Especially if she wanted to maintain any sort of control. So, she focused on his nose.

Which was right above his full, expressive mouth. Right below his big, gorgeous eyes. Good grief. She was dying.

"I took a temporary position in the history department." He must have sensed she was on the verge of breaking because his answers were simple and straightforward.

"A what? At this college?" She reeled on him, furious, but she didn't know why. Deep down she was happy to see him. A terrifying feeling since her realization from the other day was just confirmed. She wasn't over him. She would probably never be over him.

"My friend Harry—you've met him—knows the dean of humanities. She needed an acting history chair while they conduct a search for the permanent replacement. I was on sabbatical so when I was asked, I said yes."

"And you didn't consider that it would be weird for you to show up in my hometown?"

"Oh, I considered it. I did." He took a step toward her, and Nat took a step back. She couldn't get too close, or she'd launch herself at him. "But I'd rather risk you being angry with me than never seeing you again."

Damn. That just cut to the core. Didn't everyone dream of someone uttering words so romantic, so pure, like he just did?

"And..." he continued, taking a step closer, "I had to come since it seems my family had something to do with you bolting?"

Well, shit. "I don't know what to say to that." Natalie might have lost her words, but she knew what she wanted to do. She wanted to throw herself into his arms and hold on forever. She wanted to hear his words, relish in his gentle touch. But they had no future, and it didn't matter what side of the ocean they were on, that simple fact hadn't changed.

But he was here. Right in her backyard. What the hell was she going to do?

"Nat? Natalie?" Great, now things were going to get weird. Down the path she spied Doug and he was puffed up like a menacing dog. Her big brother had decided to act like a big brother. Natalie backed herself up to a nearby bench and sat down. Was he going to growl and bark and make an attempt at being intimidating?

Her brother was not quite as tall as James, but Doug was a retired Marine officer, so what he lacked in height, he made up in breadth. He drew up to his full height as he pulled up alongside James and extended his hand. "We didn't get a chance to talk. Doug Miller."

"James Phillips. Natalie spoke of you often."

"Did she? Yet she never mentioned you." That was an intentional dig. "So, you and my sister are…friends?"

James didn't respond because he was still trying to figure out the answer to the 'friends' question.

"Oh, for Pete's sake. He was my boyfriend, for lack of a better term."

"Ah. *Was* being the operational word. Is he why you ran home from Europe, Nat?"

He was, indirectly, but she had no intention of laying the blame on him. Ultimately, the decision was all hers. "It's complicated, Doug. Just let it drop."

"Maybe, but first I want to know what brought Mr. Phillips here." Her brother rarely bothered with her unless it was to tell her how much she had screwed up. Doug was all about doing the right thing.

James had folded his arms in that way he did when he was losing his patience with someone. He'd clearly had enough of Doug and his insinuations. "Doctor Phillips. Professor, if you prefer."

Feeling the need to tweak her overbearing sibling, she added something to the conversation specifically to annoy him. "Or in a pinch you may call him *Lord* Linden."

Watching Doug's mouth fall open was quite satisfying, but the title-drop didn't amuse his lordship. She could see the annoyance spread across James's face. He never leveraged his title, but she had no problem throwing her brother off-balance.

"Lord Linden? Seriously?"

James brushed off the question and the snide tone. "Do you have a point, Mr. Miller?"

"What brought you here, Professor?"

"As I explained to Natalie, I was offered a temporary position as the head of the history department. It was an attractive offer, and I accepted it."

"And you just happened to land in our backyard."

"A coincidence, but yes. They approached; I accepted."

"I don't find that plausible." Doug, as usual, was trying to intimidate. He spread his stance and locked his hands behind his back, addressing James like he was a green recruit.

James was neither green, nor a recruit. While Nat was

initially annoyed by the posturing between the two men, it was turning out to be quite entertaining.

"Mr. Miller, whether you find it plausible or not is of no concern to me. You're free to ask questions of anyone you please, but I have no intention of entertaining your inquiry or your insinuations any further. I find it all quite insulting."

"I don't care if you find it insulting or not. Look, pal, I don't know if you noticed, but that's our name on the library…"

That did it, Natalie burst out laughing. The sound rolled through the quad, echoing off the buildings. "Oh, my God. Are you really pulling the our-name-is-on-a-building card? With an actual English nobleman? He's not impressed, Doug."

James shrugged lightly. "I wouldn't say that. I think your family is impressive and the library is a testament to their commitment to the area and the college."

His words, sincere and thoughtful, surprised her. "Oh, well…"

"What doesn't impress me is someone throwing around that name trying to intimidate me. Based on what I've learned in a short time, I hardly think your grandfather would approve."

Her brother, for once, was speechless. Natalie could not believe how effectively James had shut him down, and it reminded her why she'd been so attracted to him. There was no bluster around James, just dignity and a quiet confidence that surrounded him like an aura.

"I will, however, take my leave. It's obvious there's nothing to discuss, so I'm going to call it a day. Please give Mia my best."

He turned without another word and walked toward Sailors Hall. A retreat so quick, Natalie didn't have a chance to respond to what he said. There was plenty to discuss. Her eyes followed his long, lean frame as he strode down the cobbled path, walked up the steps, through the heavy wooden doors and out of sight. Her heart broke a little. Not a surprise considering how she'd been feeling the last few days.

For a split second, Natalie thought she could hear her brother grind his teeth and she braced for the fit of temper that was sure to come. She had to keep reminding herself Doug was a good man going through a rough time, but she wasn't going to let herself be bullied. She'd had more than her share of crappy people this year, and her brother was not going to throw any of his baggage on her. Frankly, it was all she could do to keep her own shit together.

"I can't believe you were with that guy. What an asshole. He was lucky you ever gave him the time of day."

If she could only tell him the truth, Doug would see that James was an amazing man, and Natalie had been the lucky one. Okay, so she wasn't happy that he had found his way to Long Island, but that didn't make him less wonderful. Especially since he was concerned about her. She had left him without explanation, without reason.

She'd hurt him, lied to him and he'd still sought her out.

Liam had said she should talk to him. Maybe she should. The way he'd looked at it, Natalie was letting a simple conversation stand between her and the man she loved. But it wasn't simple. There was so much more going on. James didn't know about the setup, or the blackmail.

Or did he?

Sure, she could tell him, but the earl wasn't lying when he said he would file a complaint. Natalie would likely be arrested. There was no one to back up her story, and the embarrassment and the heartache it would bring on James and her family just weren't worth the risk. His stepfather had executed his plan perfectly.

While James would be outraged, there wasn't much he could do. And the ensuing battle, if he ended up taking her side, would pit him against his mother.

James lost his father at a young age, very much like Natalie did. And, like Nat, his mother was left to raise him. She was a strong woman, with a lot of opinions and even more expectations, but she loved her sons.

Tears burned her eyes and Natalie looked away so her brother wouldn't see. It was too late, she realized, when he sat on the bench next to her and looped his arm around her shoulders.

"You okay, Natty Bean?" It was the nickname he'd had for her since she was little. He used to use it to annoy her, but at that moment she found it incredibly sweet and comforting. "I can still go kick his ass."

"No, it's not his fault. I messed up." She dropped her head on Doug's arm. Tears dripped down her face reminding her, once again, that she wasn't close to being over him. Part of her wanted to go find him and tell him everything. She imagined he was in his office, angry and confused, but what she had to say would only hurt him more.

"I am no expert on relationships," her brother began, "but I think he still has a thing for you."

Nodding, Natalie couldn't speak. The last thing she wanted to do was lose it completely. James's presence, his reaction to her, brought all the feelings she'd been trying to tamp down roaring back to the surface.

"Is he really a lord?"

"Viscount," she croaked out. "Lord is how you would address him."

"A viscount," he repeated. "I don't even know what a viscount does."

Natalie felt a watery laugh escape. "That's okay, I don't think a lot of viscounts know either."

Chapter Six

NOT KNOWING WHAT to do with the rest of his day, James figured it was as good a time as any to get to know his new home a little better. He certainly couldn't go back to the football game, not after the embarrassing display with Natalie. He'd mucked that up. He knew she would react badly to seeing him. He wasn't supposed to be there; certainly, he should have told her he was in town as soon as he arrived. It was a bloody mess.

Instead of heading back to the field, which would have been disastrous, he decided to take a walk through the small, picturesque village that—according to Mia, as well as his very early research—had a number of stories to tell. Founded in the mid seventeenth century, the village had been called Whaler's Cove and Oyster Neck before the Jennings brothers made the town a destination for sailors with their compass shop.

It was renamed Compass Cove around 1725 and the name stuck.

He could see as soon as he parked that the shops on Main Street were decorating for the holidays. Thanksgiving was soon, at the end of this month, if he remembered correctly. It didn't escape him that this was the first time he'd be away from home for Christmas in a decade. He was looking forward to the change.

The downtown wasn't extensive, but it had a lot of character. Wreaths and garlands adorned the lampposts, trees were being strung with lights and store owners were outfitting their front windows and doors with silver and gold baubles and beads. He imagined when it got cold, a light snow would make the place look like it was dusted with icing sugar.

He knew Rinaldi's Café was at the center of town. He saw a bookstore, a florist…maybe he could send her flowers? No, Natalie wasn't that girl. Fierce and independent she wasn't going to be wooed by a bouquet of pretty blooms. Natalie was about actions, not gestures.

Continuing down the street, he marveled at the variety of businesses. There really was something for everyone here. Just then an empty building caught his eye. White clapboard, large windows, and a pitched roof with skylights gave the structure a clean, unfussy look. But what totally gobsmacked him was the sign in the window.

Coming soon ~ Belgravia Gallery

Belgravia? Good Lord. It could only be Natalie. Part of him felt a twist of anguish deep in his core because a business meant she was putting down roots in her hometown. The other part of him, however, was proud of her. She was going to make her own way no matter what.

James leaned in and looked through the front window. The interior was anchored by wide-planked wood flooring, which complemented white walls and plenty of natural light. When needed, modern industrial light fixtures hung from the ceiling, and spotlights were mounted along the tops of the walls. The space was, quite literally, made for her.

Pride swelled and James wondered if she was going to display her own art, or if she would be on the lookout for the latest talent. Whatever Natalie decided to do, she would be brilliant at it.

He couldn't help but think about his encounter with her earlier that day, first at the game and then on the path that ran through campus. He'd misjudged the situation badly, and he wasn't sure how he was going to manage the awkward mess he'd created. God, he should have known better.

Still, the thought of her made him smile. Wearing jeans, a blue and gold rugby shirt sporting the Jennings crest, and trainers, Natalie had looked like a first year. Except for the fire in her eyes. The wisdom, the intelligence, the breadth of her experience shined through. Guilt spread through him when he thought about how he'd upset her. He was questioning the move regularly, not usual for him. But if he had accepted the loss of her without even an attempt at getting her back, what would that say about him? The few times he had given up on things, mostly relationships, James ended up regretting it. Whether it was a friendship, or colleague he'd lost touch with, or lover with whom he'd ended things badly, James yearned for closure.

He didn't have the closure with his father either. He'd gone back to Eton after a midterm break, and he never saw him again. They had argued right before he left—James was an arrogant ass as a teen and he couldn't remember what they'd fought about—but the next thing he knew his dad was gone, claimed by a heart attack far too young. The reason for the argument was unimportant; his regret was not saying goodbye.

Knowing he was going to be on Long Island until at least June, James resolved that he was going to find a way to reach Natalie. One way or another they would find closure. Either they would be able to find their way back to each other, or the relationship would end cleanly and, he hoped, amicably.

He stopped outside of Rinaldi's Café, checked the framed menu hung in the window, and realized it would be wise to be famished before he went in for a bite. There were too many tempting items to choose from, and he had an inkling he'd want to try everything. To that end, James decided to find the compass shop first. He was positively obsessed with the compass gift left on his desk by the faculty of the School of Arts and Sciences. He found himself playing with it, looking at all the intricate details and trying to understand what it was that made the compass so special. He felt connected to it somehow.

Fortunately, the establishment wasn't far. Heading across the street, he admired the building that housed Jennings Fine Compasses and Watches. It had to be one of the oldest structures on the street, with a large heavy wooden door and paned glass windows highlighting the storefront. While some of the panes had obviously been replaced, he saw examples of crowned glass in some of the windows. The circular wave pattern was beautiful, intricate and reminded him of the old glass you could still find in the buildings in Cambridge.

Without any more delay he opened the door and stepped inside. He had no idea what to expect, but the truth of it stunned him. It was a showplace, and a miracle. A museum in its own right. This business was hundreds of years old, the craft and tradition passed through the generations. That just didn't happen anymore.

Feeling himself drawn inside, it felt like the place was breathing. It was alive with memories and James had never seen anything like it. Antique shelves were decorated with fine glass pieces, crystal, and gift items. Some were tackier than others, but he could see there was something for everybody. There were paintings by local artists, photographs, a case of jewelry, some of which looked custom-designed. On the far wall, under a map of Compass Cove that was dated 1750, was a display case that contained a stunning antique compass.

James wondered if this was the compass that Natalie had told him about, the one that inspired the town legend. When he got closer, he saw a small portrait of a man and a woman, sealed in an archival sleeve, with a little note underneath written in that wonderful old-fashioned cursive scrawl. *Caleb and Lucy. 1751, Wedding portrait.*

Marveling at the relics in the case, a bundle of letters tied with a faded ribbon, an antique fountain pen, and a piece of jewelry, James felt his smile widen. This was exactly the kind of history he loved because it was personal. It was unique. It was the story inside the story that made history remarkable.

"Hi, can I help you?"

James turned and the look on his face must have startled the other man because he stepped back. There, standing before him, was his neighbor. He didn't know the man's name but there was no mistaking that this was the man who was talking to Natalie the other day. He was tall, with short-cropped hair and a rather boy-next-door, all-American look about him. James reached out his hand.

"I was just admiring everything in your shop. Particularly the compass and the artifacts. I'm a historian, and this is my catnip."

The man smiled and took his hand. "This entire town should be right up your alley. Not from around here, are you?"

"No, I'm on loan to the college from Cambridge. My name is James. And I do believe we're neighbors."

A wide smile broke across the proprietor's face. "You don't say? You're the new guy next door? It's very nice to meet you. Liam Jennings."

"This shop is incredible. Just brilliant. It's the kind of place you'd see in London tucked away in some narrow alley that only the locals know about."

With an acknowledgment to his surroundings Liam leaned against the display case that held the cash register. "I'll take that as a compliment. This place has the years behind it. I think there're some tchotchkes on the shelves that have been here since my great-grandfather's time. Specifically, a cast-iron dog statue. The thing gives me the creeps, but I don't have the heart to get rid of it."

James found the gentleman amusing, and he couldn't ask for a more entertaining neighbor. "I received a gift for my new colleagues at the college, a compass. It had your maker's mark."

"They welcomed you to the family. It's a tradition. We always give compasses to celebrate a new stage in our lives. The most common gift would be for a couple when they get married. It's usually purchased by a family member as a way for the couple to keep going in the same direction. In your case it's probably a nod to you finding your true north."

True north? Was James looking for his ideological home. The place where his heart was?

"That sounds complicated. But it was a lovely gesture, and the instrument is impressive. Perfect for a history guy like me."

"So, you said you taught at Cambridge?" Liam's eyes

narrowed as he sidestepped James's story. "A friend of mine just came home from living in London for a number of years."

Was that how this was going to go? Hmm. Might as well just tell the truth—there was no good reason to be cagey. "Natalie? Petite, blazing blue eyes, short hair that flips up and around like a crazed pixie?"

A burst of laughter bent Liam's head back. "That would be her. And a perfect description it is, sir."

James smiled. He was going to enjoy this. "Liam, can you take a few minutes? I was going to go to Rinaldi's for some food. Would you like to join me?"

Looking around at his empty store, Liam nodded. "Everyone is at the game for the next couple of hours. I can leave my part-timer here for a bit."

"Brilliant." James decided right then if he was going to get Natalie back, he was going to need to enlist every person in Compass Cove to help him.

RINALDI'S CAFÉ WAS charming. James was glad Liam was along to direct him through the massive menu. He wasn't quite up for the coronary-inducing specialty burger, so he settled on a bowl of fish chowder, and a cheese toastie better than anything he'd ever had at home. He was told by their server that the bread, thick and hearty, was baked on site that morning. Liam, on the other hand, ate like a dying man starting with a bowl of clam chowder and diving into a triple-decker sandwich that he called a club. The turkey, tomatoes, lettuce and bacon were piled on the same hearty bread. There were also fries. He couldn't call them chips, because they were curly. Curly fries. Quite delicious.

Liam turned out to be quite a chatty lunch companion, especially where Natalie was concerned. The two had been friends since childhood, and there was a time that they had even dated. But his concern for Natalie now was almost fraternal. It seemed the woman had a pack of older brothers both biological and otherwise. Unlike Doug Miller, Liam Jennings was more subtle. He might be protective of Natalie, but James didn't feel like he would break any bones.

"So, how do you like it on this side of the pond?" Liam said it with a faux British accent, and James found it funny. While someone else might come across as obnoxious, Liam was obviously good-natured. James had a feeling he got away with a lot because of that particular trait.

"I've been here just about a week. I've spent time in New York City, but never out here. It's absolutely beautiful. Everyone at the college has been warm and quite welcoming. I find it all very refreshing. I still don't understand why you drive on the wrong side of the road, though. That's been giving me a little bit of trouble."

Liam laughed. "We have a lot going for us. People always think Long Island is the Hamptons, traffic or nosy neighbors. Well, we do have nosy neighbors, but we like them—mostly." He sent a withering look toward an older woman who had been wiping down the counter for the last few minutes. Eavesdropping, more than likely. "It's a beautiful place, with a rich history. You should have lots of material for your research."

James chuckled. "I find the library an excellent resource. Your family has donated so many artifacts, and primary source documents I thought I'd fallen into a historical nirvana."

"There is more. I have items at the shop I'd be happy to show you any time. I also have boxes of letters, maps, deeds, files... I've had some of it restored by the archives department at one of the state university libraries. I'm keeping it in a safe right now until the Maritime Museum has some open space, or the library collection has time to absorb it all."

James couldn't believe his luck. "I'd be happy to go through it with you. I love original documents. I know a lot of my colleagues are leaning into voice records and broadcast interviews and more modern record-keeping, but nothing gets me buzzing like an old letter."

Taking a long sip of his milkshake through the straw, Liam smiled. "James, I think you and I are going to be friends."

"I agree," James said. "I think we are."

SOME WOMEN, WHEN they were upset, jumped into a bottle of wine, or ate a box of chocolates. Natalie baked. After the game she stopped at the grocery store and picked up all the supplies she would need for four different kinds of cookies. Each one filled with chocolate. She was telling herself it was a dry run for the Christmas holidays when her family gathered to do the baking, but it wasn't. It was stress. Stress over the third degree she was subjected to when she returned to the game. Stress over seeing James again. Stress over the guilt of leaving James.

Considering what she was up against, Natalie realized she didn't have enough chocolate.

The kitchen at the boathouse was small, but it was modern and highly functional. It had a double wall oven, a great range top and an ample refrigerator. There was a single dishwasher drawer set into a fabulous island with a butcher-block top. It was perfect for kneading bread, cutting and rolling cookies, or just having a cup of tea and sketching the landscape outside the window.

There was a small living room, and a bedroom and bath off to the side. She knew there were closets in the main house bigger than this little cottage, but Natalie didn't need any more. One pleasant surprise she found when she'd gotten home from the game, was that some boxes had arrived from England. A friend of hers had been charged with shipping things over a little at a time, but these were the boxes she'd been waiting for. One of them included her Christmas decorations.

So, tonight was about cookies and tea. And Christmas.

The sound of voices outside the door startled her.

Before she even had a chance to stand, the door opened, and three women walked in. Mia, who was her sister now by marriage. Lilly, her best friend forever, who was engaged to her other brother, and Jordan who was so pregnant Natalie thought she might burst. Still sitting at the island, she eyed her friends.

"You don't knock?" Her reaction was grounded in her defensiveness. She was sure they wanted information, but their eyes also told her they were there for support. Suddenly, Nat's heart beat a little harder and her insides warmed. Her people.

"Are you kidding?" Lilly said. "Since when do I knock? And since when do you not tell me about Hot Prof?"

Jordan, who understood whirlwind romances, gave Natalie the best teacher side-eye she could muster. "I am also not happy about finding out about you and Hot Prof like this."

Mia nodded. "Same. I mean, what the hell, Natalie? I gave the guy a mini-tour of the library a few days ago—he's charming, by the way—but it would have been nice to know about him. How could you leave us out of the loop?"

Because facing James wasn't enough today, now she was consumed by the guilt or not telling the people in her life about him. They were right to be upset and hurt. She had kept so many details from them it was hard to even think they still consider her a friend.

But she knew these women weren't going anywhere. Even if they were aggravated, these girls had her back. She wished she'd remembered that when she first came home, instead of suffering in silence.

"I know. I should have told you about him when we first started getting serious. But there was something special about keeping it, I don't know, between us." The three faces staring back at her were not convinced. "I should have said something."

That privacy, the sense of keeping something just for herself was rooted in the well-meaning, but never-ending advice she received. It was also rooted in the guilt, the belief that she was always disappointing her mother, or her brothers, wanting to avoid the questions that came out on a breath… *Oh, Nat…what have you done now?*

She would have heard it already if her mother hadn't gone away on a quick trip with her longtime beau. She'd been interrogated at the game by Jack and Doug, and she was sure Adam wasn't too pleased that she'd been keeping secrets. She'd left before he had a chance to say anything.

Natalie wondered if the women had been "sent." It wouldn't be beyond her brothers to use those close to them to get information, but she didn't think the girls would have gone along with it. If they were here, it was for her. Natalie had to believe that. If she didn't, she really had lost everything.

Mia, who had become more sister than sister-in-law over the past year sidled up next to her on the other side of the island. Her arm looped through Natalie's, and Mia dropped her head on Nat's shoulder. Her brother Adam had been gifted with this amazing woman, and every day he questioned what he had done to deserve her. Natalie felt the same way… Mia was a gift.

"You can tell us," Mia said quietly. "We're your family. We want you to be happy. If you want him run off, just say the word."

She meant it, too. They would circle the wagons if she needed them to. Judgment would be put aside to protect her. And that was the moment Natalie realized she'd done exactly the right thing. Had she tried to fight the earl, he not only would have gone after her, and James, but her family could have been in his crosshairs as well, even from thousands of miles away. Protecting them was worth the heartache. And Lord knows she'd had enough of that.

She couldn't tell them why she left him, for almost the same reasons she hadn't told James. He would put up a fight, he would go after his stepfather, but so would her family. The Millers would not take a threat to one of their own lightly. The implosion on both sides of the Atlantic would be epic, but Natalie wasn't going to let it happen.

James would get over her. Of that, she had no doubt. It wouldn't be easy, especially now that he was in Compass

Cove, but life would go on. Natalie would dive into her new business, James would enjoy his teaching and his writing, and they would slide into a distant normalcy.

It sounded like torture. But it was the only way.

Lilly pulled the cork on a bottle of wine. "I grabbed these bottles from the wine cellar at the main house. I didn't even look at the vintage. It's very possible I just tapped into something really expensive. So, we'd better enjoy it."

"You don't have to do anything to him," Natalie said. "He's here, and while I may not like it, he hasn't done anything wrong. The breakup was on me."

Jordan tilted her head, a question brewing in her large expressive eyes. "What do you mean it was on you?"

Leave it to the teacher to ask a question that required a complete explanation. However, without the details, which Natalie wasn't willing to share, there wasn't much to tell. "I made the decision to leave. He didn't break my heart. I'm pretty sure I broke his."

She shouldn't have said that last part.

Saying that out loud for the first time hit Natalie square in the gut. She had blindsided him with her decision, there was no doubt about it. And she died a little bit inside as she thought about it. James didn't deserve it and if leaving was proof of anything, it was that she did not deserve him.

Unfortunately, he was now in her orbit. Natalie had escaped to Compass Cove to put distance between her and her heartbreak. Funny how things never quite worked out the way you planned.

Lilly hadn't said too much. She'd been through her own trials, had kept her own secrets, and had come out the other side stronger and happier. But that strength only came when she opened up about what she'd gone through. When Natalie first arrived home in August, she made light of the event that triggered the loss of her job; hell, she'd lost the life she'd built for herself. They didn't know about the threats, or the pain Natalie went through when she was forced to leave her home and her man.

She didn't have Lilly's strength. The woman had pushed back against a vicious abuser, leaving a glamorous career to build a brand-new life. Mia had found her strength, her independence, and the love of her life, when she stood up and ended the toxic relationship with her mother. These were strong women, and she loved them, but their very presence drove home the truth of Liam's statement from the other day. She was a coward.

People often asked what she was made of; the truthful answer would be not much. Natalie tended to take the path of least resistance. Coming home had forced her to face that fact. She had to change; it was time to face the things that scared her the most and to fight for what she wanted. How to do that was the question.

"I don't want to talk about James, not right now at least, but I do have some news." Maybe telling them about her plans would show them she wasn't going to disappear again.

Almost on cue, her friends leaned in, eyes on her, waiting. Natalie felt her leg start to move as it often did when she was nervous, her foot tapping rapidly on the wood floor.

"The toy store on Main Street? You know, the one that just closed? I rented the building. I'm going to open a gallery."

Collectively, the women all dropped their jaws. That was a reaction Natalie could enjoy.

Mia was the first to regain her senses. "You did? That's amazing! What made you decide to open a business? It's perfect for you. Will you curate collections? Or is this only for local artists? Will you display your own art?"

Mia's questions came so fast, almost without a breath in between, Natalie wondered if she'd had a little wine on her way over.

"So, you're putting down roots?" Lilly smiled. "You're actually going to stay."

Natalie nodded. "That's the plan. The lease is for a year. As far as the collections—I'm not sure yet. I'm going to get in touch with some of my contacts in New York City. That'll give me an idea of what to expect, who's hot, which agent is sniffing out the best new talent. Being an art dealer in the States is very different than in Europe. But I'm excited about it. Fresh starts are always good."

That was something all four of them could agree on. A little over a year ago Mia had moved to Compass Cove with her nephew to get a fresh start in her own life. A little over a month ago she'd married Natalie's brother. Lilly had come back from California, intent on forgetting what she'd gone through when she lived there. With strength and fire, she'd made a new life for herself and fought back against the man who'd brought her so much terror. Jordan had recently lost her father, but she'd found new love with a man who'd made his own fresh start.

Life may throw a bump in the road, but it was up to each person whether or not to keep driving and make the best of it or turn around and go back to safety. The gallery was Natalie's first step in her new life.

Jordan was a month away from giving birth and started toward Nat. A few weeks ago she stopped walking and instead began wobbling in the way that pregnant women do. Once she was close enough, she gave Natalie a hug. "I'm proud of you, girlfriend. I'm sorry if your heart is broken, but we're here for you. And we will help you forget all about him if that's what you really want."

"It's for the best," she said, not really believing herself. "It will be hard having him in town, but I shouldn't have run away. Maybe we'll be able to make peace with what happened between us."

Lilly was examining the lineup of ingredients on the counter near the sink. Distracted by the beach outside the window she smiled. "How many times did we gather in this very spot, before it was fixed up all pretty, and cry about boys?"

The boathouse used to be utilitarian. It still sported weathered green shingles on the outside, but the inside had been transformed. Back in the day it had been finished enough for Nat and her friends to have summer sleepovers when they were teenagers, but it was far from finished. It never mattered, as long as they were together.

Natalie shrugged at the question. "I couldn't say," she said. "A lot. But we were always here for each other. No wine—well, mostly—but we always managed to get over whatever troubled us."

"And we will do so again," Jordan said, grasping her hand. "Now, what are we going to bake first?"

Mia grinned and lifted the bottle of wine that Lilly had opened and examined the label. "Whatever we decide, it had better go well with a 1959 Bordeaux. With a vintage like this, you want to make sure to get the pairing right."

"Well, how about that?" Lilly said on a giggle. "I really did snag an expensive bottle."

The laughter that filled the boathouse lifted Natalie out of her dark mood. The day hadn't started out well, but her friends made sure it ended that way.

Lilly raised her glass. "To new beginnings," she said. "And friends who have your back."

Hear, hear, Natalie thought. "To friends."

Chapter Seven

I T WAS LIKE being caught in a windstorm: fast, furious and a little terrifying. But it was also exciting.

Natalie always loved her work. The art world was vibrant, interesting, and ever-changing. Every day brought new challenges, and wonderful new things to explore. But now? The game had definitely changed. Opening her own gallery gave Nat a rush she'd never experienced before. Why hadn't she thought to do this sooner? Capitalizing the enterprise wasn't easy, but she knew her business, and she had a great eye and a wide contact list. It was only in prepping for the first show at her own place that she realized what she'd been missing out on.

It'd been ten days since she'd taken possession of the building. Most of the leaves had fallen off the trees and the temperature had been dropping steadily, getting very cold at night, and staying chilly during the day. She could still get away with wearing a heavy sweater or knit jacket, but winter days were coming, and Natalie couldn't wait.

Compass Cove was taking the change of seasons in stride, as it always did. The town was built to weather everything nature could throw at it. Heat waves in the summer were combated by cool breezes off the water. Fall and spring storms were buffered by a coastline that protected the town. And winter? Winter brought its own magic. It started with Christmas, led into the new year, and that's when the snow came. Natalie missed good heavy snows. London was very temperate, and it never quite brought the weather Natalie was used to.

Deciding a coffee would be a good idea, she grabbed her jacket and headed out to Main Street. Happy that Rinaldi's was a close by neighbor, Natalie found herself there several times a day, even when she wasn't working, getting a caffeine fix, picking up a salad, or indulging in one of the bakery's signature sweets meant to tempt even the most disciplined eater.

As she made her way toward the café, Natalie looked back at her gallery. Everything was happening so fast it was hard to keep up. The sign had been installed yesterday and she couldn't quite believe the pride she felt when she saw it raised and secured into place. Her vision became real in that moment, and as she watched she thought of all the people she wanted to tell.

From where she stood it looked perfect. The ancient sign bracket Liam had found in the barn at his father's house was exactly what she needed. Instead of displaying the name across the front, she decided on a hanging sign, much like those she saw walking through villages in England.

Natalie cleaned up the bracket and was lucky to find a talented painter and woodworker through one of her professors at Jennings who had been more than happy to make a recommendation. The way everything was clicking into place gave Nat the impression it was meant to be.

Group texts with pictures went to her girlfriends, her family, and two former colleagues from the gallery in London. That was particularly satisfying because with the texts to England, word of her new endeavor would get back to the owners who fired her, who were complicit in the earl's scheme. They would know she had no intention of vanishing into the ether. For the first time in her life, Natalie felt empowered. For once, she was doing something just for herself, and she wondered why it took her so long.

For much of her life, crushing fear and doubt were her constant companions. Feeling like she could never measure up drove her to exhaustion, trying to be the best at everything, to please people and meet impossible deadlines.

But this? Taking a last look at the storefront, she had no doubts about what she was doing here. Yes, she wanted it to be a success, but for once, Natalie wasn't competing. The passion burned in her.

After sending the initial stream of text messages, she found her thumb hovering over James's name on her contact list. She wanted so badly to share this with him. She'd seen him on the street, and last week when she had gone up to Liam's house to look at some of the paintings he was donating to the library, she found out James was his new next-door neighbor.

Natalie didn't send that text. He would see, soon enough, that the gallery was coming to life. Her first show was set to open the day after Thanksgiving. On display would be select, one-of-a-kind glass ornaments and tree toppers, as well as sculptures crafted by master glassmaker Liam Jennings. It hadn't been easy to get Liam to agree to show, but Natalie played on his vanity, his pride, and shamelessly used their friendship to get him to take a chance on her. He wouldn't regret it. With Christmas just around the corner, the timing for a show like this couldn't be better.

What she hadn't told him was that she'd convinced two art critics to attend opening night. One, was from a local daily newspaper that would introduce Liam to his Long Island neighbors. The other critic was from the *New York Times*, and that review could make Liam famous, and his glass very valuable.

Natalie was just about to walk into Rinaldi's when her cell phone rang. The number, which came out of New York City, was unfamiliar. But with so much publicity about Liam's debut, as well as the new gallery, she picked up any call that came in. She was glad she did. "Natalie here."

"Natalie Miller? Is that you?" Oh, she knew that voice.

"Melanie Thompson, as I live and breathe. Why are you on the other end of my phone call?" Natalie had a feeling she knew. Melanie who used to work as a curator at a large auction house, was now an art agent. Rumor had it she was looking for new talent.

"I was reading the calendar updates on the local arts website and discovered that there was a new gallery opening in a little North Shore town called Compass Cove. Imagine my surprise when I saw your lovely face next to the announcement. First, I didn't know you were back from London, and second why didn't you call me as soon you decided to open your own place?"

The woman was exhausting. She could talk faster than a cartoon character on speed. Thank goodness some things never changed. Melanie was a constant. "Honestly, Mel. It happened very fast. A space opened up in my hometown and I jumped on it. A friend is a local artist and agreed to let me have his first show. If you're looking for clients, he's going to be a hot one."

Natalie didn't know if Liam even wanted an agent, but here she was setting the trap.

"*Really?*" Oh, that tone. Mel was interested. "You know I respect your opinion. When are you showing him?"

"Opening night is the day after Thanksgiving. Should I send you an invitation?"

"I would adore one." Even if Melanie decided not to sign Liam, sending her an invitation was a good move. She could put on airs when she wanted to, but the woman was well respected. She knew what separated an artist from a hobbyist, and when she found that artist, she treated him like gold.

Other dealers, museums, and wealthy clients trusted her implicitly.

"I can't wait to see you, Natalie. Are you glad to be home?"

"I am." Turmoil aside, that wasn't a lie. Natalie was making peace with her decision. For the first time in years she felt like she was seen. She wasn't in anybody's shadow, nobody was telling her how to do something better, and she wasn't afraid of trying new things. She might make a mess from time to time, but Natalie was in her element.

"Mel, I'll send your invitation right away with a plus-one. Text me your address. If you come across any of your agent friends who might like to attend, please have them give me a call."

Melanie agreed enthusiastically to passing along the information for Natalie. If Mel did manage to get a group of agents interested, Natalie would send a car filled with champagne and canapés to drive them out from the city. It was the least she could do.

Sticking her phone back in her pocket when the call ended, Natalie turned toward the café. Just as she was about to pull the door open, James stepped out, coffee in one hand and a small white bakery bag in the other. Rinaldi's had to be paradise for his sweet tooth.

He was certainly a welcome sight for her.

"Hey there," she said as casually as possible. A little voice was whispering in her ear. *Remember, this is no big deal. He's just a guy who lives in town.* "I should have known you'd find your way here."

In theory, the little voice was correct. He was just a guy, a local for all intents and purposes, and not requiring any special treatment. He might have been James, Lord Linden, a viscount in England, but that wasn't the way it went down here. Natalie could relax.

No, she couldn't. The man turned her inside out every time he looked at her.

James didn't seem the least bit startled to see her. He was acting the way she should be acting. Casual, friendly, nonchalant. "Good morning! Are you going in for your second cup or your third?" The question was seemingly innocent, but the underlying knowledge, him knowing her need for caffeine in the morning, was intimate.

Flustered, Natalie grinned while the heat rushed to her face. "It's my second cup, I'll have you know. Stop being so judgy." She nodded at the white bag. "Find something to your liking?"

"Always. In just ten days' time I've become a regular. The hazelnut tarts are divine."

"You and that sweet tooth. I'll give you the name of my dentist." Her response made him laugh, and oh, it was a beautiful laugh. She felt the tingle start at her neck and creep along her shoulders and down her spine, filling her belly with warmth and electricity. Only James had this effect on her; no other man had ever made her toes curl.

"How is the gallery coming together?" he asked. "From what I could see through the window it was almost as if the store was designed with you in mind, just waiting for you to move in."

That was true. It was perfect for her.

At first, Natalie was annoyed that her grandmother and Lina had meddled in her business, which they swore wasn't their intention. They simply wanted her to see all the *possibilities*, Grandma said. And it was true, neither of them said anything about the shop until she noticed it herself. The idea was spinning in her head before they even sat down at the café. Begrudgingly, Natalie could admit to the fact that while they hadn't directly meddled, she did feel somewhat set up. The impromptu lunch, the walk through town, seeing Liam's glass, and finally the empty storefront—they knew exactly what would get her wheels turning. Whatever anger she felt, however, had faded, replaced by a sense of gratitude and warmth that these women knew her so well.

"I'm having my first show at the end of the month. I hope you'll come." *Why had she said that?*

His mouth picked up at the corners. "If I'm welcome, I'd love to. I hear you're showing Liam's art glass."

Natalie nodded. "And I hear you two have become friends. A couple of bachelor neighbors up there on Cove Landing."

"We get on. Truthfully, it's nice to have a neighbor. The house outside of Cambridge has so much acreage there's nobody for a kilometer or two in any direction. And I never got to know the people on either side of me in London. I think they were as transient as I was."

It could also be that for a good part of the last year, James had spent more time at her flat than he did at his own townhouse.

"Are you enjoying your work?" She was sure he was making an incredible impact at Jennings. He was very good at what he did. James was gifted with people and managed them with a deft and gentle hand, but it was the teaching that was at the core of all he did. Teaching, researching, and sharing what he discovered were James's passions. It was only now that she understood how important embracing one's passions could be.

"I wasn't sure how I was going to adapt to the system in the States. But I rather enjoy it. I like the feel of the campus—the smaller size allows you to get to know the people you work with and the students. I've connected with more people in two weeks than I did at Cambridge my first two years. Maybe that's more about me than the institution, but I'm very comfortable."

"You always had a soft spot for us Yanks," she teased.

"I certainly do." With a wink and a nod, James smiled. Lord, have mercy. That smile was lethal and Natalie's insides responded by turning to goo. "I'd better get going, I have a meeting at eleven. If you need a hand with anything…"

"Thanks," she said, now feeling her nerves jangle in response to his gaze. "I'm good, but I'll let you know. Thanks."

James turned and made his way down Main Street, fishing a key out of his pocket with his free hand. As he walked away, she held on to the door of the café watching as the feeling of missing him overwhelmed her. Her instinct was to follow him, to try to explain. But how could she make him understand what happened without full disclosure? She wouldn't be able to leave anything out.

Tamping down the feelings, Natalie focused on what was immediately ahead of her. Her gallery and creating a new life for herself. She couldn't even hope that he would be part of it.

WHY DID HE do this to himself? No matter how many times he said he would keep organized, James ended up with piles of papers on his desk, unable to find the notes he needed for his meeting tomorrow. "Bloody hell. Where is that budget?"

His plan was to take the folder home and look it over with a neat glass of scotch and a sandwich. It had taken a couple of weeks, but he finally felt settled in his new home. It wasn't grand, or ancient, but it was comfortable. At the end of the day the house gave him peace. His day had gone fine. If he looked at his schedule, every appointment, every phone call, every chat with a student or faculty member went well. What had unnerved him was his unexpected meetup with Natalie outside Rinaldi's Café.

He'd behaved admirably, all considered. He'd asked appropriate questions about her new venture and hadn't once told her how he went to bed every night thinking about her, and likewise woke up every morning missing her. Remarkable restraint, indeed.

James had two choices: get over her or get her back. Otherwise, his stay in Compass Cove would be intolerable. James swiveled his chair, taking respite in the sight of the campus walk. It was getting darker earlier and earlier, but students were still out, heading to the dining hall, or just watching the moonlight on the water. It was incredibly routine, and comforting to see that despite his inner turmoil, life went on.

A rap on the door broke into his thoughts and brought him back to reality.

"Professor Phillips?"

The deep voice told him it wasn't Emma letting him know she was going to leave. Only when he turned his chair did he see the imposing form of football coach Adam Miller standing in his doorway. He had wondered if any of Natalie's brothers were going to pay him a visit. He found the male posturing in her family to be a tad archaic, but he did appreciate that they wanted to look out for their sister.

He stood. "Coach Miller. What brings you by?"

Adam, who exuded confidence with his team, didn't

seem sure of what he wanted to say. Not what James expected. Doug Miller was all bluster. Adam, with his hands shoved deep in his pockets, already seemed to regret the visit.

Still, he pressed on. "Do you have a minute? I have a couple of questions about Natalie."

Interesting, James thought. He was very particular about how he phrased the request. There wasn't a stitch of intimidation in his voice, and it was obvious Adam Miller could be quite intimidating if he wanted to be.

"Of course." Coming around his desk, James motioned toward the sofa in the sitting area, noticing Eleanor lounging on the far corner. Adam nodded gratefully. At six foot four, his large frame filled the space. James, who wasn't lacking in height himself, felt dwarfed by the former professional footballer. Adam twisted his fingers and if James didn't know better, he'd say the man was nervous.

"Can I get you a drink? Water, a soft drink…a whiskey?"

Adam didn't hesitate. "A whiskey. Neat."

James went to the cabinet in the center of the far wall and dropped down a very elegant, concealed bar. His predecessor had left it stocked with two bottles: a twelve-year-old Speyside single malt and an excellent Irish whiskey. He poured two fingers of the whiskey into a pair of crystal tumblers and handed one to Adam. He sat in the large leather armchair that faced the sofa. Adam Miller had something on his mind.

"This whiskey," James said. "Was aged for fourteen years

in a bourbon barrel and spent the last two years in a sherry cask. It's very smooth."

Taking a swallow, he could see from Adam's reaction he agreed. "It's good, thanks."

"What's on your mind?" James saw no need to mince words. "You said you want to talk about Natalie, and I'll help you if I can, but I have no intention of breaking her confidence, or intruding on her privacy."

"I appreciate that." Adam turned the glass in his hand, obviously considering what he wanted to say. "We're very happy to have her home. But—" He took a deep breath and leveled his gaze straight at James. "She loved living in London. She loved her life. Getting her home for any length of time was almost impossible. What happened? She said she left you, so I'm going to assume you either fucked up or she did."

"I wasn't happy about it, not at all. I thought we had a future." He took a swallow of the amber liquid and felt the familiar burn in his throat before the warmth settled in his belly. "I still don't know exactly what happened. But I can tell you her leaving wasn't something either of us did, but Natalie's response to an incident at her gallery."

"That thing with the customer?" It was obvious Adam didn't like abstraction. On that, he and James were in agreement.

"Yes. I do know that, unfortunately, my stepfather was involved. Though, I have little information. Natalie isn't talking, and neither is my family."

"It's always about family." Adam wore the expression of a man who understood. "My brother told me you have a title or something. Is this all some prince and commoner story?"

"Not for me," James said. "But my mother and stepfather can be awful snobs. I just don't know what could have happened that would've caused her to react the way she did."

Adam dropped back into the sofa cushion and breathed out. "She hasn't told us much of anything. She barely talks to my mother; she keeps my brothers and me at arm's length. My wife knows something, but she's not telling, which is damn annoying." Adam rolled the glass between his palms. "I want to help, but I don't know how."

This conversation wasn't going how James expected. Adam Miller was an imposing figure...someone completely larger than life. But in this case, he was an older brother who was simply worried about his sister. "Adam, I want Natalie back. But I also need to respect her reasons for leaving, even if I don't know what they are. I'm hoping, eventually, she'll tell me. In the meantime, I'll give her as much space as she needs. I suggest you and your family do the same."

That probably wasn't the answer Adam was looking for, but James didn't have anything else to tell him. His brother had clued him in to what was at the root of Natalie's flight, but details were sparse. As much as he loved his mother, he had a sinking suspicion she was involved in it too.

Adam stood, draining his glass. Once he put it down on

the table, he extended his hand toward James. "Thank you. We're worried about her."

"She's very lucky to have all of you." James took the outstretched hand, shaking it. "I suspect, when the moment is right, she'll tell you everything, but in the meantime take comfort in the fact that she's opening her gallery. It's a sign that she intends to stay. Not what I was hoping for, but your family should be very happy."

Once he reached the door, Adam nodded. "True enough. Maybe you'll like it so much here, you'll want to stay as well. Good night, Professor. Thanks for the drink."

Chapter Eight

THERE WAS SO much to do. With just a week until the opening of Liam's show Natalie had a checklist as long as her arm. The glass started to arrive, and each piece took her breath away. She'd ordered pedestals and shelves, and stark white Christmas trees on which to hang ornaments. She'd also cut branches from trees on her grandparents' property and sprayed them with white and silver spray paint.

She had learned long ago that art in and of itself was beautiful, but art presented memorably was unforgettable. She wanted to make sure the people who walked into her gallery had a visceral, emotional response to what they saw. She wanted them to feel the effect of being surrounded by color, and light, and beauty.

She positioned pillars of different heights around the walls and in the center of the room. At the entrance, just past the reception desk, was the Christmas tree. Twelve feet tall, stark white, with opalescent glitter it positively shimmered in the light.

Her phone rang, probably the fiftieth call in the last two hours, but this time she saw it was the caterer. Natalie hit the button and answered. "Hannah, it's Natalie."

"How are you holding up?" Hannah Webster was a personal chef based in New York City, preparing meals for wealthy clients most of whom resided on the Upper East and Upper West sides of Manhattan. What most people didn't know, was that when she wasn't cooking pescatarian or the latest fad menu for the rich and spoiled, she loved to do parties.

"I'm okay," Natalie lied. "Everything is fine."

"You are going to go to hell for the lies that you are telling me. Although everything *is* going to be fine. I have no doubt about that." Natalie had met Hannah when she was in grad school at NYU and was in need of a roommate. Back then Hannah was freshly graduated from the International Culinary Institute in Switzerland and was getting her start as a sous chef at a downtown eatery that featured a tasting menu that ran around $500 a person. After learning her craft and the business, she'd broken out as a personal chef to the rich and famous. Natalie loved Hannah first because she was amazing and talented, but second because Hannah made sure Natalie ate during the years she was in grad school.

They had remained good friends and when Nat needed her party catered, she'd called the best chef in the business.

"I have everything ordered for next week, but I need you to make some of the more specific choices. Which caviar, which pâté, which gourmet fried pickle."

"Oh, my God. I love you. This is going to be amazing."

Natalie laughed but Hannah wasn't kidding. Her friend never joked about food.

"I'll send you an email; get back to me today. This grazing table is going to be fabulous."

"You're fabulous, thank you." Natalie hadn't seen Hannah in nine months. The last time they got together was in London. James had joined them for drinks, and that one meeting had her friend predicting Natalie was going to marry him. They'd been together three months, but Hannah knew there was something special between them.

Lilly and Jordan were childhood friends. They were special in ways Natalie could never explain, but her friendship with Hannah was different. She didn't know Natalie Miller of the Miller family. Hannah knew the woman who was struggling to find her place in this world separate from any identity that had been bestowed on her by birth, or bank account. And it wasn't that Lilly and Jordan judged her, but the three of them grew up in a bubble—Hannah popped the bubble.

"How are you really holding up, girlfriend?"

"Oh, you know—I'm stressed. I want this to go well. It's like I have something to prove."

"To whom?" Why did people keep asking her questions?

"Just to myself." And her family. And the town. And now James was here, she wanted him to see she was moving on.

"*Riiiight.* Prove what? You've always done your job better

than anybody else. You feel every piece of art in your soul."

"I guess. It's just…well, nobody around here knows that part of me. I want to show them, and I want it to be spectacular. I want to be seen, Han. It's important to me."

"Well, if I can help them see you better with fabulous food, I'm there for it. Call me Monday—we'll finalize the plan."

"Okay, and don't forget to send me the email. I'll talk to you soon."

She ended the call thankful for the simple support her friend had given her. In truth, she'd had more than her fair share recently. Adam had come down to the boathouse last night just to check on her. He'd wanted her to know that he wasn't going to ask questions about what happened in London, but he would listen if she wanted to tell him. It was so out of character for her bull-in-the-china-shop brother that Natalie couldn't speak for a minute. After she got over the shock, all she could do was hug him. Adam held her tight and all he said, whispered quietly in her ear, was that everything was going to be okay.

She carried that with her. His simple promise… *Everything is going to be okay, Natty.*

The rapid taps at the door brought Nat to the front of the store. Maybe it was another delivery, Liam coming to check on how things were going, but no it was her mother back from the Mediterranean, tan and beautiful, and smiling like a fool. Natalie had forgotten Mom was coming back into town.

She'd been gone for a month on a private cruise with her longtime beau, Alan Gaffney, a local doctor. Technically he was Natalie's doctor, and her mother's doctor… Alan was pretty much everyone's doctor. Yeesh. The curse of small towns. She shuddered. Unlocking the door her mother burst in and threw her arms around her. "It is so good to see you. I got home yesterday, and you didn't come to see me, you rotten kid."

"I wasn't sure you were home. You didn't tell me." Natalie looked up at her mom who was almost six inches taller than she was.

Her mother's brows furrowed as she gave Natalie a bemused look. "I didn't?"

Nat shook her head and stepped out of her mom's embrace.

"Oh. Hmmm. Well, I'm here now. I can't wait for you to tell me all about the gallery, and the opening. I mean, it happened so quickly! Your grandmother filled me in, but I want to hear about it from you."

"It did happen fast. I guess that means it was meant to be."

Linda Miller took a slow turn and examined the space with a critical eye. "My dear, you have a gift. I've seen Liam's glass. But I think once it's displayed in here—" she waved her right hand "—I will see it completely differently. Are you going to decorate this tree with his ornaments?"

"That's the plan."

"Wow. I hope Liam is ready to be famous."

Natalie was taken completely aback by her mother's kind words. She adored her mother—there was no question about that, but the boys tended to suck up all the air, while Natalie felt invisible. Maybe opening her business would take what she did from the abstract to the real.

"Thanks, Mom. I'm really excited to see how it all turns out. I have a sketch in the loft. Would you like to see it?"

"I would love to."

They took the twelve steps to the upper level of the building. The ceiling, the walls, and the floor were all painted white. There were industrial light fixtures, but the most impressive features were the three large skylights with southern exposure. Natalie had easels set up, cabinets filled with supplies, and at the far end of the room, a large desk. She'd been here only a couple of weeks, and it was already cluttered with papers, catalogs and sketches. It felt like home.

"Well, it looks like your room from when you were a teenager. So, I guess that means the creative mind is at work."

"Very funny." Her mother was correct, though. Natalie always worked like this. "My desk turns into chaos during the project, and at the end I do a complete purge and clean. It's very cathartic, and it prepares me for the next project."

"That actually makes a lot of sense." Linda walked slowly around the room gazing up at one of the skylights. "Nat, this is incredible. You took a real risk, but I think it's going to work out."

"I hope so. I want it to. I didn't realize how much I needed to do this until Grandma brought me downtown for lunch. She always seems to know exactly when to throw something in my path, you know?"

"Oh, I know. Who do you think fixed me up with Alan?"

Her mother stopped in front of the easel that had a sketch of what the room would look like on opening night. She examined it for a moment, not saying a word. Natalie joined her and it was the simple squeeze from her mother's hand that told her she had Mom's stamp of approval. Natalie was almost thirty-three years old. It shouldn't matter, but when her mother squeezed her hand, she felt safer than she had in a long time. Sadly, she had no idea it was lacking.

"So, can I ask you about the guy? You know, the one who's now here in town?"

"He is here in town. No, you cannot ask about him."

"Pfft. Well, then I take back all the nice things I said." God, her mother was a pain in the ass, but Natalie was very lucky to have her.

"Too late, Mom. Too late."

Chapter Nine

THE EVENING WAS cold and a November nor'easter was rolling into Long Island Sound. It looked to be a rough night when the storm finally hit. But in the meantime, the weather was putting on a show, with whipping winds and sporadic downpours.

He was reminded of home and summer trips to the sea with his father. The English coast could be brutal, particularly near Cornwall where the Atlantic Ocean, the English Channel and the Celtic Sea came together, and smashed against the rocks while the ghosts of sailors seemed to scream their warnings. Stepping out on his deck he could hear the rushing air howling like an animal and the waves crashing on the bluffs below. The moon was peeking out, for the time being, casting an eerie light over the churning water.

It was outrageous to be outside on a night like this. The gale-force winds were fierce and James was having trouble staying upright. Just as he turned to go back in the house, he saw her. Natalie was standing on Liam's deck holding on to the rail, and leaning into the wind. If it wasn't such an insane move, he'd be able to enjoy how beautiful she looked, as fierce and as turbulent as the weather.

But Natalie didn't have his height or his weight and staying upright was going to be an impossibility once her arms tired. The woman was insane. Fabulous, but insane. He couldn't just leave her out there knowing she could be pushed over the side or thrown off the deck flat on her back.

Turning his shoulder into the gale, James made his way across the lawn damp with sea spray, calling her name.

"Natalie! Natalie!" She couldn't hear him. Grabbing on to the fence rail James guided himself to where she was standing and called again. "NATALIE!"

That did the trick. She turned, not at all startled to see him. She raised her voice over the roaring noise. "Isn't it amazing? The wind, the water… I love when nature gets bitchy."

"It's impressive," he yelled. "But will you please come inside? I'm afraid Mother Nature might decide to push you in the drink."

"Don't be ridiculous! It's fine! It's not even raining!" she said while throwing open her arms. That was the moment a huge gust caught her petite frame like a piece of driftwood and tossed her backward. Fortunately, James was quick enough to catch her before her head whacked the edge of the deck.

"That is not *fine*." He looked down at her and noticed she was visibly shaken. "Come on, let's get you warmed up."

He didn't wait for permission but scooped her up and

walked to the back of his house, fighting the edge of the storm the whole way.

"Put me down!" Natalie wriggled in his arms, but not enough to constitute an objection. And he obliged, putting her down when they reached the large porch on the back of his house. Opening the door, he gave her a little push inside.

"Oh, crap. My bag is near the deck."

"Got it." James sprinted back to the platform overlooking the bluff and grabbed her giant satchel. The thing was damned heavy. Before heading back, he glanced over the edge and shuddered to think what would have happened if Natalie fell.

When he arrived back at his house, he found her in the sitting room, looking up. This part of the house had a soaring vaulted ceiling, and one of the walls was covered to the rafters with local art. She was completely enthralled.

It might not have been raining, but Nat's hair and face were wet, obviously from the spray, and when his hand brushed hers, he could feel her skin was icy cold.

"You didn't have to carry me," she snipped at him.

"If I hadn't carried you would you have come along without an argument?" He already knew the answer, but he wanted to hear her say it.

"No." She sniffed her irritation. Whether it was for him, or for being caught off guard by the storm, he couldn't tell.

"That's why I carried you."

She grinned, barely, and circled the room forcing a

change of subject. "Very nice. Definitely different for you, though."

"It is. I like it. It's not a large house, but it feels like it is because nothing is closed in, and the ceilings are high. I was very lucky that a residence came with the job."

"You're happy here? I mean, with your work?"

Why did she feel the need to clarify?

"I am. The school is well regarded, the students are motivated, and the faculty is exceptional. I'm very much enjoying my work. I think the American system suits me."

She was still standing awfully close to the glass door. Did she think she was going to make a run for it? "Would you like to sit down? Have a drink?"

"Oh, I don't want to put you out."

"You won't. I have tea, wine, or something stronger. I could even put something stronger in your tea." He smiled trying to ease what appeared to be nervousness. *Natalie was nervous.* And James found that development quite delightful.

"Tea is lovely. Thank you."

She followed him into the kitchen and pushed herself up onto the edge of the kitchen counter, crossing her legs casually as he filled the kettle and set it on to boil. She watched while he went through the mundane steps of making her cup of tea. It felt like many of the mornings they'd spent together after endless nights in bed.

"Do you cook for yourself?" An unusual question, but Natalie knew what kind of life he had in England. He never cooked.

"I do, sometimes. I'm bloody awful at it, but I have learned how to make a fairly decent pasta dish. Wonderful thing that internet."

"You're eating at Rinaldi's a lot, aren't you?"

She had him there. "And Dock's End. The fish and chips are excellent. Like home. Complete with mushy peas."

"Gotta have those mushy peas."

It was amazing how easily they slipped into a conversation, just like the other day by Rinaldi's. Yes, there was some tentativeness, but there was an ease and a familiarity that reminded him how much they actually liked each other.

"This is a huge change for you," she observed. "You're living alone. No cook, no live-in housekeeper—only what? Two bedrooms?"

"Three. You make me sound spoiled." The country house had twelve bedrooms, and only one was in regular use.

"Maybe you are spoiled," she began. "A little."

The tone of her voice had taken on a soft and flirty lilt. James felt his gut tighten. She was here, in his house, a storm was raging and the bedroom was less than twenty feet away. Moving closer he planted his hands on either side of her hips and leaned in. "I think you have mistaken me for some other viscount. I'm the nice one."

Natalie burst out laughing, throwing her head back, the joy palpable. The jolt of his heart was proof of how much she still affected him.

"Go ahead, have your fun."

"I will." If she was bothered by her ordeal on the bluff, she'd shaken it off. "Really, are you adjusting okay?"

"I am. I certainly understand why you spoke so fondly of the place. It's rather special. And not just because you're here."

"Awww." She gave him a gentle punch on the shoulder to go along what could be described as an "aw shucks" face.

James caught her hand before she had the chance to pull it back, threading his fingers through hers. Their eyes locked and held while the room around them stilled, the only sound was the wind pounding the outside of the house, while his heart thudded against the inside of his chest. He could feel it beating for the first time in months.

Before his head had a chance to stop him from acting, James leaned in and grazed his mouth softly across hers. The shocks and tingles were deliciously familiar.

To his surprise and delight, Natalie didn't retreat, but pressed her forehead to his.

"Sneaky," she whispered when he tilted his head back to take in her face. Then she teased his lips with a little peck. "You know I can't resist you."

There was nothing quite so sweet as Natalie's kisses, and James swore he would never tire of them. The pressure, the softness, the taste of her was a miracle.

"That's good to know. It gives me hope."

He remembered the first time they met. It was just after

Christmas last year, and it took months before he had the nerve to invite her to dinner. James thought it fitting that he met the woman he considered a gift during the holiday season. He wondered if Christmas in Compass Cove would offer similar magic, and if that magic would help them find their way back to each other.

Still kissing, only their lips touched as they cautiously got used to each other again. Soft explorations and teasing sips brought back how she tasted, like vanilla and cinnamon, the flavor of warm cookies on a cold day.

And her scent…a heady combination of sage and lavender drew him closer to her warmth. They leaned into each other, her breasts brushing his chest ever so lightly, but still their hands didn't move, afraid that if they engaged them in the dance that would give them permission to explore further.

James would take whatever he could get and if these long, unhurried kisses were all she would offer, he would be thankful that she still wanted him.

His groin ached, his heart pounded, his body felt flushed. Their tongues touched briefly, still gentle, but the kiss was becoming more intense. They were caught up in the moment. There was a dreaminess in each move, each touch, each breath.

The beep from the electric kettle brought them both down from whatever cloud they'd settled on. Natalie's eyes drifted open and landed on his. The blue of her irises was dark, stormy. "Oh, boy," she breathed out. "I didn't expect that."

James knew what he said in that moment was critical. He didn't want to sound possessive, or dismissive, or needy. But he was needy. He needed her. "Neither did I, but it was quite pleasant."

Pleasant? Did he just say it was pleasant?

"That it was," she said, smiling shyly.

He could feel the longing for her consume him. It wasn't new, these were old needs coming home to roost.

"That was never our problem," she said rubbing a hand across her belly, a sign she was nervous. "It's late. I think I'm going to pass on the tea and go home."

Bugger it. He'd scared her off.

"Is it safe?" He glanced outside and saw the wind was stronger and the rain had come. He'd been told that the weather was going to make driving treacherous.

Natalie frowned when she looked outside and saw the rain coming down sideways. The storm had worsened, and she was undoubtedly spooked by her tangle with the wind. "Crap, this blew in fast. The roads are probably flooding already."

"You could stay. There are two rooms upstairs."

Her eyes fixed on his, going deep. Was she searching for the reason to say no?

"James…"

Reaching for her hand, he laced his fingers with hers. "I

can't let you leave. I'd never forgive myself. Stay at Liam's then, if you won't stay here."

"Liam is at his glass house. He'll work there all night. He said the storm inspires him." She rolled her eyes like a teenager. "Such a diva."

It was James's turn to laugh. Even when she was gripped with indecision, she could still make him laugh. "Then stay. I'll be on my best behavior."

"Like a few minutes ago?" She had him there. It might be a cliché, but he was drawn to her like a moth to a flame.

"I will…do better." He would try, but God, she was tempting. Natalie must have sensed his struggle, knowing she wielded incredible power over him. When she bit her lower lip like she was doing at that very moment, looked up at him through the veil of her inky lashes, he was a dead man.

"James?" Her voice came out on a husky whisper at the same time she leaned in. Their lips were a hair's breadth apart. He could feel the soft puffs of air from her mouth tickling his lips.

"Yes?"

"This isn't a good idea."

"No?" He knew that his heart was in deep, deep trouble. He didn't care, but she might and he wouldn't drag her where she didn't want to go.

"Nope." She looped her arms around his neck, her fingers threading through his hair.

He took her word for it and settled on accepting whatever consequences came out of their actions. James leaned in and kissed Natalie again. His beautiful, vibrant Natalie. The woman occupied every dream, every fantasy. When she pulled him the final inch, James kissed her knowing he was being consumed by the storm, and he didn't care.

THIS WAS SUCH a mistake, and it was her own doing. Natalie knew Liam wasn't home when she drove up to Cove Landing. She also knew there was a bad storm on the way. She rationalized the errand by telling herself that he needed the special boxes to transport his glass from his studio to the gallery. While she was there, of course, she had to get a look at the storm from his deck. Natalie loved nature and she especially loved storms. She always felt like there was one churning away inside her, which could be why bad weather was comfortable. The more Mother Nature raged, the better.

But if she was honest, her trip to the landing wasn't about any of those things. It was about the man kissing her. She was in a tangle with James, stranded in his house on the cliff, and heading toward the sweet comfort she found only in his bed. She should be running to save herself from the inevitable heartache, but instead she was hanging on to him like her life depended on it.

Thank God. Leaving him had been so hard, but the last few weeks just knowing he was in town, that he still cared for her, was pure torment. Now, wrapped in his arms, Natalie felt whole again. Even if it was only for a little while.

"I meant what I said about the guest room. It's not a ploy to keep you here. I just want you safe…"

"Shh. I know." She clung to him like he was the only one who could keep her safe. Natalie wrapped her legs around his waist when James slid his hands under her bum and lifted her up. He was so strong, her refuge in the midst of confusion, and she had walked away from him at the time she needed him the most. The loss she felt coming home was still fresh and raw. This moment between them, this night might give them a chance to say goodbye. If not literally, figuratively.

Natalie thought he might take her directly to his bedroom, but ever the gentleman, James went to the couch in the living room and settled with her there. He tucked her into the crook of his arm, turned down the lights and allowed them to get used to each other again. It had been too long since she felt his arms, the warmth of his body, or absorbed the scent of him.

Whatever reservations she had, he helped them melt away. He wouldn't rush her, wouldn't take advantage of her…it was enough to just be together. Natalie wondered if James was as overwhelmed by the situation as she was. She also wanted to ask him about his motivation, his intentions. What made him leave England and move to the small town where she lived on Long Island? Was it an opportunity he couldn't give up? Was it to get her back? To get an explanation? Or a combination of all three?

"I want to know everything," she said. "How you got the offer to come here, how it's been at Jennings, how you like my town. Tell me." Natalie was desperate to listen, to hear his voice, and allow it to soothe her in the way that only James could.

"I think I told you my friend Harry knew the dean, and when I talked to her it sounded like a reasonable opportunity for me. I felt like a ghost rambling around my big house or sitting alone in London. Without you, everything felt gray. It wasn't until I arrived that I realized how close the college was to your hometown. And then I discovered the connection. Your brother, your sister-in-law, you."

"You really didn't know?" She glanced up, but he wasn't looking at her. His eyes were fixed at some point outside the window.

His hand had started tracing tiny circles on her upper arm. It was something he would do when they watched TV together or snuggled in bed after sex—another little comfort that Natalie had missed. "I knew you would be nearby when I learned the school was on Long Island. I didn't make the connection until I got here that the college was a stone's throw from your hometown. I hoped I would be able to see you because I want to make sense of what happened. But I was also trying to get away from the memories. You were everywhere. The day Harry came to me with the proposition,

I found one of your hair clips in my bathroom."

It was always the little things, wasn't it? She'd had a similar experience when she found a pair of his socks when she unpacked a box that had arrived from England. They were too big for Natalie, but she wore them often, flopping around her house, letting the softness embrace her like a warm memory. Every day there were at least a dozen things that made her want to call him, or talk to him, or triggered a memory—it was undoubtedly a sign that getting over him was going to be difficult, if not impossible.

"I'm sorry." She didn't know what else to say to him, but the apology felt inadequate. Was she going to keep hiding behind this wall she'd built to keep her emotions in check?

"You don't have to be sorry. I just want to understand."

"I know." Hell, she wanted to understand too. "Tell me about your work. I want to hear everything. I went to Jennings, and you know it's special to my family."

Pulling back, James looked surprised. "I thought you went to New York University."

"I did a joint graduate program at NYU. My undergrad work was at Jennings. I studied art. Painting."

"I know you painted, but I had no idea you were trained. *A painter.* Brilliant."

Calling her a painter was a stretch, but the thought was lovely. "I hadn't made art for a very long time. I've gotten back to it a little since I've been home. My gallery has a wonderful loft. It's the perfect studio."

Only a few people knew she'd started painting again. Her mom. Liam. And now James.

"I like the name of the gallery. I knew it was yours when I walked by and saw the coming-soon sign."

Belgravia Gallery. It reminded her of her beautiful flat and the walk she took to work every day.

"Thank you. Fitting, I think, to name it after the place that gave me sanctuary for so many years. I miss it."

"Do you? You seem so happy here."

How could she not? Natalie nodded, tears in her eyes as she turned her face away, happy for the low light of the room that allowed her to hide. Belgravia was one of London's prettiest neighborhoods, filled with grand old buildings, gorgeous gardens, the loveliest shops… It was charming, and from the first moment, Natalie felt as though she belonged there.

She missed the bakery where she could get the best crusty French bread, the sweet-smelling flower shop, and her favorite grocer where the little old Turkish proprietor put aside a collection of her favorite fruits the moment they were in the store. Mostly, she missed the tiny little café where she picked up an espresso and a croissant every morning before going to work. She'd met James there. Several days a week when they were on the same schedule—she going off to work, and him catching a train to Cambridge—they would smile, exchange pleasantries, or have a short chat while waiting for their orders. It was lovely.

He was lovely.

One morning, an unexpected shower had sprung up just as she was about to step onto the sidewalk. Of course, it was the day she'd forgotten her umbrella. Just as she was about to make a run for it, a large black umbrella popped open over her head. James stood next to her, smiling.

"Which way are you headed?"

"Down to Pimlico Road. I'm a curator at Blue's Gallery."

Taking a sip of his coffee, he nodded. "I'll walk you."

"Oh, please don't put yourself out. It's exceedingly kind, but don't you have to catch a train?"

His smile bloomed wide; Natalie would never forget it. "Actually, I don't," she remembered him saying a bit sheepishly. "The last few weeks I've been working at the British Library. I only come to the café to see you."

Natalie always thought the idea of her heart going pitter-pat was absurd. Until it happened. In that moment she had butterflies in her stomach, a flush in her cheeks and her heart was hammering away in her chest. She was a walking, talking cliché, and it was wonderful. When he delivered her to the gallery door, he asked her out to dinner, and she accepted.

They clicked. It was like the universe was waiting for the right time to bring them together. They saw each other almost every day until she'd bounced herself back to New York.

She was moving forward, but her heart was still his.

Maybe he didn't notice she was on the verge of crying. If he did, he didn't say, but he did pull her closer.

"Would you like me to turn on the telly?"

"The baking show?"

He smiled down at her and nodded. It was a favorite of theirs, perfect for nights when they just needed to decompress. It also inspired some crazy kitchen escapades when the two of them would try their hand at the recipes. Natalie had gotten quite good. James, as he admitted earlier, not so much. They had fun together, and as the sweeping introduction to the show played and the white tent came into view on the flat screen on the wall, Natalie let the mindlessness of the moment lull her into an unexpected sleep.

Chapter Ten

NATALIE AWOKE, ONLY slightly, as she settled on a soft mattress. The last thing she remembered was sitting close to James on the couch and watching TV while the storm blew outside. It was very possible she had driven up to Cove Landing for exactly this. Closeness. Protection. *Him.*

She must have fallen asleep, which shouldn't surprise her considering how tired she'd been since deciding to open the gallery and having her first show in less than a month's time. Working from early morning until well into the night, Natalie was a woman possessed. She was also a woman exhausted and James gave her a safe place to collapse for a little while. She could have gone to Lilly, Jordan, or Mia— they all would have given her a place to hang out and relax. The girl time would have been good for her, but they would have asked a lot of questions and Natalie was too tired to think up any answers.

She heard James milling around the bedroom, being as quiet as possible because he thought she was still asleep. What was he planning? Glancing around the room she could see she was in the main bedroom. It was large with a high ceiling and a big window across from the bed that faced the sound. The view was spectacular, but the bed was heavenly.

"What are you doing?" she asked.

"Oh, did I wake you?" James sat on the edge of the bed but down toward her feet, not anywhere he could get into trouble.

"It's fine. I can't believe I fell asleep. Are you making a fire?"

There was wood on the hearth near the fireplace in the corner of the room. She also saw a small pile of kindling.

He nodded. "The power went out. It's a bit chilly. The fire should keep you warm."

Natalie was thinking he could keep her warm. They could keep each other warm.

"Where are you going to sleep?"

"I'll sleep on the sofa. I've fallen asleep there quite a bit since I arrived. It's very comfortable."

Natalie was not going to let him sleep on the couch. Not when he made a point to tell her he had extra bedrooms. "I can sleep in one of the guest rooms."

"The guest rooms don't have fireplaces, and as I said, the house is getting chilly."

She folded her legs, settling her back against the soft pillows. What had been her end game tonight? "I'm not very much fun anymore," she muttered. "I've been so tired."

"No worries. You have a lot on your plate." James leaned over the hearth and started to place the logs carefully in the firebox. He set the kindling, and in just a few minutes the fireplace started to put out heat and a warm glow. Natalie hadn't realized she was so cold.

"That should do the job." He slipped into the bathroom, and washed his hands, then grabbed a sweatshirt from his closet before heading for the door.

"I feel terrible about this. I'm so sorry. Maybe—"

He stopped just before leaving the room and turned. His expression was full of questions, but his eyes were heated. Even in the dim light she could see his desire. What had she done? No doubt, her need was equal to his, and it wouldn't take much to push them right over the edge. But was that a good thing?

"Nat, it's fine. I'll be perfectly comfortable."

"That's ridiculous and out of the question." Good grief, she sounded like a British governess issuing orders. "I can sleep in one of the guest rooms. I'll use extra blankets. You shouldn't have to sleep on the couch." Natalie hated that he was putting himself out like this just because she'd had a hairbrained idea to head up to the top of the bluff.

"I mean," she hesitated. "We could share. It's a very large bed and I don't take up much space."

He hesitated. The words at the end of his tongue were probably too painful to hear anyway. She had to face the fact that she'd hurt him, and he had a right to be wary of her. "It's not going to drop below freezing tonight, and the storm should be gone by morning."

She didn't want him on the couch though, fine or not.

Good Lord, what was she thinking? "But—"

"Natalie, I'm not going to suffer for it. My time in the Royal Marines sufficiently prepared me for a cold night here and there."

He was such a gentleman, a scholar, she always forgot he was a war hero. The way he told it, he'd lived in a bubble his whole life. That wasn't even close to the truth.

Natalie sat up straight and folded her hands in her lap. "Please don't be stubborn," she said her voice strained. "And don't make me ask you again."

He chuckled softly. "I don't recall you asking me anything."

He was going to make her say it. Damn. "Would you like to share the bed?"

"Are you sure?"

"I think we can handle it." Natalie wasn't sure of anything. The words she couldn't say—wouldn't say—were that she needed him. "I won't be able to sleep at all knowing my carelessness put you out of your warm bed."

She wasn't lying—Natalie would feel horribly guilty. But more than any reason or excuse, being with James calmed her. Ever since she'd come home, even with all the good things going on, nothing felt right. Most days she couldn't get away from herself. That was until James came to town. It was only then that her heart seemed to settle on a path. A coincidence? Perhaps. But she'd discovered his first day on campus was the day she went to lunch with her grandmother. The day she was tempted to hold Lucy's compass because she felt something in the air had shifted. It was the day she decided to open her own gallery.

Maybe the universe was sending her a message not just that they could fix things between them, but that they should. *Maybe he could stay…*

It was the first time that thought popped in her head. It wasn't necessarily reasonable, but it teased at something deep inside. Hope. Just like he said. It gave her reason to hope.

Natalie was certainly entitled to her dreams, but she didn't have to believe in them. What she could believe in was the here and now, and that seemed to be the much safer choice.

THIS WOMAN WOULD be the end of him. Natalie and her behavior had him completely turned around. He couldn't figure out what had brought her up to the bluffs in the first place. She grew up here, and she knew wicked storms like this rolled in every fall and every spring. Yes, most people got through them without incident; however, the unpredictability of the wind, rain and the tides made what she did incredibly risky. Driving up the twisty road to Cove Landing was foolish, but having her land in his bed? That was completely bonkers.

She was beautiful lying there her head resting on her arm as she gazed at him. Her face was free of all makeup and her eyes, bright blue and speckled with gold, dominated her delicate features without any need of enhancement. Those eyes held all Natalie's stories.

"Are you going to sleep in your clothes? Or would you like a T-shirt?"

Natalie smiled. "Do you mind if I borrow a shirt?"

He wasn't quite sure of her game. She was inching toward victory if it was to drive him crazy wanting her. He sensed it was more than that, though. Much more.

Going back to his closet he surveyed the contents and grabbed a T-shirt he hoped would elicit a reaction. When he tossed it to her, he got his wish. The peal of laughter shot around the room, lighting it up.

"The Hairy Coo!" She held up the shirt admiring the graphic. "That was such a fun trip." The shirt was dark olive green and sported a line drawing of the famous Highland cow, or as Nat called it the "*Harry Cooooo*," using a pathetic, but adorable, Scottish brogue. Their long weekend in Scotland had coincided with Natalie's visit to an estate appraisal outside Edinburgh. While she was working, he did some research at the Scottish genealogy archives. It was the perfect mix of business and pleasure, allowing him to see another side of her. Being able to watch her in action, appraising the contents of an old estate, dealing with a myriad of different people, he was sure that's when he fell for her completely. He was half in the bag for months, but that trip cemented his feelings. She was kind, open, willing to learn. Natalie understood that the items she looked at were part of history, and part of someone's life. Nothing was ever just a price tag. She would never have a stiff upper lip with that big heart of hers and that suited him just fine.

They did find time for a side trip out to the country. It was during their excursion that Natalie came across her first Highland cow at a little roadside farm in the town of Beauly near Inverness. She was in love, specifically she fell for an orphaned youngster, who was named Fraser after the character in the Outlander saga. Fraser the Cow was jet black, and at just a year old, already had an impressive shock of hair falling about his eyes.

"This is wonderful. Thank you."

James had a few sneaky bits up his sleeve, and he wasn't above using them if it helped Natalie remember everything they'd had. "You're welcome. I have very fond memories of that trip."

Their eyes met and her expression softened.

"James…" she whispered.

Before she could say something that could spin an already tenuous situation out of control, he pointed to the door to her right. "The bathroom is over there. I believe there's an unused toothbrush in the cupboard."

"Thank you." Natalie gripped the T-shirt in her hands and made her way inside, closing the door. As soon as he heard the latch click, he let out the breath he was holding. Jesus.

James wasn't kidding when he told Nat he could manage being cold. He had blankets and clothing. He'd be fine. What he couldn't handle was her.

Yanking a pair of flannel pants out of his bureau drawer and following it with a long-sleeve shirt, he wished he had a pair of pants for Natalie. Thinking about her bare under that T-shirt had his cock twitching uncomfortably. Frantically, he looked through the drawers, but came up empty. Everything was too big. He had socks to give her, grabbing a thick wooly pair that would swallow up her tiny feet.

He changed quickly and checked his phone. He had a good charge, but the signal was spotty. They were definitely on their own tonight.

He heard the bathroom door open and the patter of Natalie's feet rocketing around the room. She went past him in a flash of green T-shirt and bare legs.

"Cold, cold, cold, cold," she repeated as she ran from the bedroom into the sitting room and then came back with her monstrous Bohemian-looking tote that was more luggage than handbag. What did women carry in those things?

She tossed the bag, which landed with a thud on the mattress, then hopped onto the bed, bounced down and pulled the covers over herself. "Oh, my God. The temperature dropped fast."

James didn't really feel it, but Natalie had often said she

had no blood. She loved the idea of winter and cold weather, but the truth was she only tolerated it.

"What do you keep in there?"

"My bag? It's my everything. I always carried a large bag in London."

"Not like that you didn't." He remembered a refined, cognac-colored tote made of very expensive leather. It was a fair size, but it was very different from what sat in the middle of his bed. This was a patchwork of color, rough and un-structured, with leather handles. It looked like she could transport a small child.

"Times change. Now, with luck, I have pants in here." Natalie unzipped the top and started unpacking.

"I beg your pardon? Pants?"

One item at a time, she dug through the bag. Her phone came out, and like him she checked for a signal and the charge. Satisfied, she put it on the night table. Next came a journal of some sort, a little pouch, a bigger pouch, a hair-brush and as she plunged her arm in almost to the shoulder, Natalie said, "*Ah ha!* I knew I had a pair."

With that she pulled out what appeared to be a pair of tights of some sort. "That's it," he said. "From now on I'm calling you Poppins."

"Aw! That's one of the nicest things you could say to me. Mary Poppins is awesome. She's *practically perfect in every way.*" Her clipped English was spot-on, including the way she rolled the "r."

He would have argued Natalie was perfect—no practically about it. "You literally have everything in there."

"I guess, I mean I need to have everything with me. I never know what's going to happen, so I like having my stuff." She started to go through each of the items. "My traveler's journal holds all my notebooks. I have a planner, a calendar, a little sketchbook and a general notebook, you know, for grocery lists or things I find out at a doctor's appointment...stuff." She shook one of the pouches and he heard it rattle. "These are my pens."

"How many do you have in there?" he asked. "It seems excessive."

Natalie gave him a bad look. He'd seen Lina Rinaldi give people that look and he wondered if that's where she learned it. "My pens are my pens. I have exactly as many as I need, until I need more. So, you can just take a step back about my pens."

James smiled. "Noted."

"Obviously, this is a hairbrush, a scrunchie—because you always need a scrunchie. This pouch has my makeup. Oh!" She shook a little glass spray bottle and spritzed. "Travel-sized perfume. I have breath mints. I also have keys, my tablet and these extra yoga pants. Which will keep me warm all night."

James had a sort of reckoning while surveying the cache she'd spread out on his bed. This was who she was. How had he not seen it? The colors, the textiles, the excess and the austerity combined, made for an interesting and enlightening picture. Natalie was never the woman who should be carrying the expensive bag or wearing stilettos every day. Naturally, she could pull it off, but she was happiest in yoga pants and a comfortable shirt helping people understand the beauty of the world that surrounded them.

James took the socks he'd picked out for her and passed them over. "These should keep your feet warm."

Natalie smiled at him, clutching the socks in both her hands. "Ohhh. Yes, these will keep my feet nice and toasty. Thank you."

Without any warning, Nat lay on her back, threw her legs up toes pointed at the ceiling, and pulled on the leggings like an acrobat. Then she dropped her feet flat on the bed and lifted her bum just enough to pull the leggings into place over a pair of lacy panties.

"That was impressive," he commented, remembering her flexibility all too well.

She didn't say anything, but sent a mischievous grin in his direction.

The socks slid on her feet easily and as James suspected they were too big, but Natalie didn't seem to mind. She tucked herself under the covers and looked out the window at the storm.

"Wow. It's no wonder the power went out. I wonder what happened."

There were no trees in the back garden, which was lucky

since he'd heard hundreds of trees came down in a storm that ravaged Compass Cove the previous March. But as far as the current outage, he had no clue. It could be anything.

DRIVING RAIN AND wind slapped at the big windows, and James was relieved to have Natalie tucked safely in his bed. He'd be on his best behavior, but it felt good and right just to have her here. Maybe they could talk a little, try to find some common ground to move forward. They were good together and he had to help her see that.

"Nat, I was thinking…" He trailed off when he looked over and saw she was curled into the pillow already asleep.

How the hell had she done that? Two minutes ago she was flipping around like an acrobat.

She looked innocent, though, like nothing could touch her, and as long as he was close by, nothing would. Her skin glowed in the firelight, translucent in some spots and luminescent in others. Flawless. Her full lips were a gentle pink and her lashes were an inky dark veil on her cheeks.

Turning on his side, James brushed his knuckles over her cheek. She stirred ever so slightly and that was the moment that cemented his intentions toward her. He could not give her up without a fight. He'd wondered for weeks what had happened between them. Now that he had more information, courtesy of his brother, he was going to get to the bottom of what happened at the gallery. Getting her back—that was all he wanted.

She was all he wanted.

"Good night, James," she whispered. "Thank you for saving me."

"Good night, Nat. My pleasure."

Chapter Eleven

NATALIE OPENED HER eyes and noticed the filtered light of early morning slipping into the windows. Where was she? It took her a second to remember that she was at James's house, and that she'd slept over because the storm had rolled in a lot faster than she thought it would.

God, she was in his bed.

On her left, Natalie saw the hulking form of his lordship, on his back, arm thrown over his head, mouth slightly open. A light snore escaped with each breath.

It was like long-lost music to her ears.

Reaching for her phone on the night table she focused on a slew of messages that had come in. She was sure one was from Liam, and then there would be scattered messages from her family. Natalie had gone completely off the grid in the middle of a major storm without so much as a word to anyone who cared about her. Wasn't she just a peach? She owed every single person an apology.

She was right about the text from Liam—his was first.

Where are you? Your car is here but you aren't.

I'm fine, I'm fine. I'm next door. I'll be over in a little while.

Should I ask? he responded.

Natalie sent a one-word answer: *No.*

"Nat? Are you okay?" James. His voice, husky with sleep, surprised her, but then she realized she must have repeated that last text aloud to herself. This was awkward. Last night when she drove up all she was thinking about was him. She was reckless, which at least kept her on brand.

"I'm fine. Sorry I woke you. I have a dozen text messages from people wondering where I am. I'm just so considerate that way."

He sat and scrubbed his hands over his face. "Storm looks to have passed. What time is it?"

"It's a little after seven. I think the power is back."

"Bedroom lights on," he said to the AI device. It obliged by turning on the lights. "We do indeed have power. I'll be right back."

He headed into the loo, while Nat answered all her texts, reassuring everyone she was fine. She let them know she'd stayed with a friend when the storm intensified. That seemed to calm most people, and honestly, she would have texted if she'd had a signal, but the cell service was crap.

When he emerged, James sat next to her on the edge of the bed. He had that wonderful, musky smell she remembered when he would wake after a good night's sleep. Every nerve ending fired in response. "Have you calmed the masses?"

"I think so. Thank you for putting me up. I know you weren't expecting…"

He silenced her with a kiss that was gentle and sweet, and held the promise of whatever she wanted.

"Oh. Ah, good morning."

"Good morning." His face was inches from hers, just a tiny movement by either one of them and their mouths would meet again. "We need to talk about a few things."

"I suppose we do." She caught his essence, a scent that was deep and earthy. She could practically taste his breath, cool and minty. It was heady and beautiful being near him again. So close…so damn close.

"I mean we can. Do you want to talk right now?"

"Not really," he said right before he lunged at her and they collapsed backward on the bed.

The kiss had unleashed the hunger in them. The passion that had been bottled inside her since she left him, came out in a great rush. The first kiss this morning, chaste and probing, gave way to the crush of his mouth, tangled tongues, gasping breath, and then, James left her mouth and moved to her ear, her jaw, dragging his lips and teeth across her skin. "I want you, Nat. I've missed you."

"I've missed you, too. So much. Help me get this off." She wriggled out of the long-sleeve T-shirt and James, ever the gentleman, helped her get it over her head. Then, after he stripped to his boxer briefs, he peeled off her leggings leaving her in just her lacy panties while his hands ran over her body, touching and teasing while his eyes traveled over her as well. Smiling as he reacquainted himself with her.

"You're sure?" he asked.

She thought he might die if she said no, but it was always an option. Not that she would. She wanted him inside her, so much she burned. "Yes."

Having been granted permission, James hooked his fingers in her panties and pulled them down, and then rid himself of his own. There were so many things wrong here. They should have talked first. Established ground rules. Thought it through. But when he kissed her, she lost her mind. That's the way it had been since their first date last spring.

The man was her weakness, her madness. With his lips and tongue, James started his exploration at her collarbone. Kissing every bit of skin, sucking on her breasts, and trailing his tongue down her belly. When he pushed her knees apart, Natalie sucked in a breath, waiting for the inevitable explosion. He knew her body, where to touch, how she would respond, and he played it like an instrument. Body and mind, no one knew her like he did.

"You know what I love about this house?" His voice was gravelly, his eyes dark.

The house? "I don't know…what?"

"I can make you scream, and no one will hear. Not like your flat. Not like my house in the country with all the staff. It's just you and me."

"I hadn't thought about that." Obviously, he had. Lord have mercy. "Screaming could be fun, I mean, of course, depending how I get there."

"I think you'll like it." He lowered his head and teased her sex with his tongue. Lightning shot through her and a moan escaped.

He did it again, and she bucked, forcing him to hold her hips with his hands. She loved having his hands on her again, every touch, every tease was like coming home. "I love it when you...oh, my God!"

He licked her again, this time stopping to suck the nub, massaging it with his mouth, sending her higher and higher, closer to the bliss she'd only ever found with him. The sensations were driving her mad, from the softness of his hair tickling the inside of her thigh, to the calloused pads of his fingers, she took it all in, remembering that he knew just how to touch her. No one made her feel like he did.

Over and over, he paced his mouth and tongue in a gentle rhythm. His hands kept firm hold of her, letting his mouth do the work. He knew just when to pull back to keep the pleasure going. To get her begging for more. Her cries were of submission and gratitude. She'd have done anything for this man. "James, please...please. I need you."

He went back to work on her. "Not quite yet. You haven't screamed."

He was relentless. Her heart was thumping wildly, as he moved her closer to climax. Her body flashed hot and cold, and each touch, each caress was a command.

Natalie felt the tightening in her core, the heat radiating

from the center. The spasms started slow, moving over her like a wave, crashing and dragging her under. The rush of power peaked with her body going taut, before dropping on the bed, boneless and spent.

While she was catching her breath, James eased himself over her, so handsome and grinning from ear to ear. He was damn pleased with himself.

"I screamed, didn't I?" Nat wasn't sure; she might have blacked out.

"Like a banshee."

Natalie felt herself blush. "Wonderful."

James leaned in to kiss her, long and slow. "It was. Let's see if you can do it again."

JAMES WAS WHISTLING. He never whistled, but after the last two hours in bed with Natalie it seemed a completely appropriate response. This woman was under his skin, and he would never get over her. He didn't want to. She was his match, his mate, his future. The only thing holding them back was her hesitance. Whatever happened with his stepfather back in London it was bad enough to keep her from going all in, but now that James had opened the door a crack he intended to find out exactly what it was.

Some kind of unseen pressure was working on her—the story she was telling about the run-in with his stepfather wasn't what it appeared on the surface. He knew that much. He also knew she'd had tea with his mother two weeks prior, and while Mother gushed about how lovely Natalie was, there was that edge to her voice, something that told James the countess was hiding something.

He never would have believed his family would be involved in underhanded tricks, but his blinders had been ripped off. It wasn't that Natalie didn't care about him—she did. He only wished she would let him in.

James wished he could chuck the whole life. Everything—the title, the house, the privilege that came from simply being born with the right name. His brother could have it. He didn't care if he was the heir; all he wanted was a life with Natalie. He wasn't certain, but it appeared that his place in the aristocracy was creating a roadblock to them being together.

What if he did stay stateside? He had the academic pedigree to get a job anywhere. He'd already had offers from American universities. He could work at the British embassy, as a liaison or he could just write. He wasn't destitute or without the means to support himself. He'd thought about it a year ago when a tempting offer had come in from a prestigious university. He'd stayed put mostly because his damned sense of duty got in the way. But staying with Natalie was outweighing any tradition or obligation.

HE SMELLED FRESH coffee and when he walked by the French door that led to the rear deck, he caught a glimpse of Natalie out by the stone wall that faced the bay. She was a sight. One of the wool blankets he'd had on his sofa was draped around her shoulders while she clasped a white china coffee mug in her hand. Her hair was a bit messy, the strands tossed by the gentle breeze, but it was her face—serene, flushed with color—that drew him in. Even from here, he could see Nat's eyes as the sun caught the fire in the blue depths. The water had barely a ripple, everything was calm, which was a relief after a rough night. The temperature had dropped, almost as if the storm had allowed the colder weather to invade the northeast. Thanksgiving was in a little over a week, Christmas in a little over a month. By New Year's he wanted to put his great-grandmother's ring on Natalie's finger.

He was in love with her. He'd dodged the fact for months. They kept telling each other they were keeping things casual, but there was nothing casual about their relationship. It was passionate, intense, but more than that they were the other's best friend. James was a nobleman, a scholar, and an officer—he didn't deal in sentimentality.

But with Nat, his heart was lost.

He poured coffee into his travel mug and debated breakfast. He should be ravenous, but he was too preoccupied to think about food, so he'd leave the decision until he got to the office.

When she came in, her smile flashed wide when she saw him. His heart tripped in response.

"You look very handsome, Professor." Natalie approached and put her hands flat on his chest. Rising on her toes, she planted a kiss on his cheek—it was sweet, almost platonic. Which didn't feel right to him.

Natalie had gone quiet. Intimacy swirled around them as she stepped a little closer, and proceeded to button his collar, before looping his tie around his neck. He watched as she focused on the knot, looping one end over the other several times and tucking it through before adjusting the length and sliding it up. She turned his collar down and once she was satisfied with her work, she looked up.

"Thank you," he whispered.

"My pleasure."

The air was thick with anxiety and anticipation, as a newfound awareness drifted over them. James wanted to drag her close and kiss her, but what would she do? How to proceed from here was complicated, at best. They'd crossed a line last night, and he didn't know what came next for them.

"Dinner?" he asked not knowing why he blurted that out. "We could go out, or I could bring you something at the gallery."

"Oh, I don't know…"

Grasping her hands, he pulled her close. "Just dinner. Don't run away from us again, Nat. Please."

"You don't understand," she forced out, her voice cracking.

"You're right, *I don't*. And I won't unless you tell me." Normally calm, James was tamping down his rage; not at her, but at the situation. "I know something more happened at the gallery with my stepfather. I also have a sneaking suspicion my mother had a hand in upsetting you. But I can't fix anything without information."

She'd turned away from him, swiping at her eyes. Damn. He'd made her cry. She didn't resist when he wrapped his arms around her. "Don't cry. I'm sorry."

"You have nothing to apologize for. This is on me." Her eyes were filled with tears when she turned and locked her gaze on his. "I'm not telling you anything because there's nothing to tell. I screwed up."

"And I don't believe you." The long exhalation allowed him to think for a moment. "All right. What if I promise not to bring up any of the former unpleasantness? Can I bring you dinner at the gallery?"

Natalie considered him for a moment before responding. "Only if you bring me a burger and onion rings. I've been craving them."

"Rinaldi's? I thought Lina was closed during the week for dinner."

"It's the holidays. Town is open late for shopping. Lina knows people get hungry when they're running up their credit cards."

"I'll come by the gallery about six thirty? Does that work

for you?"

She sighed. "Yes. But we're only talking about sunshine, Santa and puppies."

"So many rules. May we talk about Liam's show? And your work? I really want to hear about it."

Tears threatened again, but she nodded. "Okay."

Every instinct told him to stay with it. The sex this morning was unexpected, but she'd been more than willing. That was a sign Natalie still trusted him, giving him cause to hope. While he didn't want to spook her, he wasn't going to drop off quietly, either. They were too good together.

It was probably a good time to change the subject. "I was thinking about getting a Christmas tree. Do you have any suggestions?"

"You have a lot of room for a tree," she said, letting her artist's eye survey the space. "You're going to be here for Christmas? Not going back to England?"

"No. I decided on a proper American Christmas. I have a few invitations from colleagues, so there's no need to fight jet lag. I'll just stay here."

"How do you usually celebrate?"

"Some years it's very quiet with the immediate family, and just a few parties. Other years it's madness. Last Christmas I was invited to the annual lunch at Sandringham."

"With the queen?" She smiled.

"Indeed," he replied.

"I didn't know that. I guess there are a lot of parties."

"There are always parties. My stepfather has a house party for New Year's Eve at his place in Sussex." James had attended the party only twice because it wasn't at all about family or celebrating. It was only about being seen. "It's a massive affair, with hundreds of people. He shoots off fireworks."

"Hundreds of people and fireworks. Wow." Knowing how she felt about his stepfather, her response was admirably measured. "Are there pony rides, too?"

The rumble of laughter exploded from his chest. Based on what he'd learned about the Millers, he could see Natalie wasn't impressed. "It sounds more remarkable than it is. I don't like going."

"Okay, then. A Compass Cove Christmas it is. If you want a real tree, the fire department sells them as a fundraiser. The trees are very nice. There's also a good tree lot that opens the day after Thanksgiving. It's a little farther east, going toward Angel Harbor. They will have bigger trees. You do have a lot of height in here."

"You'll come with me? To choose a tree?"

She tried to shake off his request lightly, but he could see she was taken aback. "Dinner and tree shopping? You're pushy."

James grabbed her hand, pulling her in. "I'm *determined*. I'm going to show you that I deserve you, Natalie. I won't let you down."

Reaching up, she laid a hand on his face. The emotions

between them, deep and strong, were palpable. "I know that. You are not the problem, dear James. I am."

Natalie grabbed her bag before rising on her toes to kiss the cheek that was still warm from her hand.

"Nat, I'm not giving up. I'll see you at half past six."

"Right. Till then."

He followed her with his eyes as she walked across the big lawn toward Liam's house, disappearing as she rounded the corner.

He would find a way to get through to her. He had to, for both their sakes.

Chapter Twelve

THE STORM DIDN'T leave a lot of damage, which was a relief considering downtown was fully decked out for Christmas. There were a few stray wreaths on the ground, some garlands drooped off rooflines, but it wasn't anything that couldn't be fixed. There had been a wicked storm the previous March, and it took the town weeks to clean up the downed trees and damage from the flooding.

The wind last night had taken down the rest of the leaves, and the air felt clean and crisp in her lungs. Winter was coming—*Christmas was coming*—and Natalie couldn't have been happier. The tingle that jumped across her skin and the ache between her thighs were also contributing to the happy glow.

Spending last night with James was unexpected, but not unwanted. For the first time in three months, she slept all the way through. For the most part they'd stayed on their own sides of the bed keeping a healthy distance between them, but twice they'd inched toward each other. She'd felt his breath on her neck, the touch of his warm hand. The familiar sound of his breathing was like a lullaby. And unlike the times they spent in London, Cambridge, or even Scotland, this felt different.

Maybe it was being in a new place with him, the situation of being stuck together—isolated from the world—that dictated who he was and how he was supposed to act. He often said his title and lineage didn't define him, but she didn't necessarily agree. Natalie understood tradition and roots. She loved her family to bits, but even though she was a grown woman, they had a role in her life here, just like James's family played a role in his. His standing, his job, his title were all part of him. They helped make him into the wonderful man he was today. But they did come with expectations, as well as privilege. And attachments.

*Lunch with the queen…*she had nothing for that one.

Fortunately, she didn't have to think about it, not right then. There was work to do. Her gallery would open in a little more than a week, and Natalie still had ornaments to hang and sculptures to arrange. She'd gone from one Christmas tree to five. The additional trees were white and silver and of varying sizes, and they were positioned at the corners of the gallery. The large tree would be a focal point and she would decorate it with white lights and Liam's most spectacular ornaments.

The heavy cardboard boxes she had given to Liam were stacked along the wall waiting to be opened. Natalie's stomach clenched. The minute she hung the first ornament or set up the first glass sculpture, this show would be a reality. All aspects of a show were important. The planning and promotion, the selection of individual pieces, the theme...it was all part of the process. But setting up the physical space was something altogether different. Having a vision was one thing; seeing something come together was a completely different vibe.

When Natalie set up a show she had a rough plan on paper, a sketch—or thirty—of how she visualized the room, and the wisdom to know she might change direction completely as the pieces started to speak to her. The vibe of the collection, the personality of the artist all had to come through. That was the whole purpose. It might have been Natalie's gallery, but it was Liam's show. It was about him and his work.

As she carefully placed the first tray of ornaments on a small cart, the door opened. She loved the tiny jingling sound the bell made when someone entered. It was a small and silly thing that reminded her she was in her own store. Her business. Something she was creating. Glancing around the big Christmas tree she saw Lilly, Mia, and Jordan walk in. While she was happy to see her friends, she knew there were going to be a lot of questions. A lot. Because as much as Natalie loved her hometown, it was afflicted with serial nosiness. Everybody knew everything about everyone. It was hard to stay out of the loop, even if you wanted to. Lilly was the first to speak.

"I need to know everything."

Natalie shrugged. "I don't know everything. I can't help you there."

Lilly wasn't amused. "Don't be a smart-ass. You know what I'm talking about. You spent the night at James's house."

Natalie wanted to know how she'd found out. When she got home this morning no one was around. She went right to her cottage, showered, changed, and came here. She didn't talk to her grandmother, her mother, any of her brothers. She stopped in at Rinaldi's and got a coffee but didn't see Lina. It was like Compass Cove was shrouded in some cosmic gossip cloud raining information on everyone.

"I went up to the Landing last night to see Liam. He has some larger pieces that require special packing. I brought him the boxes. He wasn't home, but James was. We visited for a while, but by the time I was ready to leave the storm had kicked up and it wasn't safe." *That was the honest truth.* "It was completely innocent." *That was a lie.* The things he did to her this morning were not innocent.

The way her friends were staring back at her, she could see they didn't believe her. Why should they? She wouldn't believe them if the situation were reversed. "I'm going to hang these ornaments. If you would like to help, you're welcome to stay and I'll send out for lunch. My treat. I would love to spend time with the three of you, but if you start asking me about James, I'll feed you gruel and crackers."

Jordan's big blue eyes widened. "Even me? You'd starve

your pregnant friend?"

"You're a Rinaldi now. You will never starve." Jordan's new husband Nick was a local pediatrician, and Lina Rinaldi's grandson. When Jordan delivered the baby, she wouldn't have to cook for two months. Nana Lina would handle everything.

Annoyed as she might be, Natalie was still happy to have them there. It was a great comfort to be able to lean on her friends. On paper, Natalie knew she could handle the opening, but her anxiety wasn't listening to reason. Opening a new gallery in a small town was risky. And even though she understood art, and marketing, and the creative world, that didn't mean she felt prepared for what was coming.

All that meant Natalie felt out of her depth on two fronts: the gallery and her relationships. Neither one was currently a disaster, but there was that potential. How Natalie handled either of those things was anyone's guess. She surveyed the three faces in front of her and decided to come clean. She couldn't lie to them.

"Everything started out innocently. We did sleep in the same bed. However, in my defense, he insisted. It was getting cold, and it made more sense than making him sleep on the couch."

Lilly was leaning against the wall, arms folded conveying her suspicions. Jordan's expression was bright and hopeful. Mia looked sympathetic. Like she understood the power a man could have over the woman who loved him.

"Was it amazing?" Mia asked. "He looks like he would be amazing. Those brainy guys…"

"Mia! Settle down." It was funny watching Lilly worry about decorum. She had a habit of not following rules. But whatever she had heard about Nat staying over at James's house it didn't seem Lilly was ready for the truth. The whole sordid truth.

"He was amazing," Natalie confirmed. "But that's all I'm going to say. The situation between us is so complicated… I'd like to think we could work it out, but I don't know."

"What's holding you back? I imagine the two of you would complement each other so well."

Jordan was exactly right. They did complement each other, and she was holding herself back.

Lilly looked down at the tray of ornaments and picked up one in sapphire blue that caught the light and refracted it around the room. "Oh, my God. There are flecks in the glass that make it look like stars. It's like a tiny galaxy."

"You have no idea. Each one is gorgeous. Every line is unique. He has some that are mercury glass. I swear, he's going to be famous. His work is special and accessible. Families can own a piece of fine art. That is truly spectacular and I'm so excited to get his career off the ground."

"Natalie, I have never seen you this excited about…well, anything!" Jordan looked at the sketch she had on the cart with the ornaments. "Should we follow this guide?"

"Yes. I will end up rearranging but getting the ornaments

on the respective trees is a good start. You all don't mind helping?"

"Are you kidding?" Mia shrugged out of her jacket and headed for the cart. "Just tell us where to start."

THERE WERE FEW things James enjoyed more than feeling like he belonged. Lina Rinaldi had a way of making everyone feel like family, sometimes to their delight, other times to their peril. He entered the café to order dinner for himself and Natalie, and Lina was engaged in a raucous conversation with three other ladies in a booth. They were talking and laughing in the way old friends do—all at once.

"James! Come here. I'd like you to meet my friends." Lina waved him over to the table and he happily obliged. The ladies all looked to be about the same age, but each was different.

"Girls, this is James Phillips. He's an English import at Jennings for the rest of the school year. James, these are my oldest friends." She nodded to each as she went around the table.

"Ladies, it is indeed a pleasure." He smiled wide sensing how important this particular first impression was going to be. He tried to get a feel for the group, but each of the ladies presented quite differently. They were as diverse as the little town in which they lived.

Present were Mia's grandmother, Janet Lang, as well as Lilly's abuela, Clarita Vasquez. Interesting. Lina was Jordan's grandmother by marriage. There was definitely a theme.

Finally, Lina motioned to a proper and refined elderly lady, with high cheekbones, radiant skin and bright, bright blue eyes. He'd know those eyes anywhere.

"This is Anna Miller, Natalie's grandmother."

James bowed his head slightly as if he were greeting Her Majesty. "Mrs. Miller, it is a pleasure to meet you, finally."

"Lord Linden, the honor is all mine." Her speech was clear and light, not at all tinged by the fatigue one often heard in a woman of her years. What did surprise him was the use of his title.

"There is no Lord Linden here, just James. This seems to be a meeting of the minds. Are you all enjoying your supper?"

"We always do," Lina responded. "We've been friends for over fifty years. There aren't many things that last that long."

He could see from their body language that these women knew each other better than they knew themselves. Lina was right: not much lasted as long as these women had been friends. It seemed to be a theme here in Compass Cove, one he envied. The grandmothers had been friends for decades; Natalie and her friends had known each other since childhood. The men seemed to have strong bonds. This community fostered relationships that lasted. He had no idea what was in the air or the water, but he found he wanted to be a part of it. Hearing his title for the first time coming from Anna Miller's mouth made him uncomfortable. He didn't want to be Lord Anyone, and he didn't want a large country home, or land, or privilege unless he earned it. His stepfather's house in Sussex had 125 rooms. No one needed 125 rooms.

He wondered if the colonial spirits, the rebels who fought for independence, were influencing him somehow. He respected where he'd come from, and the monarchy had a place in British society. Her Majesty was an honorable woman, who above all else pledged herself to service of the country. But looking at England from across the pond, James saw complications that shouldn't be playing a role in his life. Things were simpler here. It wasn't that America didn't have its own problems, but the truth for him was plain: Natalie was here, and if she wanted him to stay, he would find a way to do so.

"What brings you in, James?" Lina asked. "Do you want your usual soup and sandwich?"

"No, actually I'm bringing dinner to Natalie. She's been working all day and I convinced her to take a break."

"How did you manage?" Mrs. Miller wondered, her wry smile tilting her lips. "I feel like I haven't seen her for days."

Oh, cheeky. The woman was fishing for information. "I know she's been quite busy. The gallery is opening in, what…about a week?"

"Yes," Janet Lang interjected. Her soft, easy demeanor reminded him of Mia. It was easy to see the familial connection. "It's opening right after Thanksgiving. Are you looking forward to spending holidays with us in the States?"

"I am. It will be my first."

"Where are you spending Thanksgiving, James?" Lina's inquiry had a probing nature about it.

What he didn't expect was the answer that came from Mrs. Miller.

"Well, of course he's spending it with us." She looked at him with those eyes and he knew he had no choice. "We would be honored to host you. The house is full, and a little unruly, but it's a wonderful day. You are not allowed to say no, by the way."

The three other ladies laughed. He'd been snagged. His first thought was how Nat would feel about it.

"She means what she says," Lilly's abuela interjected, her Spanish accent light and musical. "You cannot say no."

"Then I humbly accept." Instinctively, James dropped his head. This woman really did have a queenly air. "I appreciate your welcome."

His eye caught the hostess at the register, who waved and held up a white paper sack. "It appears dinner is ready, so I'll be off. The proprietor of Compass Cove's newest business is waiting for her burger."

"Do give my granddaughter my love," Mrs. Miller said. "And tell her to give her old granny a visit at some point."

"I'll do that." He said his goodbyes to the rest of the table and picked up the bag at the front door. He was proud of himself for not divulging too much information, as these women were master inquisitors. They could ask more with a single glance than most people could with a flood of words. And they were more intimidating than most.

It was obvious that steel spines ran strong in the female population in Compass Cove. Even the softest of women possessed one.

Once he left the café, it was a short walk to the gallery, which was conveniently placed just a few doors away. There was brown paper covering the windows, hiding the preparations going on inside, but he could see all the lights on inside telling him Natalie was still at work on the main floor. He hoped the day hadn't been too difficult. He remembered how intense she became when she was setting up shows at the gallery in London. It was all-consuming because she was a perfectionist who obsessed over the tiniest details. With new artists she was particularly nervous because she knew a poor showing could end a career before it started.

That Liam was a friend probably compounded every emotion that normally consumed her. James had no doubt the show would be spectacular, but that wasn't going to change how she worked, or how she dove into each task. He found the best thing to do during stressful times was make sure she ate, make sure she slept, and listen as necessary. He made the mistake once of offering advice. He learned quickly that she didn't want anyone to solve her problems…Natalie would solve them herself. What she needed was support.

That is what he intended to give her.

He was about to knock on the door when he heard a burst of laughter from the inside, and Mariah Carey's "All I Want for Christmas is You" playing in the background. This was not what he expected. Instead of knocking, he pushed the lever and found the door unlocked. When he walked in, he was absolutely stunned.

The first thing he saw was a Christmas tree, white and looking like it was frosted with castor sugar. It was at least fifteen feet tall. Around the sides of the gallery were pedestals, shelves and tables all holding beautiful pieces of glass, but it was the tree, the massive tree in the center of the room, which caught his attention and held it. It was covered in ornaments of all shapes and sizes, a rainbow of colors and a world full of gold and silver. It was, in a word, magical.

Art was supposed to affect you on a visceral level. You were supposed to respond to it emotionally. What James felt when he walked into the Belgravia Gallery was overwhelming. He was astounded by his new friend's talent. He was amazed by the beauty and the color of each piece of glass from the larger sculptures, to the tiniest suncatcher. Finally, he was overcome by his feelings for a woman who knew and understood what this kind of art meant to the world.

If he didn't already love her, he would have fallen at that moment.

Mariah Carey had stopped singing, and instead he heard the stunning melody of Pachelbel's Canon in D wafting through the room. It was then that he spotted Natalie. Clad in black leggings and a flowy white shirt she stood in the middle of the room next to the tree. She should have blended in; nothing about what she was wearing or how she presented was remarkable, yet she was radiant. Her eyes twinkled, her smile lit up the room as brightly as all the lights on the tree, and her body language was asking him a wordless question. She wanted to know what he thought.

He would have hoped his stunned silence told her how much he loved everything he saw, but James needed to say it as much as she needed to hear it.

"I am beyond impressed with what you've done in so short a time. I expected to come in here and find you completely stressed, but you're dancing. Natalie this entire display is brilliant. Just brilliant."

"You really think so?" She didn't move but twisted her fingers together nervously. *What he thought mattered to her.* That revelation, that simple truth, gave him more hope than sharing a bed with her.

He wanted to hold her. They were frozen in place, acutely aware they weren't alone. But connected, nonetheless. Her look told him all he needed to know about where they stood. Natalie was his again if he wanted her. And while her acceptance of him may have been tentative, he would convince her he was worth the risk. It would take time, but they would do it without the interference of his family, or the static of London, or the toxicity of her former job.

They would talk, and spend time together, while trying to find common ground. And James was fully prepared to get to that common ground even if it was here in New York rather than in England.

"Mia, don't you have to get home? I know I have to get home." Lilly finally spoke, breaking the trance that had absorbed them.

He noticed Mia standing off to the side, her hands clutched to her chest. Hearing Lilly's voice snapped her out of the moment. "Oh! Yes. Right. I have to make...um, eat dinner. Adam and Ben have a team dinner tonight. I'll go see my nana."

James enjoyed the way her friends were scrambling to leave them alone. Good people, these women. "Your grandmother is at Rinaldi's, Mia; as is yours, Lilly. I met them both when I was there a few minutes ago."

"It must be dinner night." Lilly grabbed two coats from a chair nearby, handed one to Mia and started toward the door. "Thank you for the intel, James. Nat, I'll call you tomorrow."

"Bye!" Mia called as the door shut behind them. It was as rapid an exit as he'd ever seen.

The speedy retreat made Natalie laugh. "That was funny. You know how to clear a room."

Depositing the sack on an empty tabletop, he went to

her. "It takes years of practice." James settled his hands on her waist. "You must be so happy. I did not expect to come in here and see that you'd not only finished, but that you're also happy with it. Natalie, it's beautiful."

"It's not quite done. There are still several pieces to place, and Liam is working on something that he says will take everyone's breath away."

"He's not telling you?"

"Not even a hint. I told you, he's a diva." Natalie stepped away from him and grabbed the bag. "Flip the lock on the door. We can eat upstairs."

Not one to get between a woman and her onion rings, James did as she asked. Natalie was already on her way up to the loft as he made his way through the exhibit. His eyes darted around as he marveled at the use of color and light.

"I feel like I've stepped into a snow globe. He looked up at the icicles and snowflakes hanging from the ceiling, all at varying heights, they seemed suspended in midair. It was only when he looked closely that he could see the almost transparent fishing line holding them up. "I don't want to know how you managed to hang all these," he said mounting the stairs to follow her. "How big is the ladder?"

"Pretty big, but I wasn't alone when I hung them."

"Good to know."

"I always make sure somebody is with me before I do something that could result in me breaking my neck. Feel better?"

"I don't know about *better*..."

"Stop where you are. Watch this." From her position on the second-floor landing, Natalie played with some controls on the wall and James watched as the bright lights went down, and the exhibit lighting came up.

"My God. You are magical." She'd aimed spotlights, floor lighting and hung twinkle lights in just the right arrangement that the glass popped, casting colorful prismatic effects all over the walls.

This wasn't just going to make Liam famous, but Natalie as well. When the word got out about what she could do the gallery would be a destination for artists from around the world.

Finishing the climb, he pulled her to him at the top of the stairs. "Magical," he whispered.

"Oh, I don't know about that," she said. "But I'm glad you like it. I hope everyone else does."

"I don't think you should be worried about that. Everyone is going to love it, and your family will be very impressed."

At the same time she pulled him the final few steps into the loft, he heard her stomach growl.

"Hungry?" he asked.

"Very," she said taking the bag. "Speaking of my family, I assume you met my grandmother at the café since she was out with her posse."

He chuckled at the name she gave to the group of sage

women who'd questioned him. "I did. She's lovely. Very, I don't know, European? I mean I know she's American…"

"Very astute, and an apt description. My grandmother was raised on Nob Hill in Boston, summered on the coast of Maine, and attended boarding school in Switzerland. She is a Lowell, an old Brahmin family that ran in the same circle as the Cabots and the Lodges."

"My goodness. I'd love to speak with her about her lineage. It sounds like she has quite the pedigree."

"She does, and the stories to go along with it. Ask her how she met my grandfather. It was scandalous."

"Was it now?" He helped her unpack the food and spread a drop cloth on the floor, picnic style. "Your granny invited me for Thanksgiving dinner. I am flattered, of course, but I will decline if you feel it's not…appropriate."

Natalie sat cross-legged on the floor and patted the paint-spattered canvas next to her. He obliged and watched her mind circle around this new bit of information. "If my grandmother invited you, it would be rude to say no."

"I have other invitations. William Harris, one of my colleagues in the department invited me to dine with his family. I could say I already accepted."

"Oh, Dr. Harris! He's such a kind man. He's a big reader, and not just history. He has a thing for romance novels. I always loved that about him. He said once, 'Genre fiction is where you find out what people were really thinking during an era in history.' I've never forgotten it."

James loved when Natalie's stream of consciousness came flooding out, but he needed to know what she thought about Thanksgiving. "I could see him saying that, but the invitation…"

"My grandmother sits on the Jennings College Board of Trustees." She dropped that bit of information like a bomb.

"Ah. I see. Well, that's it then." There was no way he could decline, and Natalie knew it. He just didn't know how she felt about it.

"I guess you're in for the Miller Thanksgiving."

"I guess so," James replied, not hiding the hint of nervousness in his voice. Natalie unwrapped her burger and breathed in the smell of spices, grilled meat and onions. "That looks good," he observed. "I've yet to try one. My stomach screams yes, but my arteries scream no."

"It's amazing. Want a bite?"

"No, thanks. I have a turkey club I've been thinking about all day." He really had. He'd become quickly addicted to Lina's sandwiches.

"A warning about my family and the holidays: it's insane. We eat from morning until we drop into bed. Drink way too much, tease each other, sing, watch football, scream at the TV, argue, and decorate the Christmas tree. It's loud and messy. We play midnight Wiffle Ball, no matter how cold it is. It's completely bonkers."

"All good to know. I will send her a note thanking her for the invitation."

The concern on her face was priceless. This was a woman who knew where she came from, and while she was certain he would be horrified, it was obvious Natalie embraced the craziness, and all the love that went with it. James hoped she knew how fortunate she was. Natalie's family was a gift, and honestly, he was looking forward to the whole experience. He had no idea what Wiffle Ball was, but the entire day sounded like a great time, bonkers or not.

Chapter Thirteen

"**Y**OU'RE PREGNANT."

The words hung in the air. Had she heard the doctor correctly? *Pregnant.* Like having a baby? "I'm sorry. I'm pregnant?"

"Based on what you've said about your cycle, I'm guessing ten weeks or so. How are you feeling?"

Nat didn't know how to answer that question. She'd been feeling okay when she came in, tired but okay. She'd mentioned to a few people she was fighting exhaustion, but she was adjusting to a new routine, opening a business. She'd had an upset stomach here and there since arriving home from England, but that had passed. Oh, and the heartburn. Wicked heartburn—but she was stressed.

Pregnant had not crossed her mind.

How was she feeling? Like she'd just been hit by a bus. Ten weeks gone meant it happened right before she left London for good. "I can't...I can't be..."

Wasn't this exactly what James's mother had accused her of trying to do? *"I know your type. You'll get yourself pregnant to get your hooks in him. To get a title."*

"Are you sure?" she asked. "I mean, really?"

"You most certainly are. I know you've only been back in the States a few months. Do you have an ob-gyn?"

"What?" Her doctor was talking, but she barely heard him. The roar in her head was deafening. It was like standing under Niagara Falls.

"A lady doctor?" Alan Gaffney had been her family physician since he took over for old Doc Gilligan when Nat was just a wee one herself. He had patience that went on for days. Thank God, because Natalie wasn't able to focus on anything.

"Right, of course. I don't. I haven't found one yet."

Turning he grabbed a pad from the counter behind him and scribbled something before tearing off the sheet and handing it to her. "Kerry Dryer is fantastic. Call her. Today."

"Today?"

Alan raised an eyebrow. "You want me to call her today?"

"No," Natalie sputtered. "No. I'll do it. God, how did this happen? How did I not know?"

"You're young and healthy, but you've been under a lot of stress since you've moved home. It's easy to brush off the signs."

Nat rubbed her hand across her belly and drew a deep cleansing breath. "You won't tell my mother, will you?"

She sounded like a teenager. *God.* Why did being home bring out her inner sixteen-year-old?

Alan and Mom were probably going to get married.

They spent all their free time together, and she didn't want anything to slip out. The last thing she needed was for her mother to find out before Natalie had a chance to sit with the idea for a while.

"Of course not. You're my patient, and that means what happens in this office is confidential. I couldn't tell Linda even if I wanted to."

That was somewhat of a relief. However, Nat didn't know if she wanted to tell her mother either. Or her brothers. It would just be one more check in the *Natalie-is-a-flake* column. One more reason for them to worry about her.

And James. Oh, my God. How should she tell him? They weren't together, not really. Mind-blowing sex aside, it still wasn't official. But this? A baby wasn't on the playlist. Oh no. *The sex.*

"Can having sex hurt the baby? I mean, am I okay? Am I too old? My mother had kids so young…"

"Sex is okay. You're not too old. Everything seems fine," he said, calmly ticking off her concerns. "Your blood pressure is good and your blood tests came back in normal ranges. I mean, except for the pregnancy thing…"

"That's good. But…how? We used birth control. I thought I was careful…"

She was always careful. *Obviously not.*

"Call Kerry. She'll have answers to all your questions."

"Okay." Nat hopped off the table and smiled as best as she could at the tall lanky form of the man who had known her longer than she could remember.

Shit. "I had wine. I just remembered. Oh, my God. I'm already a bad mother."

"Natalie, it's going to be okay. Try not to let this spin out in your head before you talk to Kerry. In the meantime, pick up a prenatal multivitamin."

Her brain was way past spinning and on its way to a crash landing. Natalie had been fighting waves of anxiety since she got home, combating the panic with yoga, meditation and a full to-do list every day. But a baby? She was a hot mess. How was she going to take care of a baby?

Natalie tucked the paper with the OB's information into her bag and made her way out of the office in record time, not stopping to chat with the receptionist and the nurses like she usually would. Dr. Gaffney's practice was a few blocks outside the official downtown area of Compass Cove, but close enough to be considered in "town." It was cold, but not uncomfortable and only a little over a month to Christmas, which meant walking through town back to the gallery was out of the question. She'd see at least a dozen people she knew.

Pregnant. If that didn't beat all. She'd left England, along with everything and everyone she'd known there, without a look back. She thought she'd made a clean break, but now? The baby in her belly was a tangible link to James—the man she loved, but couldn't have.

Over the last week, they'd spent more time together and

it was a solid reminder of how good they were together.

Alan's practice was housed in pale yellow clapboard Cape, sitting neatly on the corner of Shipyard Path and Cove Road. The street ended at a pretty dock overlooking Compass Cove.

There were about a dozen of these little lanes spread around town. Each one contained three houses, maybe four, and they all ended at the water. Some had a tiny stretch of beach. Others, like this one, had a dock where the residents could tie up their dinghies or store their kayaks and paddleboards. It was one of the things she loved most about her town. Everyone was connected to the sea, and to each other.

And right now, that connection was the last thing she wanted. She needed to think without all the togetherness. She was just about to turn down the little street, hoping the walk and the water would calm her, when a voice called out.

"Hey, Nat!"

Crapola. That didn't take long. Looking toward the voice, she saw Jordan pull to the side of the road. "Are you okay? You look like you're lost." That was a pretty accurate assessment.

Just then her phone pinged. Looking down, she saw it was James.

How are you feeling? Did you go to the doctor? James knew she wasn't feeling well, and had urged her to have a checkup.

I'm fine, she texted back. *Just a little bug in my system.* That was a flippin' understatement. It was also an outright lie. But she couldn't tell him now.

God, she needed to talk to someone, but unlike Dr. Gaffney who was bound by privacy laws, she was at a loss.

"Natalie? Are you all right?" Jordan had gotten out of her car and placed a gentle hand on Natalie's arm. "Honey, what's wrong?"

A tall, blonde model of maternal perfection, Jordan was calm and caring. She was ready to be a mother. Natalie was a hot mess.

"Oh, Jor…I…I…" Tears clouded her vision. "I…can we go to your house?"

Alarm spread across her friend's face because of all of them, Natalie was the least likely to cry. "Oh, Natalie! Of course. Come on." Ushering Nat into the car, Jordan didn't hesitate, she didn't ask questions, she just helped.

In addition to being pregnant herself, Jordan was a vault. She wouldn't tell anyone Natalie's business. That's what she needed right now.

Fortunately, they didn't have to go far. Jordan and Nick had a pretty house on Cove Road. They'd bought it last spring and had been renovating it ever since. It was a big house and she fully expected them to fill it with kids.

Jordan ushered Natalie into her bright, sunny kitchen, settled her at the island, and placed a tray of cookies in front of her, followed quickly by a cup of tea. Jordan did all this without speaking, giving Natalie the time to organize her thoughts.

Her friend possessed a remarkable gift. She was a caretaker. Whether it was her students, her Navy vet husband, or her dying father, Jordan's big heart knew exactly what to do. When she sat next to Natalie, she took Nat's hand in her own. "Now, tell me what it is."

"I'm not like you. I can't just take this in stride. I mean, I'm a mess. I…"

"Natalie, I have no idea what's going on. Can you start at the beginning? Where were you before I picked you up?"

"I had a doctor's appointment."

Jordan's face froze and she squeezed Nat's hand a little tighter. "Go on. Are you all right?"

"No, I'm not." Dropping her head, Natalie sniffled. "I got some news today, and I don't know what I'm going to do. It's a little scary."

Jordan's eyes were wide, concerned. "Scary? Oh, God. What's wrong? How can I help?"

Her questions came out in a gush.

"Oh, I'm not sick or anything. There's nothing *wrong*. Not really. It's just…" Saying the words to someone else was going to make this baby real. But it was real, whether Natalie wanted to admit it or not.

"Just what?" The poor woman was panicked. Natalie was a horrible friend for scaring a pregnant woman like this.

"I'm pregnant."

Jordan eased up on Natalie's hand, but she didn't let go. "Pregnant? I didn't expect that. I mean, thank God it's not actually bad, but I was not expecting *that*."

"Me neither, but it's not great news. I'm getting myself together. How can I take care of a baby?"

Jordan could so easily judge her. Natalie's life had been a cakewalk compared to the things Jordan had gone through. There were times Nat wished she were made of tougher stuff. Her mind was racing, but she didn't cry. Nope, she wouldn't. Inside, though? She was jelly.

"Is it James's baby?" Jordan asked without a hint of judgment.

Natalie nodded. "I have no idea what to say. Before I left England his mother said I would try just this kind of thing to get him to marry me. *You'll get pregnant and try to trap him*," Natalie said in her best clipped British accent.

Trapping him was the last thing she wanted to do. Did she want him? More than ever. But force a marriage? Hell no—she ran away from him.

"How far along are you?"

"Three months? Doctor G. did a sonogram today, but he wants me to have a more advanced one to really determine the baby's age. I mean, I know when it happened. It was the day before I left London."

Jordan was still holding her hand, steadfast in exactly the way Natalie needed. A port in the storm. "Well, you have to tell him."

"Sweet baby Jeebus. He's going to be horrified."

"Horrified? I don't think so. He did follow you to the

States… That has to mean something."

"I don't even know how to broach the subject. *Hey! You remember that time we got together before I ran away from my life, and you? Surprise!*"

Rolling her eyes Jordan gave Natalie "the look." Compassionate, yes, but Jordan didn't take anyone's crap. "There are a few things you should do for your own piece of mind."

"Go to the doctor, I know."

"You have to tell your mother. You need to tell her before she finds out."

"My mother? Are you serious?" Natalie couldn't wrap her head around how she would approach that conversation. "How would she find out?"

"Mothers always know."

The thought of telling her mother was terrifying. How many times was Natalie supposed to disappoint her? And why was Natalie, at almost thirty-three, still letting her inner teenager get the better of her?

"You know you have to tell James." Natalie nodded. She knew. "That's more important than telling your mother, truly. But Nat, a baby. A baby is magical."

Natalie laid a hand on her tummy. It still felt flat, but she had the sudden sense she wasn't alone anymore. As much as she wasn't sure what she wanted, Natalie couldn't believe how protective she felt. She was worried about everything, every morsel of food, every sip of beverage, her sleep, her stress… Could she be a good mother?

She had no idea how James would react. He was a wonderful man, and she had no fear that he would belittle, or make any demands of her. But it would turn his life upside down. She knew she couldn't go back to England—not with him. But maybe, just maybe he might consider staying in the States.

At least for a little while. The thought stopped her in her tracks. Would he? Is that what she really wanted?

"I'm sure it won't be an easy conversation to have with him considering, but it will be okay. I'm sure of it."

The thought of it made Natalie's stomach turn somersaults. She knew Jordan was right. Her friend might have been an eternal optimist, but she wasn't wrong about James. But as Natalie knew, the right thing—especially in this case—was not the easy thing.

JAMES HAD GOTTEN only a few cryptic text messages from Natalie. He was glad she went to see the doctor, but he didn't know if there was anything actually wrong.

I have a bug in my system. What did that even mean?

He would guess she was exhausted. The woman had been working nonstop on Liam's show and it was sure to have worn her down. But there was something else, something off about her. She'd unexpectedly dropped by his house the other night, falling asleep almost immediately, the same way she did the night of the storm. The woman had been completely beat, and he couldn't shake the thought that it wasn't just tiredness.

He left work not wanting to go home right away, so he stopped at the pub in town. The place felt like home with warm wood walls, scarred tables, and an impressive set of bottles on the wall as well as a line of beers on tap. Also like home were the Christmas decorations. Gold garland framed the windows, red and green ornaments hung over the bar and a really horrid-looking Father Christmas, rendered in plastic, sat near the entrance to greet patrons.

James figured he could get something to eat, have a pint and relax for a little while. Hopefully, he could get his mind off the woman who had fully occupied his thoughts.

He enjoyed his meal, the steak sandwich accompanied by thick-cut *pommes frites* hit the spot. His doctor had told him to watch his cholesterol as it ran on the high side in the family, but an occasional indulgence wasn't going to kill him. He'd run it off. Thinking about whether it was too cold to run outside tomorrow, he started when Liam popped into the empty chair across from him.

"Hello, mate," Liam slurred. "I haven't seen you in a week."

Mate? Seriously? Liam was drunk.

"Well, you have been holed up making all that glass. I expect you haven't gotten more than an hour of sleep a night for the past month."

"Two hours, but not much more than that. That woman is a slave driver."

"That woman? You mean Natalie?" He couldn't imagine how *That Woman* might react if she heard him.

"Are you done eating?" Liam picked a tiny bit of potato off James's plate and popped it in his mouth. "Come join us at the bar."

The bar? Turning, James saw the Miller brothers—Adam, Jack, and Doug—all lined up watching a hockey game on the large telly. He didn't know if he wanted to do this. It would be nice to have a beer at the bar, watch a game. It wasn't something he'd really done since he'd gotten here, or before he got here for that matter. But the Millers? He didn't know if he was ready for them before Thanksgiving dinner.

"I don't know. I should probably get home." He felt the pair of big hands drop on his shoulders.

"Nah. I think you need to hang out with us."

Looking up and behind, James saw Doug Miller standing over him. Doug was a little drunk as well, based on the glazed look in his eyes. It must be the theme of the night.

"Right then."

He wasn't openly hostile, so James took that as a good sign.

Well, why not? He'd have a drink, maybe a few laughs and head home. Perhaps he could find out exactly how to play Wiffle Ball. He paid his check and walked to the bar, taking a seat next to Jack Miller. He was the brother with whom James hadn't spoken. An FBI agent, currently on leave, Jack was back at university getting a PhD in psychology. That meant they would either have a lot to talk about or nothing because James had no intention of allowing himself to be analyzed.

Adam extended his hand first, while Jack and Doug nodded noncommittally. However, there were no growls coming from the lot of them, so that was a plus. "I hear you got snagged in our grandmother's Thanksgiving net? She is ruthless."

"I wouldn't call her ruthless…persistent, maybe."

"Ha," Jack said, tilting a bottle of pale ale to his lips. "Don't let that sweet old lady act fool you. She wants you at the table, you'll be at the table."

"Nope. Gram is calculating." Doug tapped a finger to his forehead and missed, almost taking out his own eye. *Cripes.* "She knew you couldn't say no."

"Natalie said as much." Well, that was a mistake based on the way the three of them had locked him in their sights.

"So," Jack began. "Speaking of Natalie…have you seen her today?"

"I haven't, no." He wanted to avoid giving too much information.

"Heard from her?"

"Just a text. She's been very busy getting ready for Liam's show. By the way, where is Liam?" He looked around the bar for his friend, and spotted him chatting with a lovely woman three tables away who possessed an impressive mane of black curls. She looked familiar. James hadn't met her, but he had definitely seen her around town.

"Aw, shit." Adam grimaced. "Drunk Liam is on the loose."

"You'd better go rescue Maddy," Jack said to his brother.

James wanted to add that Maddy didn't look like she needed rescuing. She was rather enjoying Liam's attention, drunk or not. Dare he say they were flirting? Their concern was rendered moot when Maddy shooed Adam away with a flick of her hand.

"They're going to sing," he groaned when he returned to the group. "They got Bobby to fire up the karaoke machine."

"Sing? Oh, for Pete's sake," Jack whined. "What are they singing?"

"Something Christmassy." Adam wiggled his fingers in the air. James wasn't sure if the other man was annoyed because his friend had ditched them on their boys' night out, or that there was going to be karaoke.

"Kill me," Doug mumbled as he downed the shot of whiskey the barman had just poured.

"You'll have to forgive our brother—he's not into Christmas this year." Jack seemed to be the most personable of the brothers, possibly because of his law enforcement work.

"I'm never into Christmas," Doug said. "So back to Natalie. What's going on? Are you going to make her a princess or something?"

Was this really happening? Did he have to explain himself? Not to mention the man talked like an idiot, and he knew for a fact he wasn't. Doug Miller taught military history at Jennings. He was an adjunct and James was, technically, his boss. The man had two master's degrees and an impeccable military record.

"You know that's not going to happen," James retorted. "I do care about Natalie, but she has her own mind. If you want to know what *she's* thinking, you should ask her."

Doug tried to stare him down, but it wasn't going to work. "She makes us crazy, you know. We never know what she's going to do next."

"Next? She's opening a gallery that's going to be the talk of the New York art community, and she's going to make Liam famous." James accepted a beer from Adam. "Other than that? She's going to be brilliant at whatever she does."

He could see the concern on her brothers' faces. Each of them worried about her, probably for different reasons, and he found it rather touching. The bond between the Miller siblings was strong. However, he didn't care for the way Natalie's brothers underestimated her.

Pointing with his beer bottle, a smile broke across Adam's face. The annoyance had obviously passed. "They're getting ready to sing. I think he really likes her."

"Maddy is something special. Liam couldn't do better.

She's older than him, I think..." Jack smiled, apparently happy for his friend.

Doug was quiet, looking reflective and serious as he rolled the bottle between his hands. It must be a Miller thing. He'd seen Adam do the same thing with a glass. "Your sister is the strongest person I know," James said. "I know you may not believe it—hell, she doesn't always believe it—but she's resilient. I do think she's happy to be home."

"Thanks for that. We worry about her. She keeps her feelings pretty close to the vest." Doug nodded appreciatively.

"That she does." James wished she didn't.

"So, are you looking forward to Thanksgiving tomorrow? Come early—brunch is the best part."

"I am actually. It's my first time celebrating the holiday and I'm doing so in grand style apparently."

"You are. My grandmother goes all out. It's a good time, though. Good people."

James was the one with the question now. "May I ask you something?"

"Shoot," Doug replied.

"What is Wiffle Ball?"

Chapter Fourteen

NATALIE EYED HERSELF in the bathroom mirror. First, she looked at herself facing forward, then she looked at her profile on one side, then on the other. There was no apparent difference. Her stomach still flat, her boobs didn't look any bigger—they were flat, too—so she could probably relax and stop worrying that everyone would be able to tell she was pregnant.

She was pregnant. There was no good reason for this to have happened. They'd used protection, but as her doctor said sometimes protection failed. Still, Natalie wondered why she hadn't noticed. Was she that out of touch with her body? Had she been that preoccupied?

Rubbing her hand across her stomach, she sighed. It was amazing how she got used to the idea so quickly. It surprised her a little that she was not only adapting to having a baby, but part of her was excited.

It was managing a baby that had her mind spinning. She'd just opened a new business, she was on her own, she was living in a tiny boathouse on her family's property. Granted, Natalie could *afford* a baby. She could manage alone, her family was here and she had a great support system, but she never thought she'd be doing this alone. She'd always imagined having a baby with her partner. Someone she loved.

How would any of this work? He was going to go back to England, and that wasn't in her plan. And what if she had a boy? Her son would inherit James's title. It was crazy. She could be carrying the heir. Natalie's big decision now was when to tell him.

And how to tell him she wouldn't marry him when he asked.

There was a knock at the cottage door, and Natalie looked at the clock she had on the bathroom counter. Crap. It was after ten. She should have been at the house already.

"Natalie?"

Dammit. Mom was there.

"I'll be right out." She was going to have to stay in the bathroom, or let her mom get an eyeful of her in her underwear. *Here goes.*

"Sorry. Sorry," she said as she left the bathroom. "I'll get dressed and be ready in five minutes."

"It's okay," her mother said calmly. She looked casual but pulled together. Her brown hair was pulled back in a clip and her jeans and sweater looked comfortable and cozy. "James just got here though, and he brought a big box of pastries from Sweet Chemistry Bakery in Angel Harbor. I think there are apple fritters."

"What? You should have led with that, Mom. By the time I get there, the boys will have inhaled everything." Lina was a master baker, and her breads and tarts were to die for, but apple fritters from Sweet Chemistry were worth fighting over.

Natalie jumped in a pair of fleece leggings, pulled on her shearling boots and threw a sweatshirt over her head. She was at the door ready to leave, when her mother laid a hand on her arm.

"Mom, come on. Sweet Chemistry?"

"Stop. Look at me." Her mother was frozen in place. Serious.

Natalie felt her whole body stiffen. "Mom…"

Her mother's turquoise eyes weren't quite the same as hers, but they were big and bright, accented by little crinkles at the corners which were more pronounced when she smiled or when she was considering something seriously. She was beautiful, tall and lean. She looked down at Nat, taking in her face and then scanning her body. After a few seconds, her mother's expression changed. Her mom was gaping, open-mouthed and searching for words. It hit Natalie that Jordan was right.

She knew. Her mother *knew*.

"Oh, my God." Her mother's hand flew to her mouth. "Natalie, are you…are you pregnant?"

"Uh…I…"

"Are you? Honey, tell me." Her mother, who was normally calm and collected, was shaking.

God, Nat, what did you do now? Her mother was going to have a stroke.

Normally, a conversation like this would require alcohol, but Natalie couldn't drink. Time to power through. "I...*am.*"

The tears in her mother's eyes that had been threatening spilled over. At first, Natalie couldn't tell if her mother was upset, angry, or thrilled. When she lunged, throwing her arms around Natalie's neck, she knew the answer. It seemed nothing was more important than a grandbaby.

"I am so happy." Her mother was still holding on, while she gushed and sobbed. "I know I should be telling you all the reasons this will be difficult, but you're almost thirty-three—I think you're ready."

"I don't know about ready, but I am having a baby. And I'm not unhappy about it. Surprised? Absolutely. But I'm not unhappy."

"Nor should you be. Things sometimes happen when we need them to, not when we expect them to. Oh...tell me...what did James say? You could be carrying the heir! Oh, my goodness. Have you thought about the gallery? What happens if you move back to England with James?"

Her mother was ecstatic because she thought Natalie and James were together. That explained her enthusiasm. How did she break it to her? "I haven't told him yet. Things are still a bit tentative with us. I don't want to go into this with unrealistic expectations."

"Unrealistic? It's his baby, isn't it?" Her mom seemed to realize how horrible that sounded as soon as she said it. "I'm sorry. That was crass."

"Yep. Just a little." Natalie dropped her head on the cool surface of the kitchen island. "I'm still trying to figure all this out. How to tell him, what to do…it's a lot. And it's complicated. I left London for a reason."

She felt her mother settle next to her and drop a gentle hand on her back. "Want to share? I'll listen, and I won't judge."

"Thanks, but I'd rather not. Today is supposed to be fun." When she looked up, Natalie saw her mother wiping her eyes on the sly. She really was trying, and Nat appreciated it. "Let's go back to the house. If I miss the apple fritters I'll be really cranky." Cranky was probably an understatement.

"I'm here if you need me," Mom said as she wrapped her in a hug. "I did this four times and I still remember each pregnancy like it was yesterday."

"Really? I thought women forgot so they could have another without the trauma."

"That's delivery. Yours is the only one I remember. Which is why you were my last."

Natalie snorted a laugh, but sobered quickly. "Promise me you won't tell anyone."

"Not a soul. Now let's go. I don't want to have to fight

you for the fritter."

"I'd win," Natalie boasted. "I'm meaner."

"You got me there."

When James pulled into the entrance of the Millers' estate, he had no idea what to expect. The drive was more of a private road set at the edge of the area known as Jennings Bay, lined with trees still shedding their leaves, and perfectly landscaped with vast expanses of lawns and gardens. Natalie had told him the property used to encompass over forty acres, but now it was around ten, with the rest of the land designated as protected wetlands.

The first building he saw looked like a small caretaker's cottage. It was made of stone, and well kept. There was a car parked next to the structure. There was a stable with paddocks behind the cottage, but no horses. *That was a shame*, he thought. He knew how Natalie loved horses.

The tires crunched on the gravel drive and finally it opened up into a cobblestone courtyard flanked by several buildings.

To his right he saw a large white mansion in the Georgian style, three stories, large windows, porticos on each side, and a grand entrance. The house was beautiful, and he couldn't wait to hear the story of how it ended up in the Miller family.

Ahead of him, there was a four-car garage. For some reason he was expecting it to be larger. On his left was a lovely home, made of clapboard and brick, that looked like it had once been a carriage house with high-pitched roof lines, arched doors and windows, and a long profile. Based on what Natalie had told him this was the guesthouse where she had been raised. *The guesthouse.* He marveled at the architecture and size of the lovely building.

Leading away from the house, and down next to the garage he saw a path disappear into the trees. He expected if he walked that way, it would take him down to the beach, and to Natalie. She told him she was staying in the converted boathouse. It was small by her own admission, but she liked it that way. Cozy, she'd called it. It gave her some space from the chaos and kept her near the water. *"I can think there,"* she'd said.

Last night, when he was having drinks with her brothers, the alcohol had loosened their tongues. They were worried about their sister, and not just in the *her-old-boyfriend-came-to-town* kind of way, they sensed something was wrong and they had no idea how to help.

James wished he could have given them some insight, but he wasn't going to. He hadn't broached the subject with her since he'd come to the States, not wanting to send her reeling again. With Liam's show opening tomorrow he had to do his best to help her stay calm.

After parking between a pair of large SUVs, James took the two boxes, and a small bag from the bakery in Angel Harbor off the seat, not knowing what awaited him inside. He was sure this was the kind of house where people entered and exited through a side or a garden door. But he was a guest, a newcomer, so the front door it was.

On his way to ring the bell, he was met by a tiny elfin creature. She had dark, olive-green eyes, a spray of freckles across her nose and silky, dark brown hair that fell to her shoulders like water. James imagined this is what Natalie looked like when she was a child, and he was enchanted.

"Good day," he said to the child. "Are you guarding this dwelling?"

"You talk funny." That wasn't what he expected but he almost laughed aloud because the little girl sported a stronger New York accent than most of the adult New Yorkers he'd met recently. "You are mistaken," James corrected. "I speak the Queen's English. Now I ask again...do you guard this dwelling?"

Her eyes narrowed and a tiny grin tipped the corner of her mouth. "Who's askin'?"

"Lord Linden, but you may call me James."

"What's in the box?" This was serious. It appeared he was in the midst of a negotiation.

James leaned in, realizing he had a bargaining chip. "One box contains donuts and pastries."

"And the *other* box?" This youngster was formidable.

"Apple fritters." That did it. Her eyes widened; her mouth dropped open. Even the little one knew the value of what he carried. "Ahh. Will you help me then? Facilitate my introduction to the inhabitants of this castle?"

"I guess…but I get dibs on a fritter before my uncles, my dad or my cousin Ben."

"Agreed. As I said, I am Lord Linden." He bowed. "What is your name, elf?"

She giggled and it was delightful. "I am Rosie, at your service." The small one executed a near perfect curtsy.

Rosie, it turned out, was the ideal person to escort him inside. Doug's youngest, she was chatty and had her father, her uncles and everyone in the immediate vicinity totally cowed. He was greeted warmly by the Millers, but Natalie wasn't yet there. Her mother offered to fetch her daughter from the boathouse.

As he expected, the apple fritters disappeared, and after one bite he found out why. The pastry was doughy, sugary, apple-filled bliss. He stayed at the fringes of the family, accepting coffee from Doug, who was surrounded by a pack of little girls that included Rosie. It gave him new insight into the man. He was a protector.

Nat had told him how her sister-in-law had left the girls with her mother for what was supposed to be a long weekend to regroup, and never came back. Doug, a career Marine, had been assigned as a military attaché at an embassy in the Middle East, and got home as quickly as he could. When he did, he found three brokenhearted girls.

If they were brokenhearted now, it didn't show. They loved their father, and if James ever thought badly about the man, he was sorry for it.

Natalie burst into the kitchen, trailed by her mother, who he knew had to be in her mid-sixties, but looked like an ingénue herself.

"Apple fritters? Did I miss them?"

Her brothers and her nieces looked at her sheepishly. Her grandmother even averted her eyes. There wasn't even a crumb left in the box. Lilly, who had arrived early with Jack, handed her a half-eaten fritter. "You can have this."

"Are you kidding me? All of them?" Natalie was visibly annoyed, but based on what she'd told him about the coveted treat, it shouldn't have been a surprise.

Walking to him, she looked dejected. "Of all days for me to oversleep… I'm usually up with the sun."

"That you are." Her face, when he took a small white bag from the counter, was confused. "Maybe this will make you feel better."

Skeptical, she took the bag from his hand and felt its weight. "Hmm. What's in here?"

"I remember what you told me about your brothers inhaling all food that came through the house, so I figured I'd get you your own."

Natalie's eyes widened when she noticed the brightly colored sticker on the side telling her the contents were also from Sweet Chemistry. "You didn't. Did you?" She looked in the bag and a wide smile bloomed across her face. James would bring her surprises every single day if he could keep seeing that smile.

"You brought me my own apple fritters. You are amazing. And very sweet. Thank you." She went up on her toes and kissed his cheek. It was a sweet kiss, and he could feel the warmth of her appreciation seep through him. These were the moments that mattered—simple ones when all a person needed to know was that someone was thinking about them.

Natalie looked at her brothers triumphantly. "He puts you guys to shame. This is what a gentleman does."

"The gentleman is going to find himself with a wedgie," Doug said.

"Give it your best shot," James retorted, thinking no one had threatened him with a wedgie since primary school. "You won't even get close."

Jack and Adam seemed content to stay out of the trash talking, leaving it to the two Marines in the room. It was possible he and Doug Miller were becoming friends. They did have a lot of common ground. Maybe this was an unlikely outcome of his time on Long Island.

Natalie was sitting at the kitchen island chatting with Mia, Lilly, her mother, and grandmother while blissfully enjoying her apple fritter. It was good to see her like this: comfortable in her skin, and happy being with the people around her. As much as she loved living in London, he sensed Natalie knew she didn't quite fit. Of course, she had friends, but it wasn't her place. Not like Compass Cove.

Being welcomed by this family had churned up James's

desire for his own. For the longest time he wasn't sure if he wanted to marry, or if he wanted children. He knew what was expected of him, but whether or not a family was in his future was never sure.

Until now.

Chapter Fifteen

H ER GRANDMOTHER HAD officially gone over the top.
Natalie thought about the table set for dinner and
couldn't remember the last time there were almost forty
chairs. Instead of the dining room, Grandma had the staff set
up the ballroom, a rarely used space next to the large formal
dining room. The extra room was a good idea. It wouldn't be
very polite to elbow her neighbor while she was trying to eat
her turkey and stuffing, but she wondered if it would be
overwhelming with its high ceilings and ornate decor.

That was until she walked in the room and her breath
caught. If Natalie had ever wondered where she got her
artistic talent, she realized it was from Grandma. The room
had been transformed. It was filled with plants and fall
flowers, and café lights were strung across the ceiling.

The entire room was awash with brown, deep red, gold
and yellow. Bushel baskets of gourds, pumpkin, and dried
native corn overflowed in some of the corners. There were
potted trees and the tables were styled with burlap runners,
bouquets of fall leaves and dried flowers. At each place there
were deep brown place mats, red chargers and the loveliest

scrolled stoneware, turning each place setting into an elegant, but simple, invitation to come together and break bread.

The tables weren't folding tables. No, these were fine wood tables that were kept in a storage room and brought out when lots of seating was needed. There were four, fifteen-foot-long tables arranged in a rectangle. It would be a loud and wonderful gathering. Definitely something to be thankful for.

Natalie circled the tables and found her name; breaking with normal protocol, James was seated next to her. She knew her grandmother had worked on the seating for a week before she got just the arrangement she wanted. It made Natalie happy that she would experience his first Miller holiday with him. Lord help anyone who switched seats.

"Wow. Just when I thought I'd seen everything, this house surprises me again."

James walked into the room; his attention was immediately drawn to the tromp l'oeil on the ceiling that was painted to give the illusion of the sky at dusk. Then he examined the wall of French doors that led out to the formal gardens. His eyes finally met hers.

"I'm so glad I came. Your family is wonderful. Every last person has been so welcoming. I feel like a bit of an interloper, but I'm grateful to be here."

"I'm glad you're here," she said going to him. "You fit right in."

"I can't help but fit in. You are very lucky, Nat. I know

no family is perfect, but your family's devotion to each other is very special."

She knew. Sometimes it helped to hear it from someone on the outside, however.

"Did I tell you that you look beautiful today?" he asked.

She felt her face heat at the compliment. After inhaling the two fritters he'd saved for her, Natalie went back to her cottage to change. She was wearing a simple black shift dress with black boots, but she did rather like the scooped neckline on this dress. She guessed James did as well.

"Thank you." The exchange was so simple yet laden with meaning. What was she thanking him for? The compliment? The pastry he remembered to bring just for her? His kindness toward her nieces, her mother...everyone? For the opportunity to become a mother?

She guessed it was all of it.

"You're wearing the necklace I gave you for your birthday."

She touched her neck and felt the cool tourmaline beads roll under the pads of her fingers. They'd gone for a weekend in Paris last June and although they'd only been together for a couple of months, she knew their relationship was getting serious. It was a perfect late spring day, and the city was bright with flowers and activity. They'd just left the Tuileries after a lovely walk through the gardens, and he steered her into a pretty little shop on Rue du Mont Thabor. He'd noticed her admiring the necklace earlier, and when he had the chance he brought her back to the store and bought it for her. Natalie wore it back to the hotel feeling special—not because she had a lovely piece of jewelry, but because of the thoughtful man who wanted to make her happy.

"I love this necklace."

And I love you, she thought. *I walked away from you, but I love you.*

His face dropped into concern. Could he sense what she was feeling?

"Natalie? What is it?" He came to her and pulled her close. "Is something wrong?"

He cradled her body gently against his. They fit together perfectly, despite being so different. She snuggled into his warmth, his sweet protection. She settled there. Content. Safe.

"I'm fine," she finally responded to his question. "Just hold me a little longer."

"Of course."

Natalie had to figure out a way to tell him about the baby, and she needed to do it soon. She was almost three months gone, and there was no telling when her little belly would pop. Sure, it could be another two months, but Natalie had a feeling as she rubbed her hand across the flat muscle of her stomach that it wasn't going to be that long. She just didn't know what to say.

"Hey there, so how do you feel about having a family?"

His first instinct would be to propose, and Natalie's first

instinct would be to accept. She didn't want to trap him into marriage, but was it a trap? It didn't feel like one. It felt right. Natalie had never felt so right about anything.

Looking up, her gaze locked with his. His mother be damned. Gossips be damned. James deserved to know everything. After Liam's show opened tomorrow, they would talk.

"There you are!" Grandma's voice echoed in the massive room and the two of them stepped away from each other. "What do you think?" She waved her cane like a wand. "Not bad for your old granny, is it?"

"Grandma, it's beautiful. I was worried about the space, but it's perfect."

"I wanted to make it like eating in the garden. It's much warmer than I expected today, so we might open some of the doors and let the fresh fall air inside."

"Mrs. Miller, thank you so much for inviting me to join you today. I can tell you that it is going to be something I long remember."

"James, we will expect you back every year."

Placing his hand on his heart he dropped his head. "You honor me."

Grandma just ate him up. All that good breeding made her patrician heart happy. Natalie did love when he went all regal, though. He was so good at it, and the best part was he meant every word.

DINNER HAD BEEN overwhelming, for his taste buds and his eardrums. The large room echoed, the sound bouncing off the plaster ceilings and walls. But it was a wonderful time. James had never been with such an eclectic group of people, all of whom got on with each other.

There were professors from the college, friends from town, relatives who were local, and some from away. Children sat among the adults and participated in the conversations around them. He had been warned about this, but Anna Miller was clear—the only way young ones learned how to behave was to participate in the behavior. There would be no banishing to the kitchen or the children's table. They were family and they would be treated as such. He was completely enamored with Doug Miller's daughters. He'd met Rosie on the way into the house, and when he delivered his bakery goods, he met Rebecca and Rachel. The girls were sweet and well adjusted. Considering what they'd been through he considered it a minor miracle.

After brunch at which he had indulged in something called mulled cider Natalie gave him a quick tour of the house. The Georgian-style mansion was built in the 1920s by her great-grandfather who had come into money when he expanded his businesses. Seeing technology as the wave of the future, he invested in communications, transportation, and aerospace.

The house had eight bedrooms, twelve bathrooms, a solarium, formal gardens, this ballroom and downstairs was an actual replica of a speakeasy. None of that included the guesthouse, the caretaker's house, the garden cottage or the boathouse. In all anyone who was present at the table would probably be able to find a bed for the night on the grounds.

He was sitting in one of the chairs on the flagstone terrace in the garden watching the light fade over the horizon when Natalie stepped outside. She had found a plaid blanket and wrapped it around her shoulders, pulling it tight as she sat in his lap.

"This is nice. You and your blanket can keep me warm."

"As long as you don't speak above a whisper, you've got it."

He laughed. "I have never had a dinner like that before."

"I told you it was madness, and we're not done. We're decorating the Christmas tree next. The kids are downstairs prepping their Christmas show. Because you cannot decorate the tree without Christmas carols."

"It sounds fantastic." He pulled her close and flinched a little because he was sure he was getting harder by the second. No doubt Natalie could feel it pressed into her backside.

Her lashes fluttered and the corner of her mouth twitched.

"Oh, Professor. What are you thinking?" She ground her hips into him, and James's mind went blank.

"You're wicked," he whispered into her ear. "How am I going to resist you?"

"You only have to resist me now. Later you can take me home."

"Home?" He wasn't sure what she was talking about. His home? Hers?

"Uh-huh. Wanna sleep over?"

"Are you sure? You have a big day tomorrow." He was obviously drunk. Why would he try to dissuade her from letting him in her bed? He'd been hoping for this. He'd even thrown a bag together and left it in his car.

"I'll be fine," she purred. "Say yes."

"Yes."

"Good," she said, standing up. "Now, go take a walk and meet me inside when you won't scandalize my grandmother. I have to give her a hand with something."

She didn't give him a chance to answer, but he was content to watch her head into the house, her little bum swaying as she went.

It took a few minutes but he was able to go back inside and join the festivities.

He reentered the kitchen and found a hub of activity. The giant refrigerators were being emptied of leftovers, which had been packed into takeaway tins. Cardboard boxes were filled and there was an assembly line passing the boxes out the kitchen door.

Mia appeared to be directing the operation. "What's going on? Can I assist?"

"Oh, yes! We're sending the leftover sides to the home-less shelter. Can you help Adam load boxes into the van?"

"Of course. No turkey?" he asked, realizing there wasn't much turkey left.

"The restaurants in town roast turkeys and send them. Families provide sides and desserts."

"That's brilliant. What a great community effort."

She handed him a loaded box. "Natalie put the whole thing together. The season is hard for many, and we have so much. Hopefully this helps people feel a little more, I dunno, festive. Happy."

He rolled up his sleeves and got to work, marveling once again at the generosity of these people. It really made him reflect on his own upbringing. Personally, he had projects and charities he supported. He lent his name, his influence, and money, but he rarely got his hands dirty. What was happening in this house is what brought joy to the holidays.

It felt good.

When James finished helping to pack the food delivery, he wandered off on his own to the sitting room where one of the trees was waiting for decorations. Sparkling with what looked like a hundred thousand lights, the tree had to be close to twelve feet tall and it still didn't brush the ceiling. It was set in a bay of windows that had been decked with pine garland, berries and crimson bows. He was the only soul in the room, grateful for a few minutes of quiet.

Ornaments sat in large boxes on the floor—hundreds of them—carefully wrapped in tissue or plastic. Reaching into a box he lifted a glass globe, inlaid with delicate red and green foliage, out of the tissue. He held it up to the light. The ornament was obviously an antique, which made him wonder about the story that might be behind it. Stories. The room was filled with them. The boxes contained memories and that was why Mrs. Miller included the Christmas trees as part of Thanksgiving. The decorating wasn't about lights and tinsel, but about history. About family.

"Oh, you picked a good one." Linda Miller entered the room and sat next to him. It seemed he was going to have conversations with all the Miller women today.

"It's beautiful. It does have a story, then?"

She was holding out her hand, so James placed the ornament in Linda's outstretched palm. "Oh, yes. Theodore Miller—my husband's great-grandfather—was a wild romantic. He was also very determined. The apple of his eye was Elizabeth Perry, also one of the original families in Compass Cove, but the Perrys were of the well-heeled variety. It was the Gilded Age and all the best families were jockeying for a good match." The affection in her voice was touching. He hoped one day people remembered him with such fondness.

"You passed the Perrys' Victorian house right before you turned onto Jennings Road. Anyway, Lizzie's parents didn't want their debutante to have anything to do with a boy like

Teddy Miller, but he was smart, and he loved her. Eventually they convinced her parents to let them marry. Lucy's compass actually helped, but that's another story."

"I need to get Liam to show me that compass. I want to know what makes it tick."

"You and everyone else." She smiled before continuing. "The Millers were craftsmen. They had one of the biggest boatworks on the North Shore. Teddy knew that the money, real money, was to be made by expanding the enterprise. So, in addition to boats they made inroads in rail, communications and eventually, aviation."

"I love hearing family histories. When did they build the house?"

"The house was built in the thirties. Teddy had picked up the property years earlier for a song. There was a run-down house, lots of outbuildings, marshlands. He and Lizzie didn't do anything with it—they had a house in town—but when he died his son, Ethan, began work on it for his family."

"Amazing. Where does the ornament fit in?"

"Ahh, yes," she said. "The ornament was the first gift Teddy Miller gave Elizabeth Perry. He went to visit a friend of his father's, an artist who had built a house and a school not far from here. Teddy asked the gentleman if he had something special for a girl he was sweet on. She was fourteen; he was sixteen."

"Teddy was a smart young man. So, this must be from

around the turn of the century."

"Around there, yes." Linda handed the ornament back to James and he carefully examined the intricate design. It was reminiscent of fine stained glass, and that's when he saw the mark. *LCT.*

Louis Comfort Tiffany?

"This can't be..." If it were a Tiffany piece it would be priceless.

"It could. Mr. Tiffany lived around here. Built a mansion on the water around the turn of the century. Now, we can't be sure..."

"But everyone is sure." James finished her sentence.

"Yeah," she drawled. "Pretty much."

"That's a wonderful story." James was fascinated. He had so much to learn.

"Every ornament in this room has a story. The one you're holding is the first. Teddy promised to find Lizzie a special Christmas ornament every year. His son Ethan, who built this house, did the same for his wife. James gave ornaments to Anna, and John found beautiful ornaments for me. When he died, I started the tradition with the kids."

"So these boxes are filled with love. Your love stories are going on the tree."

She nodded, her blue eyes twinkling just like Natalie's. "That's a lovely way to put it. I think that's why Natalie is so excited about Liam's show. She knows one of his ornaments could be the start of someone's love story. Just like the ornament you're holding."

In all his life, James had never experienced tradition in quite this way. His family was steeped in it, but the more time he spent in Compass Cove, the more he understood that tradition meant very little without an understanding of the people who were at its core.

The Miller family had roots, as did the Jenningses, the Rinaldis and the Velsors. Here, there were generations of people committed not to a tract of land, or a title, but to each other. It was humbling, and it was no wonder that when she needed to run, Natalie ran home.

Good acts, kind people, hospitality, warmth and acceptance…this was where Natalie came from. These gifts were at the heart of who she was. Whether or not she believed it, her family understood her very well, and they loved her.

He loved her, but only now did he find the nerve to admit it.

The voices started low but grew louder and louder as they came down the hall. There was excitement building as they got closer to the sitting room. The children came in first all in matching Christmas pajamas, and Rosie bounced on the sofa next to her grandmother. Everyone filed in quickly, taking a seat wherever they could find one. While there weren't forty people like at dinner, there was still quite a crowd.

Jack escorted his grandmother into the madness, and it was then that he could see the absolute delight on her face.

Natalie squeezed in next to him. "I was looking for you. Where have you been?"

"I've been here. Your mother told me the story of Teddy and Elizabeth."

"Oh, that story gives me the warm fuzzies. Still, I want to get the ornament collection appraised, but my grandmother won't have it."

"I wouldn't let you either. You can't put value on what's in this room. All I can tell you is that it's priceless."

She must have felt his emotion because her eyes filled with tears. Could she know how much she meant to him? That he would go anywhere, be anything she wanted if it made her happy? James's heart was bursting, like it had been freed from a long sleep. He couldn't wait anymore. Slowly, he leaned in, and whispered so only she could hear, "I love you, Natalie."

"Oh, James." Her breath escaped, the tiniest noise that sounded like relief and fear at the same time. "I don't know what to say."

"Nothing. When you're ready, you'll know exactly what to say."

James always imagined that when he confessed his feelings to Natalie, he'd do it privately, someplace where the two of them could allow the idea to settle around them. Instead, he was in a room teeming with people that was anything but quiet.

Even so, it felt right.

Everything with her felt right.

Chapter Sixteen

NATALIE DRIFTED AWAKE when the cold air hit her face. She had the sense of being weightless, floaty, but still secure. Safe. Eventually, her eyes drifted open, and she realized she was on the path to her cottage. James was carrying her. Why was he carrying her?

Because when she'd left the madness in the family room, she'd fallen asleep in a comfy chair in the library.

Several questions raced through her mind. Still, it was nice and she snuggled close to him, being rewarded with a kiss on the head. "You're awake?" he asked.

"Mmm hmm." The lights along the flagstone path through the woods would lead him to the boathouse, but she wasn't going to let him carry her down the stairs. There were too many steps, even for her big, strapping viscount. "This is very *Bridgerton* of you, Your Lordship."

James laughed out loud at the reference to one of Natalie's favorite shows. "Is that how we're playing this?"

Natalie giggled. One of the things she'd tried to put out of her head was how much fun they had together because she missed it so much. Teasing and joking, they truly enjoyed one another's company. He had a wonderful sense of humor, a wry wit that was observant and smart. The most obscure things would set him off, and he could find humor almost anywhere.

It's one of the reasons his students loved him. He was a marvelous teacher, well read and interesting. When they traveled to Scotland last spring, she had a wonderful time listening to him as they explored Edinburgh and the Highlands. He felt the history in his bones. Respected it. That's what came through. For him it was a story in a story, a tapestry of people, places and things that came together.

"You can put me down." Natalie was awake now, having enjoyed a lovely nap. She was perfectly able to walk by herself, but James didn't seem too eager to put her down.

"I don't think so. I rather like walking with you in my arms. At least I know where you are, for the time being."

"Well, you're going to have to put me down when we get to the top of the bluff. I'm not going to let you carry me down the stairs. There are fifty-two steps—too many for even you."

He grinned, his eyes ablaze at the challenge. "You think so? We'll see about that."

"Seriously, James. Don't. I'll walk."

She saw they were entering the clearing at the edge of the bluff, the water spread out before them, and Cove Landing was awash in moonlight, the lights in the houses twinkling in the distance.

"Oh, God," he said it like a prayer. "It's beautiful. That's where I live?" He nodded toward the Landing.

"It is. That's Liam's house up there. The one on the most distant point, next to the lighthouse. Yours is on the other side of his. We can't see it from here."

He smiled down at her, and Nat's heart flipped. "That's too bad. I could wave at you every morning."

For the first time in months, Natalie thought about being with him. Truly being with him. Not friends with benefits, tentative lovers, or two people pining at a distance, but all in. Partners for life. It didn't feel impossible. He loved her. He'd said so, and if Natalie was honest with herself, she knew she loved him right back.

For the first time since she came home, she didn't think about loving James as an impossibility. It didn't trigger thoughts of the threats leveled by the earl, or the disapproving sniffs from his mother. There was only him, and now, their baby. No doubts.

Reaching out, she pressed her hand on his cheek, warm and rough with stubble. She was consumed by the feel of him, by his intense gaze.

"Natalie…" Her name slipped over his lips, a whisper that hit her like a thunderbolt. She tried to run away from the feelings he stirred in her, tried to run away from the struggle, from the conflict, but there was no escaping what was in her heart. James was her soul mate, and that meant she had two choices: she could end this with him and never look back, never know the kind of love they could only find together, or she could be brave for the first time in her life and go all in.

She'd have to tell him everything. Not just about the baby, but about what happened at the gallery, about his mother. She'd have to reveal her fears and reservations. He deserved to know it all, even the stuff she'd hidden beneath a carefully crafted façade.

Amazingly, she wasn't worried. Peeling back the layers of her life, being vulnerable, was necessary if they were going to step over that threshold. She wanted everything with him. Absolutely everything. Gently pressing his forehead to hers, Natalie could feel him. His devotion, his loyalty, his love was hers if she wanted them. How could she say no?

"I meant what I said. I love you. So very much."

Did she say the words? Could she break herself open before him and let all she was rush out? This was James—he deserved nothing less. "I love you, too. And I've missed you."

His arms tightened around her, pulling her into his warmth. This is where she was meant to be, not running from herself, but running to him, embracing this amazing man who had the ability to make her feel whole.

"I thought I'd lost you. Please don't run away again." His voice was deep, desperate. "Whatever is going on, whatever problems crop up, we're in this together. No more secrets."

"I promise," she said with a nod. His mouth settled on hers, breathing her in, stealing her breath. His kiss was sweet, tender. Natalie didn't hold back as she felt the tears roll down her cheeks. She shivered when his lips lightly grazed the corner of her mouth, her temple, her forehead…in that moment her heart, quite simply, ached for him.

"I need to get you inside; you must be freezing." How did she tell him that she'd never be cold in his arms?

"Put me down first. The steps are very steep." Natalie didn't want to lose the connection they had, but it would have been too dangerous for both of them if he insisted on carrying her to the cottage. No matter how romantic it sounded.

James stepped toward the wooden staircase and Natalie saw his eyebrows shoot up. "Damn," he said. "That is steep."

When they were teenagers, she, Jordan, and Lilly would sneak out of her house during sleepovers and head to the boathouse so they could gossip without her brothers listening in. It was a miracle they didn't break their necks running through the woods and down the steps in the middle of the night. The place held memories, wonderful memories, and now she would be making new ones with James.

"Your cottage?" He was eyeing her little home at the edge of the water. "It's adorable."

She agreed. The house still sported the weather-green cedar shingles that she remembered from her childhood. It had a small porch encircling three sides of the house, and a ramp that went directly to the beach. When the tide was high the entrance to the cottage was about five yards from the water.

"I'm quite partial to it," she said. "How do you like the lights?"

Natalie was pleased with her decorating efforts. Last night when she'd gotten home from working at the gallery, she was such a nervous wreck after learning about the baby, she broke out the strings of outdoor Christmas lights and hung them along the low roofline. It was an unusually warm night, and she only needed a step stool for the highest points, so she didn't have to feel guilty about the risk.

The activity had done the trick—Natalie calmed down. The brightly colored lights and the boxes of Christmas decorations instantly put her in a good mood. It was doing the same for her now. The lights and the springs of pine she'd tied to the porch rail made her feel like Christmas was only days away rather than weeks.

"I like the lights," James said as he gazed down at her. "I like everything about this place. Mostly I like you."

His smile had turned wolfish, and Natalie's insides responded immediately. God, what that man did to her. All it took was a pat on the arm for James to put her down. Hesitating was not an option, so she grabbed his hand and headed down the steps. Yes, she should have gone slower. The temperature had dropped and the spray from the water could have made the steps slippery. But luck was with her and the next thing she knew James was following her inside her cottage.

As soon as the door closed, Natalie was pressed against it. His hands, his lips, the weight of his body filled her senses. His lips found hers and teased. Tasted. Finally, the tip of his tongue teased the seam of her mouth, and they dove into the kiss with the passion only lost lovers could know.

Grabbing James by the front of his shirt, Natalie held on. Unlike the frenetic tangle from a few weeks ago, this kiss was slower, lazier…a sensual dance of their lips and tongues. His mouth was soft and warm, lulling her into a peaceful rhythm. His hips ground into hers, and the weight, the sensation, was like a sexy welcome home. God, she'd missed him.

He was so gentle with her, but times like these—in the true heat of passion—reminded her that he was a physical man. Big, powerful, and almost a foot taller than she was, he had a bearing that reminded her of an auburn-haired Celtic warrior with his ruddy skin and stormy hazel eyes. His body against hers was such a comfort, such a relief. *Such a thrill.*

Natalie wasn't going to go without him for another minute. Before he could object, her hands went exploring, slipping easily under the sweater he'd worn today. His skin was heating under her touch. Hearing him groan, she did even more, running her hands over his taut behind, before grinding into his most impressive erection.

"Don't you dare be a gentleman," she commanded.

"Whatever you say," he responded. With that, he picked her up and threw her over his shoulder. She whooped and laughed as he turned around, obviously searching for the bedroom.

"Where is it? The bed?" He was a man with a mission.

"That way." Natalie pointed but had to contort herself so he could see where to go. It was awesome. She hadn't had this much fun in months.

Hitting the light switch inside the door with his elbow he tossed her right in the middle of the bed and followed her down, bracing himself, so he stopped the momentum just inches above her.

James lifted his head and took in his surroundings. He first settled on the large window that faced the beach. Even at night the sea was a presence. That she could catch the glow of the Christmas lights she'd hung on the roof was even more wonderful.

The second thing he examined at length was her large, scrolled iron headboard. The look on his face was scandalous. What was he planning?

Natalie couldn't wait to find out.

"This has potential."

"Is that so? What are you planning, m'lord?" Natalie affected her best British accent.

Kissing her hard, his tongue slipped into the warmth of her mouth. Teasing, tasting, and setting her on fire.

She continued to move against his erection until he broke the kiss. "Natalie, I haven't had sex in weeks. And before that it was months. Please stop so we can get this done properly."

The giggles that threatened were wicked, and could possibly kill the mood, so Natalie tried desperately to keep them at bay. *Properly?* His formal tone, his language—the accent—made him sound like he was an old English butler. She couldn't help it.

Right as he started to nibble his way down her neck, Natalie lost it. The fits of giggles that rolled through her were more than likely a result of nerves. Being with him again, knowing they still had something special, was hard enough, but hearing his clipped speech and his proclamation about getting things done "properly," she lost it.

While her body spasmed with laughter, James pushed himself off her and stared. Much to Natalie's dismay, there were no more delicious nibbles anywhere, just one very annoyed viscount hovering over her.

"Why are you laughing?"

"Oh, I'm sorry," she choked out. "Really. It's just when you said we had to get this done *properly*...oh my God. You sounded like a stodgy old Brit. *Prrrroperly,*" she teased in her best mock accent.

James was still balanced over her, scowling. This was everything, and she'd missed it. Sex for them had always been a mix of hot, coma-inducing passion, and fun. Pure fun. Natalie figured she laughed out loud with James as much as she screamed his name.

"You're asking for it, you know?" His growl was low and

seductive. Natalie scooted her way back from the edge of the bed, settling with her back propped against the pillows.

"Oh, no," she teased. "Is his lordship angry?"

"His lordship is going to teach you a lesson." His grin was ravenous. "*Properly*, of course."

"Oh, really?"

He lunged at her, shackling both wrists over her head with one hand while his other was busy ridding her of different pieces of clothes. "Really. Now hold on to the headboard, love. I have some things to attend to."

Those things were her clothes, and most of his, leaving Natalie deliciously naked.

"That's better." With a light smack on the ass, he spread her legs wide, settling himself between them. His mouth came down on one nipple, licked it, and pulled gently.

Natalie, who had taken his advice and was holding on to her wrought-iron headboard, arched and moaned in response.

"Do you like that, darling?"

"Uh-huh." Yeah, she was getting stupid already and he hadn't gotten below her waist.

"Oh, good." He chuckled. "Now hold on tight."

That's when he started working his way down.

His hands stroked her, traveling over her skin in a gentle caress. "You are so lovely, Natalie. You have the body of a goddess. Soft, lush, perfect."

Lush. Soft. Had he noticed the extra weight she was carrying? Natalie was naturally small, very petite, which was unusual since she came from a family of Amazons. She never felt as though she fit with her gorgeous family. She was often called cute or adorable, but never beautiful. James, however, never failed to tell her she was beautiful, or lovely, or brilliant. And she knew he meant every endearment.

"I love touching you. Having you naked like this. I just want to keep touching you." He moved his hands to her hips and then her thighs. His mouth was a miracle, and it seemed he licked or kissed every inch of her belly as he eased his way between her legs. His fingers ran over her mound and separated the warm folds at her center. He didn't say another word as his mouth came down on her and his tongue flicked and teased her into oblivion.

He was gentle, thorough, and oh so very skilled. There was harmony between them, a safe and secure space where Natalie's fears slipped away.

"James," she whispered. It was all she could muster as her brain clouded.

In her head she heard him mutter soothing, sweet words. His deep voice surrounded her, and that was all that mattered. Threading her fingers through his hair as he tended to her, Natalie felt beautiful and wicked, like the kind of woman who could tempt a man away from his family, his country, and his position. Inside her, the heat built. A low pulse in her belly became more intense, radiating out to every nerve and muscle. She watched James, his long lashes hiding his eyes as all his attention was focused on her. Biting down on her lip, Natalie stopped thinking as the waves of the orgasm washed over her.

Light exploded inside her eyelids while her hands gripped the headboard again. Her hips were bucking wildly, and that's when James shifted his position and slid into her.

God, he felt good, filling her perfectly just like he always did. He moved in such a way that the gentle friction between their bodies aroused her once again.

Her frantic movements slowed in time with his. Long strokes and deep kisses took her into a dreamy plane. A place where titles and status didn't matter. A place where only the two of them existed.

Natalie wrapped her arms and legs around James, clinging to him as he plunged deeper into her. Their bodies fit, melting together to become one.

"Lovely Natalie. I'll not lose you again. I wasn't whole without you."

His words went deep, boring into her heart and filling it from the inside out. Every touch, every movement brought them closer together. But his words, honest and sweet, undid her.

Her heartbeat for him, her very existence was made better when she and James were together. How had she not seen that?

Quickening his pace, James held on to her with one arm and kept himself from crushing her with the other. He was so strong—a protector, a leader, a scholar, and all Natalie wanted was to be with him.

She felt her body start to crest again. Like a giant wave of amazing sensations, hot and powerful, it consumed her. But through all the heat and emotion Natalie was aware of the connection between them. It was the kind of connection that made forever seem real.

She felt James as he surged into her, all his strength propelling him forward, as she received all he had to give. They were meant to be together, and they had to find a way. Their baby needed this amazing man in its life.

Finally spent, he eased himself down, still not separating from her. She was fine with that, loving the way he held her. His head had settled in the crook of her shoulder, his breathing hard and heavy. This was everything. He was everything.

"I love you, Nat. So much," he said when he rolled on his back and pulled her in.

"I love you, too," she said quietly. The words still shocked her, but it was the truth. She'd never been so certain of her feelings. She also knew it was long past time for her to be honest with him.

I LOVE YOU. It was the last thing he heard as sleep claimed her.

Watching Natalie sleep was certainly no hardship, and neither was seeing her practically orgasm into a coma. The woman went out like a light right after she came. Stroking the hair away from her face while he held her, James worried about how he was going to sort out the mess that had driven them apart. He still didn't have details, but his brother had called when he'd stepped away from the party for a little air. One word stuck in his mind. One ugly word: *blackmail.*

He expected the incident at the gallery provided his step-father leverage to get Natalie out of his life. James knew his mother disapproved of "his American girl," as she'd taken to calling her, but he never thought they would stoop to something as low as blackmail to keep his somewhat minor title from being *sullied.* It was awful. They were insufferable elitists, and he was having none of it. The gall of it all was one thing. He could run his own life, but the thought that they had done something to hurt Natalie, a person who had done nothing but make him happy, enraged him. He'd done his best to avoid his stepfather. The man was a pompous arse, but if Edward's information about what happened at the gallery panned out, James would be on a plane to pay the bastard a visit.

"Why are you scowling?" The husky-from-sleep voice surprised him. Natalie's eyes were wide open, but still hazy.

"I'm thinking." Adjusting their position so he could see her better, James smiled. "How are you feeling?"

"Very…content." She burrowed closer. "I don't believe I

have any bones."

"Ha! I'd say so. You drifted right off."

"I must have fainted from the orgasm. You did that. You're a god."

He laughed. "Is that so? Do people snore when they faint?"

Natalie was making small circles on his chest with her finger. "Snore? Why do you ask?"

"Because you were snoring."

"I don't snore," she snapped indignantly.

He chuckled at her feigned offense. "No? Could have fooled me."

Turning to face him, she smiled. "I like being with you."

"And I you. Being apart just isn't an option for me. I think it's time for us to have a serious conversation."

She seemed to freeze for a moment, looking away to contemplate what he'd said. Slowly, she inched away from him and sat up. Her face was somber, serious.

"You're right." She swallowed, the words catching in her throat. "I haven't been honest with you."

"About what happened at the gallery, about my stepfather? I have a sense I'm going to want to lock him in the dungeon of his own house after you tell me."

The silence settled between them as Natalie thought about what she was going to say. He admired her thoughtfulness, her care when choosing her words. James had learned not to rush her.

When she turned her eyes back to his, they were on fire. That was the last thing he expected.

"Personally," she growled. "I think the dungeon is too good for him."

Chapter Seventeen

"I HAD NO idea he was such an insufferable prick. I mean I never liked him, but…shit."

James was digesting everything Natalie had just told him about what went down at the gallery and his stepfather's involvement. They'd moved from her bed to the sitting room where he nursed a scotch and she sipped on some herbal tea.

God knew she wanted a scotch.

"I don't know what he'll do now that you know. I'm assuming you're not going to stay quiet about it."

He tossed back the scotch and stood. "Quiet? Hell no. My gut is telling me to get the next flight to London and make him pay. My brother tipped me off that he was the one behind your leaving, but I never suspected…I mean this is full-on Shakespearean cloak-and-dagger bullshit."

"Please don't get on a plane. Not until you've thought it through. I took off before I thought about the consequences and look where it landed me. Thank God you're stubborn."

"You're exactly where you should be." He rose, pulling her out of her chair and into his arms. "I do wish you'd told me. I hate that you suffered through this on your own, but I don't know if staying in England was the right thing for us. I needed to come here, for you."

The gentle movement of his hands on her back soothed her. In a conversation that should have been fraught with emotion, peace settled between them. It was a problem to be solved, but it was no longer a crisis. He did that for her. Someday, she hoped she could do the same for him.

They stood together, quietly, the gentle sounds of their breathing filling the space. The colored lights were the only thing left illuminating the outside of the cottage because the moon had dropped below the horizon. She should be exhausted, but Natalie just wanted to spend time with James. She wanted to make memories. They'd met right before last Christmas. She found out after they've been dating a few months that he'd made a point to stop in that coffee shop every day just to see her. Maybe, he hoped, they would strike up a conversation. It was such a James thing to do. He wasn't pushy, or overly flirtatious, he was friendly. He made her laugh.

If Natalie were to admit it herself, she looked forward to their short bursts of conversation. Sometimes seeing him was the best part of her day.

Was his behavior a little bit stalkery? Perhaps. But she couldn't fault the outcome. His little fib about stopping on his way to work were the stuff of which romances were made.

"I'm glad I came here. I understand more about you than I ever did. You are remarkable. Determined, forward-thinking, and your family...you are very lucky."

Natalie had wondered how he would react to the chaos that was the Miller clan. They could be overwhelming, but James didn't just enjoy his day, he'd embraced the crazy. He'd done that with Compass Cove, with Jennings College. James fit here, and she wondered again if he might consider staying.

She should tell him about the baby. She knew she should, but the timing seemed off since she'd just dropped the big bomb about his family.

"Are you tired? I should be," he said. "But I'm not."

"No. I was just thinking that. I should be exhausted." Between the baby, the holiday, and the mind-blowing sex, she should be deep in dreamland. "I feel like baking."

That surprised him. "You want to...you want to bake?"

"Just like Mary Berry." The mention of the star of the *Great British Bake Off* made him smile. Like the night at the house on the landing, it was another little reminder of the life they had been building. They had slipped into one another's lives so easily, it felt like they had always been together. Old souls who had found each other. Like Caleb and Lucy.

They liked the same kind of TV, and they loved the outdoors and travel, but there were differences too. He read thrillers and history, but Natalie loved romances and stories about women and families.

Of course, they had disagreements—they were both strong-willed—but even if they retreated to their own apartments after an argument, they didn't let the bad blood stew all night. One of them always called, sometimes it was both of them.

The excitement, the ache, the desire wasn't all-consuming, but a steady presence that allowed the relationship to grow in its own way. The path led to quiet acceptance. To deep friendship. To love.

Taking his hand, Natalie dragged him to the kitchen.

"You're serious, then? We're baking at three in the morning?"

"We are. I'm not going to be able to sleep—for a variety of reasons—so Christmas cookies seem like a good idea."

"I can think of a few things we can do other than bake," he said scandalously. With a little tug, he pulled Natalie into him. The giggle that escaped was only the tiniest indication of how happy she was.

James backed her into the edge of the island and kissed her soundly. A large smack escaped when he broke the kiss, confirming he was in as playful a mood as she was.

"Come on. I love to bake and I barely did it when I lived in London. I think I made you peanut butter cookies one time."

He nodded. Natalie suppressed a laugh because she remembered he didn't like those cookies very much. "All right.

You want to bake biscuits for Christmas? Any particular kind?"

"Lena taught me to make Italian Christmas cookies, but those are a little labor-intensive, so I'm thinking plain old chocolate chip will do. You don't have a problem with chocolate chip, do you?"

James was such a good sport. He'd eaten several of the cookies and didn't complain once. She could see on his face, however, that he had not enjoyed them. She had no idea why—they were her best batch ever—but there was no accounting for taste with some people. Really, who didn't like peanut butter cookies?

She'd have to accept it, and if that was his only flaw, she'd take it.

"I like chocolate chip. What do you need me to do, chef?"

SHE WOKE TO the smell of cookies. Buttery and sweet, the aroma lingered in the air. Slowly, her senses were waking up. When her eyes fluttered open the beach was bathed in gray light right outside her window, signaling another day was about to start. Rolling over, she expected to see James lying next to her, but instead he was sitting on the edge of the bed, staring at the phone in his hand.

He wasn't moving; he just sat frozen, thumb poised over

the screen. He was thinking about calling home, confronting his family, protecting her. It had to be incredibly difficult for him to even think about, and she didn't know if she wanted him to do it. Because as much as the earl and the countess wanted Natalie gone, they had betrayed James, and he wouldn't take that lightly.

When they first started dating, she'd had no idea about his title. All she knew was that he was a history professor at Cambridge. That he consulted for museums and libraries. She'd often hear him on the phone discussing any number of topics in just as many languages. Nat knew he'd served his country in the Royal Marines, and that made her a little homesick for her brothers. James's brilliance, his confidence, his sense of duty had always attracted her, but it was the way he dealt with his students, how he intuitively knew how to get the best out of them, that helped her fall for him.

The whole viscount thing popped up one night when he asked her to escort him to a formal gala, and they were announced as "The Right Honorable the Viscount Linden and Miss Natalie Miller of New York."

He obviously forgot to tell her something. *Men.*

After the gala she'd returned to his flat, and while she prepared cheese toasties, he sat on a stool at a small table in the kitchen and told her about his life growing up, about his parents and about his brother. He'd had a nice childhood. Special in many of the same ways Natalie's was special. James's world was small, insular, but he'd had an almost normal childhood growing up. His father wasn't the most attentive man in the world, but James never doubted his father's love for any of them. It was when he reached his teens that his role changed. Expectations changed.

That's why watching him agonize was breaking her heart. James was furious. Hurt. How did one come to grips with that kind of betrayal?

"I can hear you thinking back there," he grumbled. "You have something to say?"

Snuggling up to him and resting her cheek on his strong back, Natalie wished she could make everything better.

"Not really. I mean, I don't want you to ruin relationships over me."

"I'm a born decision-maker. I've always been comfortable with pressure. When I was in the Marines, and I was given my first command, I wasn't intimidated; I was ready. Now, I don't know what to do. It's hard to make sense of it all."

"They went behind your back. I guess it's understandable."

He turned. "It's more than that. They didn't care one bit for my happiness. They don't respect me. It's sobering."

Moving, she shifted her position and settled on his lap. Looping her arms around his neck, Natalie kissed him. "Could you talk to your mother? Leave Stepdaddy out of it?"

"Yes. Probably."

"Maybe that's a place to start." Natalie was giving the

woman more grace than she deserved, but people made mistakes. She wanted to believe a mother's love was at the root of her decisions.

"What if she asks when I'll be back in England?" James tightened his arms around her. "I don't know what to tell her."

What was he getting at? "You don't? Isn't the end of spring term your end date?"

"It is. But I'm thinking about staying."

That was the last thing Natalie had expected him to say. "Stateside, or at Jennings?"

"Jennings if they'll have me. I think they will. How would you feel about that?"

His eyes were locked on hers. Just hearing he wanted to stay calmed all her fears about the baby. They would be in it together. "Really? I mean…oh, my God. How does that work? Do you keep your title? Does your brother become viscount? Can you leave?"

He laughed. "I can leave, and the title stays with me. I teased the idea to my brother." James shook his head a bit and grinned. "He wasn't surprised. He and his family will move to the house in Cambridgeshire, if that's what I decide to do. He can work from home part-time and take the train into town a few days and week. But he won't get my title. It doesn't work like that."

"I see." Giddy at his news, Natalie felt her blood heat up. Leaning in, she nipped at his ear, then his chin before moving to his mouth. She lingered there, savoring the taste of his lips. There was sweetness from the chocolate, and an earthiness from the scotch he'd had earlier.

She straddled him, loving the wide-eyed surprise on his face. "This is nice."

Natalie loved sex with James. It had always been good between them, easy and fun, but while she would flirt and tease, she was never this aggressive. She found she liked taking control, and based on the hardness pressed against her thigh, he did too.

"What is it you're after, Ms. Miller? Perhaps I can be of assistance."

She giggled, taking another nip of his neck. "No worries, Professor. I've got this. You just hang on for the ride."

It was so easy to get lost in his gaze, in the way he focused on her. His eyes darkened as she moved against him, his breath catching. Natalie groaned as he slipped his hand under her T-shirt and caressed her body with precision and skill. He knew all her spots—everywhere she liked to be touched.

They moved in sync, melted into each other. He pulled her shirt over her head and when they were both naked, Natalie leaned in. She shivered when her nipples grazed against his, the heat coming off both their bodies tangled in an invisible dance, pulling them together.

"You are my heart, Natalie. There's no one else and there never will be. It's only you."

His hands encircled her waist, and tenderly, his thumbs grazed over her belly, right where his baby was growing inside her. Natalie was moved, incredibly moved. Her eyes flooded with tears. Slowly, she shifted her hips and took him inside her.

What had started out as heat and need, had settled into a bonding of their souls. His thrusts weren't hard or fast. This was a gentle worship that dared their past selves to be open to the melding of hearts. He was hers…her love and her future.

JAMES WAS BACK to sitting on the edge of the bed with the phone in his hand. He wasn't looking to dial, instead his eyes were fixed on Natalie who was in sweats, fuzzy boots and a hat she'd made herself, doing yoga on the flat of a large stone at the edge of the water. He'd seen whitecaps when he woke earlier, but now the bay was smooth as glass. It was as if Mother Nature knew Natalie needed the quiet.

His mother had to be his first call, even if he wanted to avoid the confrontation. After hearing Natalie confirm what Edward had told him, along with all the additional details of what happened at the gallery, he didn't know how he was going to go through with this.

But even if he didn't want to talk to his mum, he owed it to Nat. They had put them both through hell, but she deserved better.

Still, he watched her. She was calm and focused, appearing to let nature inside. He'd seen Natalie's storms, when she was out on Liam's deck the night of the nor'easter, when she was fighting back the demons of her own anxiety; when she was protecting the people she loved she was fierce. The least James could do would be to find some of that nerve to protect her.

Scrolling, he stopped at his mom's contact information and pressed the button to connect the call. She picked up on the second ring.

"James, darling, how good of you to call. When will we see you? You'll be home for the holidays?"

"No, sorry. I have no plans to come for Christmas. I'll be spending it in Compass Cove."

"*Compass Cove?* How quaint. A typical New England town I suppose? Not quite the same as Christmas in London."

He had no intention of getting into a sparring match with his mum where she put down his choices and he went on the defensive. James wasn't the one who had to explain his actions. This was all on Mum. "I don't want to talk about where I'm living, or my job. I want to talk about Natalie."

"Natalie?" His mother did her best to feign indifference, but there was a crack in her voice, something that let James know this was not a topic she wanted to talk about.

"Yes, the woman I was seeing. Of course, you remember her, you and Rutherford went to such lengths to destroy our relationship. To destroy her."

Silence. There was nothing but silence coming from the other end of the call. Finally, she spoke.

"I have no idea what you're talking about, dear. You would do well not to listen to people like Miss Miller. Isn't it obvious that she has designs on you? Did she track you down in New York? We could speak to the authorities."

"She's the one who should be speaking to the police, Mum. Did you think you'd get away with it?"

"You're talking nonsense. Get away with what?"

"Blackmail."

"*Blackmail?*" she sputtered. "I—I never! That's absurd. Did she tell you this? Are you with her?"

He had no intention of telling her anything about Natalie. This was about his wildly dysfunctional family, and her god-awful husband who was going to be held accountable. His mother would have a choice: accept his relationship with Natalie and keep her husband in check, or she would be out of his life.

If he couldn't trust her, there was no reason to pretend.

"James? Do you want to explain to me what you're talking about? I had tea with Natalie this past summer, a week or two before her *assault* on your stepfather. I won't lie, I told her I didn't think she was suitable for you. No offense intended, but we live a different kind of life than an art dealer from the United States. So, if you're angry with me for telling her I didn't approve and I didn't trust her not to do something underhanded like get pregnant, you'll have to deal with it. I'm not sorry."

God, she needed to climb down off her pedestal. "Mother, you need to google the Miller family from Compass Cove, Long Island. I think you'll find it interesting reading." If nothing else she would stop thinking that Natalie was after the family fortune. "But you still haven't answered me about the incident at the gallery. The setup, the threats—how could you do that to her?"

Again, she didn't say anything. He wondered if anything he'd said was getting through. "Mother? Do you have anything to say about it?"

"You have me at a disadvantage, my boy. The only thing I know regarding what happened at the gallery is that there was a disagreement and your Natalie hit the earl in the nose with a very expensive statue. It's unfortunate, but at least you don't have to worry about having someone so prone to violence in your life."

It didn't seem possible, but it became obvious that his mother didn't know about the scheme. She didn't know about the actress, or the earl's plan to get Natalie out of England. But why? The earl couldn't have his title, hell, even if James wanted, he couldn't pass the thing to his brother. The family money was locked up tight in investments and trusts.

"Are you sitting down, Mum?"

"Yes, why? Are you going to accuse me of being in on a plot to steal the Crown Jewels?" His mother had clearly grown tired of his anger and accusations.

"Because I have a story to tell you."

Chapter Eighteen

NATALIE WAS READY.

The gallery was picture-perfect, looking like a Christmas wonderland, and with seven o'clock closing in, for the first time in weeks she felt like everything was going to work out. And she wasn't just thinking about the show. Her personal life, specifically her love life, had taken an unexpected turn into the wonderful.

She and James had covered a lot of ground the night before. They had gotten little sleep, but every conversation, every kiss, every touch, every orgasm brought them closer together. She told him everything—well, almost everything. His fury about what his stepfather had done, as well as his mother's complicity, left him reeling. That's why she hadn't told him about the baby yet. But this weekend Natalie would make a plan, a grand revelation to let him know he was going to be a father.

In the meantime, this was Natalie's secret. Well, Natalie and Jordan, and her mother...

Okay, maybe it wasn't a secret, but it would still be a surprise. Natalie could only hope he would be as happy about it as she was. It surprised her that she'd gotten used to the idea so quickly. She loved kids, but motherhood seemed so far off. Setting her hand on her still-flat tummy, she felt a tickle of warmth from deep inside. She would work to be a good mom. Her goal was to raise her child to be happy and healthy. How could it not be with family and friends, and a daddy like theirs in the picture?

The bell over the door tinkled, reminding Natalie that it was showtime. Smoothing her hands over her black cocktail dress, she turned to see James standing in the doorway. He held a beautiful bouquet and flashed a smile that made her toes curl. Memories from last night washed through her. If it weren't so close to opening, she'd drag him upstairs and make a few more memories.

"You are stunning." His words were everything because they were more than just words. As clichéd as it was, James wore his heart on his sleeve. He really loved her and for the life of her, Natalie couldn't figure out what she did to deserve him.

"So do you," she said as they closed the distance between them. His dark blue suit was coupled with a crisp white shirt he'd left open at the collar. He wore the family signet ring on his right hand along with a gold Rolex watch. "I've never seen this."

Natalie lifted his arm to look at the timepiece, which was obviously an heirloom.

"It belonged to my grandfather, the tenth Viscount Linden. It was given to him by his grandfather when Grampy returned from the war in 1945. I'm named for him."

"It's beautiful." Natalie examined the timepiece for a few more seconds before taking his hands in hers. "It suits you. I love the connection to your family."

"It seemed appropriate to break it out for the evening. This entire show is about family, really." He looked up and took in the space. "Natalie, this is spectacular." Before a uniformed server could get past him, James grabbed two flutes of champagne off the tray and handed one to her. She smiled even though she had no intention of drinking it.

"To Belgravia Gallery and its lovely curator." James clinked his glass to hers and took a sip. "You've created magic here, Nat. Magic."

The lights hanging from the ceiling seemed extra twinkly tonight, just like the ones on Main Street. The town was awash in holiday spirit. Ask any local, and they would tell you Compass Cove came alive in the summer, but Natalie disagreed. Christmas here was moonlight sprinkled with stardust. It was a child's smile, a wink from Santa, and a favorite cookie hot from the oven. Compass Cove was every good thing in her life.

It had taken her a while to see it, but now it was her turn to give something back to the town and the people who gave her courage she never knew she had.

It was a lot of work opening Liam's show, but if ever there had been a community effort, this show was it. And it made her happy, so happy to be able to showcase her friend's brilliant work. That James was here with her made it all the more special.

They were more alike than she'd ever realized. His family could be just as overwhelming as hers, and the titles and trappings of the aristocracy didn't change that. But deep down, she knew she was loved, as was he.

James laid a hand on her cheek, cupping her face ever so gently. His touch set her heart skipping wildly and her mind racing. She had no idea how they were going to make a relationship work, but she had to believe they would. For their baby she had to have faith in James…and in herself.

"What's wrong, Nat. Are you crying?"

Crap. Was she? Dabbing at the corner of her eye, Natalie sniffed. No matter how hard she tried, she had no poker face. "I…I love you and I don't want to mess it up again."

There was no hesitation as he pulled her in. "You won't. All we must do is be honest with each other. We can get through whatever life throws at us if we have trust."

He was right—trust was everything. The little twist in her chest reminded her that they needed to have a long talk, and it had best be sooner rather than later.

A blast of cold air surrounded them as the first guests entered the gallery, including the featured artist. Liam was accompanied by his father, Jordan and Nick, and Maddy King who had her arm linked with Liam's. Wasn't that a lovely surprise.

Natalie handed the champagne to James, and rushed to greet her friends. She hadn't let Liam see the exhibit before it opened, begging him to trust her.

There was that word again.

"Holy shitballs, Nat," Liam exhaled. "I can't believe this. The exhibit is art."

If she squeezed her fingers any tighter, she'd cut off circulation. "You like it?"

Over the last week she'd tweaked the placement of at least a hundred ornaments. Liam had been stockpiling the glass for two years. His production was inhuman.

"Oh, my God. *Yes.* Thank you." The bear hug he gave her was all the approval she needed. Natalie was thrilled he was happy with how she'd showcased his work. Liam was so much more than a friend; he was a fourth brother. Sometimes she felt he was the only one in Compass Cove who understood her.

Maddy had a wide smile. She pulled Natalie away from Liam to give a hug of her own. "This is going to be a beautiful night," she said, her chocolate-brown eyes shining. "For both of you."

It made Natalie happy to see her two friends were on their way to becoming a couple. Then again, the way Liam leaned in and whispered in Maddy's ear—and her very flirtatious response—made Natalie wonder if they were already there.

Her family arrived just as the light piano music filled the

space. Everyone looked around when they heard "I'll Be
Home for Christmas."

NATALIE BARELY HAD time to breathe before the door
opened and she saw three well-known art agents step inside.
They were followed by the art critic from the *Times*. As her
brother Doug would say, *Shit's gettin' real.*

Natalie wasn't sure if she should run right over to greet
them, which is what she would normally do, or if she should
let them take in the atmosphere first. These were serious
women, and they were rarely affected by the environment.
Their jobs were visual, driven by emotional reactions to what
they saw, which was what made Natalie hang back until she
could gauge their response. They stood for a long time,
tilting their heads, talking among themselves, leaning toward
the Christmas tree that was right at the front door. One step
in the room, two steps in the room, and finally, with the
third step in the room smiles broke across three of the four
faces. That was a good day in the art world.

"You can breathe now." Natalie glanced back over her
shoulder, and saw the smiling face of her mother who was
perusing the gallery with Dr. G. "I think they like it."

"Eh," Natalie said, skeptical. "We'll see." She knew that
while her guests might appear delighted, that didn't make
the work marketable. However, from what she could see, the

agents were enjoying themselves. The art critic? That remained to be seen. Having just returned to the States, Natalie didn't have deep contacts in the media like she did in London. But that didn't mean she couldn't be charming. Yep. It was time for some charm.

Before she could make her way over to her VIP guest, Melanie Thompson rushed forward, dark hair flying behind her. "Natalie, this is fabulous. I adore what you've done! It's enchanting." After the perfunctory air kisses, Mel leaned in conspiratorially. "I *need* to meet Liam Jennings."

Boom. She was hooked. Melanie had impeccable taste. This was an exceptionally good sign.

Natalie managed to hold on to her composure, even as the urge to high-five everyone in the gallery swamped her. She'd celebrate later. It was time to make Liam famous. "Right this way."

AT MIDNIGHT, JAMES took Natalie's hand as she spun her way out of the gallery. With her stilettos tucked safely in her tote, and a pair of warm boots on her feet, she locked the door and threw herself at him. "I can't believe we did it! Did you see everyone gushing over Liam? He sold so many pieces, and I think he's going to have an agent by next week."

Natalie rubbed her hand across her middle, something he

noticed she did when she was dealing with stress.

Granted, she was riding high on adrenaline, and there was satisfaction in her smile, but she still seemed on edge. Just on the cusp of happy, but not quite there. "You did it, darling. You did. You set up a smash show in weeks, not months."

"Liam made it happen. His talent, his energy permeated that room. All I did was decorate."

Taking her hand he pulled her back to him. "Stop selling yourself short. No doubt that Liam is brilliant, but if I've learned anything it's that he would have blown all that glass and given them away as patron gifts at the shop. You saw the potential. He knows it."

As pleased as she was, as successful as the opening had been, she had doubts. He'd seen this before. Two sides of the same coin as the saying went. Natalie was breathtakingly talented, an astute businesswoman and she had incredible instincts. She knew these things to be true, yet still she felt she wasn't enough. Wasn't deserving. It was no wonder his mother and stepfather had been able to chase her off.

"Natalie, look around." With steady hands, he turned her in his arms. The view down Main Street was idyllic, awash in Christmas lights and decorations. It was a Norman Rockwell painting come to life. People were still out, lingering after the party at the gallery, grabbing a drink at the pub, a hot chocolate at the café, or just lingering in town to hold on to the joy she'd unleashed. Couples, families, groups of friends had been infused with the Christmas spirit and it was all a result of Natalie's creative light. Yes, the show was about Liam's art, but Natalie gave it wings.

He was so proud of her.

"You are at the center of what you see. Look at how happy people are; the happiness is rolling off them in great waves. Like the lighthouse that brought sailors home safely, like the compass that gives direction, you've made your mark."

"But it wasn't about me…"

"No, and that's what makes it so remarkable. Everyone knew Liam blew glass, but you showed them why it was extraordinary. Why it was something to celebrate. You released so much joy. I wish you could see that."

Nat turned and buried her face in his coat. It was moments like this that his protectiveness welled up and he realized he would do absolutely anything for her. He wondered if she understood the power she had over him, that he was completely lost to her.

"I always feel like I'm trying to prove something. That I have to be perfect."

"You are perfect—"

She cut him off. "I don't want to be perfect. I push for perfection all the time. I stress over it, I lose sleep over it. It consumes me, and all I want to do is just…I don't know…*be*. I want to stop turning myself inside out."

James could feel the tension in her as she clutched his

shirt. She still hadn't looked up, but he had a feeling when she did, her eyes would be flooded with tears. He didn't understand what drove her. By any standard, tonight had been a success. Liam was overwhelmed and eternally grateful to her, and there wasn't one person who wasn't impressed. That included Lina Rinaldi, and even a newcomer like James could see Lina didn't impress easily.

"I'm happy," she whispered. "I am. And I'm humbled by the response, but do you know where my mind went just now?"

"Where?"

"Right down the rabbit hole. *What will I do next? How will I top this? Is there more talent? Will artists who don't know me still want to work with me?* It's awful. It's worse when I'm home because, you know, *I'm a Miller.* I want to enjoy doing things without wondering how I'm going to keep topping myself. But that's what we do."

"Is it?" He tilted her face up to his. He'd been right—her eyes glistened with tears, but they also sparkled with the brilliance of the Christmas lights surrounding them. "Adam went from professional footballer to small college coach. Jack is back to being a student, certainly not glamourous…"

"Yeah, don't let what you see now fool you. Adam was a lost puppy until Mia came along, and Jack would vanish for weeks. He's a recovering danger junkie. Doug…I don't know what he's going to do. He lost his identity. I mean, he'd do anything for his girls, but I see the pain he's in.

Though, if I try to broach the subject with him, he shuts down."

Doug was a tough nut, guarded and oftentimes quite gruff. However, considering what he'd been through, James understood. When Natalie referenced "his girls" she'd meant Doug's daughters, of course. But James knew he also had a soft spot for his younger sister. He was a protective man, and churlish exterior aside, he felt things deeply.

That was how he saw the Miller family. They were people who faced life as best they could. Kind, generous to a fault, and devoted to each other, they did their best.

"It's pathetic, really," she sniffed. "The poor little rich girl whining about her art gallery. Out of touch, much?"

"The simple fact that you'd say that tells me you're not quite as out of touch as you think you are. And believe me, where I come from, we know a bit about being out of touch."

They'd begun walking again, her hand resting lightly in the crook of his arm, her body leaning toward his. He wanted nothing more than to reassure her, but maybe he needed to let her be, like she wanted.

There was a sea of emotion churning inside her. An energy that James could feel. In London, her work could be stressful, but not like this. For Natalie, the show, her business, her connections in Compass Cove were personal. That made the stakes much higher.

As they walked, she received congratulations from people

passing by. Natalie accepted each accolade graciously, but they also made her uncomfortable. Maybe it was time to get her home.

"Are you tired?" he asked.

"I'm getting there. It was a full day."

"It was. I hope you know how proud I am of you. I believe your family is as well."

"Because I exceeded expectations…"

"No, because you were brilliant regardless of any reservations you had, deciding to open a business and claim your space here. You didn't let your misgivings, or your fear, define you. You're a damn warrior princess. Imperfections and all."

She stopped, frozen in place, her crystal-blue eyes locked on his. "Oh, wow. I…"

"You know who else knows that about you? Your brothers. I do believe you're their hero."

She was stunned silent, and he was glad. Maybe she would hear him. James didn't expect years of self-doubt to be vanquished with a single pep talk, but he wanted her to know he believed in her. Her family did as well.

There was no doubt about that.

"So many people think bravery is physical," he began quietly. "It's not…it's mental. It's having the strength to push forward, to move on, to make decisions even when they're hard. Especially then."

"I don't know what to say."

"You don't have to say anything. Just know that when you feel that doubt—that fear—even though you can deal with it on your own, you don't have to. I am here for you. I love you, your family loves you and so does everyone in this exceptional town. Trust us."

She drew a deep shuddering breath. "I do trust you. And I know my family loves me, but they've been tough on me. I don't think it was on purpose, but that whole 'pull-yourself-up-by-your-bootstraps snap-out-of-it' kind of mentality doesn't play nice with my anxiety."

"Well, then, let me help."

"Help?"

"Yes." They'd arrived at his car. The beep of the alarm signaled him to open the door for her, but instead, he leaned on the roof, continuing the conversation. "I'll be your wingman."

She mouthed the word. *Wingman.* Then she did it again pinching her eyes shut as she processed. It took only a moment for the shock on Natalie's face to be replaced with a smile and then a peal of laughter rang out in the cold night air, surrounding them with the kind of lightness that they both needed more of. He understood the pressure she was under. He understood it better than most people.

Gently taking her face in his hands James kept his gaze steady. "I've got your back. You needn't have any doubts about that."

Natalie's face sobered as she went up on her toes and

kissed him lightly on the lips. Just as she did, a drop of cold landed on his cheek. Then another, and another. Natalie felt it too because she broke the kiss and looked up.

Tiny white flakes swirled around them, frosting her dark hair and eyelashes like sugar. This was one more memory for him to tuck away. A night of triumph and promises, twinkling lights and the first snow of the season. And Natalie.

Always Natalie.

Chapter Nineteen

"RIGHT THERE. YOU see? There's the head." Kerry Dryer, baby doctor, was proving to be everything Dr. G. said she would be. Competent and kind, she explained what Natalie could expect from the exam, and how the office would partner with her through her pregnancy. Everything about the woman was calm, but there was a giddy excitement in her voice when she pulled up the picture of the tiny embryo. Obviously, Kerry loved her work.

"I can't believe it." Natalie heard the words come out, but it didn't sound like her. There was awe and wonder in her voice, something she'd missed for a very long time.

"Believe it." Kerry pressed some buttons on the keyboard of the ultrasound machine, freezing the frame. "I'll give you a picture."

"Does everything look okay? I mean I wasn't planning on getting pregnant and I didn't even know I was until right before Thanksgiving."

"You mentioned that six or seven times, Natalie. Take a breath." Lord, she could probably smell the anxiety in the air. "Okay," Kerry said. "Relax and sit up."

The exam was over, but Natalie had another twenty or thirty questions to ask. Her brain was racing.

Kerry patted her arm. "Based on the baby's size you're between eleven and twelve weeks pregnant. Technically, you're still in the first trimester. You said you haven't had any nausea?"

She'd been blessedly spared morning sickness. She'd had one or two days when she didn't feel great, but nothing like Jordan had apparently experienced. "I've been tired. I thought it was overwork, you know, stress. I just opened a business."

Kerry nodded. "Any food cravings?"

"Anything edible? I've been eating a lot. Based on your scale I've gained six pounds over the last two months."

"Weight gain is normal. The most important thing is to eat healthy. Protein, good carbs, lots of veggies. Dairy is good, yogurt especially. Keep sweets moderate, if you consume a lot of caffeine, cut back. One cup of coffee a day. Avoid alcohol."

Nat felt her head bobbing up and down in acknowledgment. She'd done a bucket of research when she found out she was pregnant. She'd read everything she could find on the internet, and had interrogated Jordan thoroughly. Natalie's nervousness had kicked into overdrive. At this point she knew so much she felt like she could give a prenatal exam.

"Are you on any medication?" Kerry leveled a firm gaze

in her direction. Yep, she knew.

"Not at this time." That was true. She'd been managing her anxiety without medication for over a year. Not that she faulted anyone for needing help. She certainly had. Thinking about it, it was kind of a miracle she hadn't gone back on her meds after everything that had happened. She was thankful, considering, that she hadn't.

"Blood pressure is little high, so we'll want to watch that. I'll let you know if anything is going on with your blood-work, but as of now, everything looks okay."

"Just okay?" Somehow, she didn't feel comforted by that.

"You're fine. Any questions for me?"

Of course, now that she had the opportunity, Natalie's mind went blank. Did she have any questions other than, *So, any suggestions on how to tell my baby daddy about his off-spring?*

It had been over a week since she'd found out she was pregnant, and she still hadn't told James. Every day it was becoming more difficult. She wanted to make it special, for both of them.

But keeping the secret definitely didn't feel right, and she knew it could come back to bite her the longer she waited. "I had so many questions, and now I can't seem to think of anything to ask."

Kerry smiled. "Totally normal. Look, this can all be overwhelming, but you can call and ask a question anytime. Get a notebook and write down what you want to know, and then at your next appointment, or sooner if needed, you ask."

Once she'd made her next appointment, Natalie was on her way with a new mom kit and a knot in her stomach.

If there was ever a reason to feel overwhelmed, this was it. Especially when she considered the circumstances. She and James were together, tentatively finding their way, but she still didn't know how this was all going to play out. For the longest time she only had herself to think about: what she ate or how much she slept, but now? It wasn't only about her.

One thing was sure, it was time to tell James. There was no good reason to put it off.

She turned the car out of town and headed toward the college.

Damn, she had to let Gram know she would be late. She was supposed to head over there after her appointment to help with some of the smaller trees around the house. She was already a little late. She spoke to the AI in the car, instructing it to call her grandmother's cell phone. The call went straight to voicemail.

"Hi, Gram. It's me. I'm running a little late. I'll be there in about an hour."

It was the middle of the afternoon, but she couldn't wait to see James tonight. Along with the nerves, she was excited for the two of them. It was best to get this part done. He would be happy; she was sure of it.

Jennings was only about ten minutes outside of town, but it felt like a world away. Driving up Shore Road with the water of North Harbor on her right, and the rolling lawns of several large homes on her left, Natalie took the time to absorb how pretty everything was. The trees were mostly bare, with just a few leaves hanging on to the branches. Normally, she'd see a lot of wildlife along the road, but the deer, squirrels, and rabbits were hunkering down for winter.

Natalie didn't appreciate the campus when she was a student. Between being a clueless teenager and spending all her time in the art studios, the beauty was lost on her. Originally, she was planning to go away to school, but after a particularly bad summer she decided last minute to stay home. It had been good for her, and faculty and resident artists prepared her well for graduate school.

Parking her car in the visitors' lot near the library, she rubbed a hand over her chest where her heart was beating so hard she could hear it in her head. One deep breath, then another. The tension felt different. Whatever was going on, she had to calm down. What could she do? Count backward. That was a trick her therapist taught her.

Deep breath. One hundred, ninety-nine, ninety-eight, ninety-seven… Exhale.

This wasn't good for her or for the tadpole.

*Deep breath. Ninety-six, ninety-five, ninety-four…*a knocking on the window snapped her out of her calming trance. Natalie jumped to see Mia smiling and waving at her. Right.

Not a surprise. Her family was everywhere.

Maybe talking would calm her down. She was always better with someone she trusted, and she definitely trusted Mia. But now she'd have to be cheerful. Nat didn't feel like smiling but she did anyway.

As it turned out, Natalie didn't have to say much. Mia was in a chatty mood and walked with her from the parking lot right to the front steps of Sailors Hall. It didn't seem to matter that Mia completely bypassed the library, content to keep her sister-in-law company.

Every time she was in Mia's presence Natalie marveled at her openness, her kindness—everything about the woman screamed nurturer. It wasn't a word Natalie would have used to describe herself, so maybe she could learn a little bit about nurturing from Mia.

She barely remembered where the history department was, but signage and a helpful security guard directed her to the second floor, east wing. When she entered, the eyes of all the women sitting at the desks in the middle of the reception area turned to her. One woman, who was sitting near the archway that said Chairperson's Office, approached.

"Can I help you?"

"I'm here to see Doctor Phillips," Natalie said in her most efficient voice. "I'm Natalie Miller." *Way to name-drop, Nat.*

The woman who was lovely, and beautifully dressed, smiled knowingly. Yep, he'd told her about them. "Miss

Miller, I'm Emma, Dr. Phillips's assistant. I'll see if he's available," she replied. "Why don't you have a seat by the window."

Natalie didn't realize she'd have to run the gauntlet to get to see James. But why wouldn't she? This was his job. He had things to do. It hadn't dawned on her that he might be with a colleague, or with a student. Not her best moment.

She waited longer than she expected, and finally the nice woman reemerged. "I'm very sorry Natalie, but he's tied up right now. He said he will call you in an hour or so."

Those words took the wind right out of Natalie. Like a punch to the gut. She had no right to feel this way, but it deflated her. Natalie didn't know if she was disappointed that she couldn't talk to James or if she felt foolish that she'd so misjudged the situation. She was savvy enough to know that she shouldn't just show up at somebody's place of work. Yet here she was looking needy and feeling silly.

"Of course. I should have realized."

"He wanted to see you, but he's, ahh, engaged. An out-of-town guest."

"No explanation needed. I'll see him later on. Thank you, Emma."

Emma nodded, and Natalie covered her unease with a smile. Trying to corral her runaway thoughts was like playing whack-a-mole. Not surprisingly, it gave her a headache.

On her drive home, Nat decided it was time to tell her grandmother the news. The nice thing about talking to

Granny was, like Liam, she was a vault. And she would be happy. So happy to have another great-grandchild.

Decorations were popping up on houses around town. While Main Street had been decorated for the better part of a month, the homes in Compass Cove were only just getting into the spirit. The Millers didn't wait, though. The day after Thanksgiving her grandmother was directing her brothers on all things Christmas. This year was no different. Adam, Jack and Doug were outside stringing lights in trees and hanging wreaths on doors, post lights, and pillars all over the estate. Grandma could have hired a service, but she thought it was more fun if the family did it themselves. Her brothers didn't think it was fun, ever, at least until they started hiding flasks in the trees. Doug's idea. He said it was about survival. The booze was necessary to keep warm.

While the boys took care of the outside, her grandmother liked to decorate the inside with all her keepsakes. Up until two years ago, when she had a knee replaced, she climbed the tall step stool without an issue.

Gram would be so happy about the baby. Natalie loved watching her with Doug's girls, and with Ben—Mia and Adam's adopted son.

Once they were all over the shock, Natalie knew her entire family would be happy. They'd have a lot of questions, of course, but babies were always welcome, and every one of them would have her back. James would too. He'd promised, and he wasn't a man who broke his word.

The cobblestone courtyard that occupied the space between the two main houses and the garage looked like a winter wonderland. She suspected her nieces had rummaged through the loft above the garage and found a collection of old—sorry—*vintage* decorations. Natalie remembered many of them from her childhood including the candy cane stakes that were stuck all through the garden beds, a plastic snowman, a giant Santa, several reindeer including one or two with missing antlers, and more Christmas lights than anyone could need. She suspected they could light all of Compass Cove and North Harbor with what they'd hung in the trees.

Double-checking that the photo from the doctor was still safely in her tote bag Natalie made her way into the house. She was ridiculously excited to tell Gram about the new addition to the family. Natalie surmised her stress was coming from keeping a secret from the people she loved. It was high time they should celebrate with her.

The kitchen, where she always entered, was quiet and lit only by the late afternoon light coming through the big windows over the sink. In fact, the whole house was quiet. Looking outside she noticed Valentina's car was gone. Val was Grandma's companion and housekeeper. She'd been with the family for forty years after coming over to the United States from Russia. Gram called her a youngster, but in truth Valentina was only about ten years younger than her grandmother.

"Gram? I'm sorry I'm late." *Nothing.* Did her grandmother forget she was coming over? It was possible. She'd talked about going Christmas shopping sometime this week, but Natalie was sure they had a date for this afternoon. Putting her bags on the island, Natalie tucked the phone in the back pocket of her jeans and walked through the bake-house.

She really did love it here. As large as the house was, it always felt like home. Natalie believed it was because the old building was infused with love. It was meticulously main-tained, and decorated with pictures, paintings, and children's art. Her grandmother still kept a clay sculpture of a dog Natalie had crafted when she was only eight years old in a place of honor in the hallway. She had many such pieces from her children, grandchildren, and great-grandchildren. She called the wall of shelves and cabinets the Miller Muse-um and deemed the collection priceless.

Natalie poked her head in the living room, a warm memory of decorating the Christmas tree on Thanksgiving night washing over her. Moving down the hall, she looked in the library, the dining room, and still didn't see her grand-mother. Finally, she got to the end of the long main hallway and stepped inside the room that her grandmother used as a sitting room and office.

That's when Natalie's heart stopped. In the corner was a Christmas tree, small by Miller standards, but still close to seven feet tall. Next to it was a stepladder, and on the floor, still as stone, was her grandmother.

Natalie had never been in an ambulance before. The EMTs tried to tell her she couldn't ride with them to the hospital, but there was no way she was leaving her grandmother alone. Finding her there, lying on the floor, was absolutely terrifying. For a split second she didn't know if her grandmother was alive or dead. Thankfully, Grandma groaned a little, and Natalie heard her name come out on a whisper.

The ambulance arrived quickly, faster than Natalie imagined it would. They burst into the house with Valentina right behind.

The best they could tell was that she tried to decorate the tree herself and fell. It looked like she had a broken hip, and they were taking precautions because nobody knew if she'd hit her head. Gram was lying on the stretcher drifting in and out of consciousness, her neck in a brace, her face pale. All Natalie could think was that it was her fault.

She'd tried to call the family, but no one was answering. Mom was in a meeting, Adam was on his way back from a recruiting trip, Jack and Lilly were in the city, and she had no idea where Doug and the girls had gone. Finally, she did the most insensitive thing, hoping for a response.

She sent a group text.

Gram fell. In an ambulance on the way to Harbor Hospital. Likely broken hip, probable concussion. Be there in 10 min.

It only took a few minutes for a flood of text messages to fly into Natalie's phone. Thankfully, the first one was from her mother.

I'll meet you in the ER. Her mother was a patient advocate at Harbor Hospital, which meant Gram wouldn't just get the best of care, she'd be watched like a hawk.

The next text came from Adam, then Jack, and finally Doug answered. All of them indicated they were on their way.

She was relieved and terrified. Relieved because she wouldn't be alone, and nervous about being peppered with questions about their grandmother's fall. Natalie had no idea why her grandmother went up on that ladder without anybody in the house. It was very unlike her. Gram relished her independence, but she wasn't foolish. She knew her limitations. At least everyone thought she did.

"Natalie?"

Her grandmother's voice, weak and thready, pulled her attention away from the phone. "Don't talk. Just take it easy."

"I have to tell you something," she struggled to breathe. One of the EMTs thought she might have a broken rib. "I have a living will."

Oh, no. No. No. No. They were not having this discussion. "Gram, you're going to get excellent care. I don't want to hear about a living will."

"Well, that's just too bad. You're going to hear about it."

One of the EMTs who was riding in the back chuckled. "I guess you're going to hear about it," he said.

Her grandmother was tough, and she wasn't going to let anyone forget it.

"Okay, what about it?"

"Your mother knows about the will. But I need you to make sure they follow my wishes. Do you understand?"

"They who?"

"Your brothers. I love them dearly, but I need you to take charge."

"Why would anyone listen to me?" Had her grandmother not been paying attention? Natalie's judgment was always questioned. It was like a family rule or something.

"Because, my dear, you are my health care proxy. You make the decisions if I can't."

Well, shit.

Gram took a wheezy breath, and the EMT patted her arm. "Please stop talking, Mrs. Miller. Just rest until we get to the hospital."

This was bad. Her grandmother was badly hurt, and Natalie was in charge. There wasn't anything she wouldn't do for her grandmother, but would her family let her?

Chapter Twenty

THE SMALL PRIVATE waiting area was suffocating her.

Her mother was talking with a nurse about Gram's health history. Adam and Mia were cuddled together on a small love seat. Doug and Jack were playing cards at a café table in the corner. Natalie, however, was pacing.

She'd hoped some of the kids would be there to distract her, but Lilly had the three girls and Ben at the guesthouse. It was the right thing, of course. The hospital was no place for them, especially on a school night, but Natalie felt oddly alone in this roomful of people. Her nieces and nephew would have been good company.

There was still no word from James. It had been hours since she'd stopped to see him at his office. She thought she'd at least have a text, but nothing. Whomever had come in from out of town must have monopolized him quite thoroughly.

It wasn't that she doubted him, but right then she was feeling abandoned. Her brothers were looking at her like she'd pushed her grandmother off the step stool. None of them were saying anything, but their eyes spoke volumes.

Her mother came from behind and wrapped her arms around Natalie. "Are you okay? That must have been horrible for you finding her like that."

Thank God for her mother.

"It was. I held it together, but I'd never been so scared in my life. She was so still, Mom…"

"Aw, baby. I'm sorry you went through that. I have no idea why she didn't wait for someone to help her."

Natalie shrugged. "I was late getting over there, but—"

"Maybe you should have been on time." Doug didn't look up from his cards. "Then she wouldn't have been alone."

Natalie's heart squeezed tight at the accusation.

"Douglas," her mother snapped. "That was uncalled for."

Natalie appreciated her mother running interference, but it was time for Natalie to speak up for herself. "It's okay, Mom."

"So, this is my fault, is that it? Natalie screwed up again. That is what you're insinuating, right?"

He looked up then, his eyes cold. "I don't think I was insinuating it."

"I—I can't believe you said that." Her throat closed, partly with rage, partly with grief that this is what her oldest brother thought of her. The rage won out. "You are such a hypocrite. On one hand you try to play the protector. The big brother. But you have never missed a chance to tell me what's wrong with me. Which is it going to be, Doug?

Because I have whiplash from your indecision. Pick a bloody side."

"Gram is going to need surgery. She was left alone. Whose fault is that?"

"Gram knows what she can do. She made a bad choice. God help me, I wish I'd been there. But I wasn't. Neither were you, by the way. Jack wasn't there, or Adam or Mom. None of us were there. Is it your fault?"

"That's it, Nat. Deflect. You're always making excuses."

"Jesus, Doug," Jack chided. "Chill out."

Natalie spun away, looking for an escape. She didn't trust herself not to go off on her brother more than she already had. The things she wanted to say would destroy their relationship.

Squeezing her mother's hand, she turned and walked out of the room. A left turn would take her toward the small café, a right turn would take her outside. She opted for outside. Her boots clicked on the polished white floor as she made her way to the exit. It echoed. An audible representation of how she was feeling. It was cold outside, and windy. But it was exactly what she needed. Time to cool off.

Harbor Hospital was set on a piece of land shared by Compass Cove and the adjacent hamlet of North Harbor. Like its name indicated, it was very close to the water. Subsequently, that meant the late fall winds were even more fierce. Right before she went out the door, her phone buzzed with an incoming call. *James.*

"Hi," she said, her voice on the edge of breaking. "I'm so glad you called."

"Hey. Yeah, I'm sorry I'm just getting back to you. Emma told me you came round today."

"I did. I had something to tell you, but—"

"Good. I have something to tell you, too. Can we meet for breakfast tomorrow? Rinaldi's at eight?"

"Tomorrow at Rinaldi's? James…"

"That would be perfect. Where are you? You're cutting in and out."

He hadn't let her get one word in. He was plowing through the call like she was a list to be checked off.

"I'm at Harbor Hospital with my grandmother. She fell, broke her hip and probably has other injuries. I'm sorry if it's making it hard to hear me."

"Hell, Nat. Why didn't you say anything?"

"I guess I didn't want to interrupt you. You were on a roll." These men were going to be the death of her. Love them as she might, they could really be assholes.

"I'm on my way. Where are—"

The three beeps told her all she needed to know. The call had dropped. Well, James was a smart guy; if he needed to find her, he would.

Natalie blinked and leaned into the wall. Her head felt like it was being split open by an axe. Fresh air. She needed fresh air.

She finally stepped outside and was immediately assaulted by the powerful wind whipping off the harbor. It was bone-deep cold, the kind of cold that could make you shiver on contact. Of course, Natalie was in a chunky sweater and a pair of leggings. She had no coat, no hat, no gloves. Her cheeks stung and the skin on her hands tingled. She knew the temperature was about forty-five degrees, but it felt a lot colder. She had to wonder if it was the wind or her heart just freezing over.

The sea air wasn't helping. Her head still hurt, and now her back was getting in on the fun. An ache formed the base of her spine, crampy and uncomfortable. Freezing to death wasn't going to solve any problems so Natalie went back inside the hospital. Back in the corridor she saw Adam was on his way toward her.

"Nat, we're getting news soon. Mom said you need to be there."

"Yeah, apparently I'm Grandma's health proxy."

Adam grinned. "Not surprising. She always knew she could depend on you."

"Really? Tell that to Doug."

"Honey, he was out of line. When this is over, I'll get him to back off you." Adam put a hand on her shoulder. "Hey, are you okay? The color just drained out of your face."

Natalie stopped. She couldn't move. Pressing her back into the wall, she slid down, wrapping her arms around her knees. "Adam, I don't feel good."

Crouching next to her he pressed the back of his hand

against her forehead. "You're ice-cold, Nat."

"I was outside."

"No, that's not it." Like she weighed nothing, Adam picked her up and started walking. Natalie was only vaguely aware of the movement. She felt light-headed, weak. It all happened so fast. What was ever-present was the headache. The throbbing, blinding headache. That hadn't gone away.

He was moving faster now, the sights and sounds getting fuzzy. Color flashed and she realized she was back in the waiting room. Her mother was there. She could smell her perfume. It was one of Natalie's favorite things. *Mom.* Her mom was saying something. She felt herself going down, falling. But then she realized Adam had set her on a chair.

There were more voices, more people, and all Natalie wanted to do, was close her eyes. Just for a minute. She needed to rest. For one minute...

THE STEADY BEEP, beep, beep seeped into her consciousness. Around her, Natalie could sense sheets, a blanket, a pillow... She was in bed. It wasn't her bed, so where was she?

Beep, beep, beep.

"Natalie?" A voice. It was James. "Nat? Can you hear me, love?"

"Uh-huh." The light hurt her eyes, so she shielded them with her hand. There were tubes in her arm. What had happened? "What? Where am I?"

"Yes. But let yourself wake up first. Take it slow. I'll pull the curtains so you'll not be blinded."

"Okay. Am I allowed to sit up? My back hurts."

He picked up the bed controller and raised her head a little bit, then put up her knees. "That's better. Thank you." When she was fully conscious, everything flooded back.

"Oh, my God. Gram. My grandmother. What happened? Where... Is she okay?"

"She's fine. Stable. They're operating on her hip later today. She's lucky. She bumped her head, but there's only a mild concussion, and other than some bruises, she doesn't have any serious injuries."

"Oh, good. I need to see her. I have to talk to the doctor." Pushing herself up, James pressed a gentle hand on her shoulder.

"Not right now. You need to wait for *your* doctor."

Her doctor. "Doctor Dryer?"

He nodded. "I think we need to have that talk, don't you think?"

"I wanted to have it yesterday."

"I know. I'm sorry about that, and about not listening last night, but Natalie you should have told me right away that you were pregnant. Right away."

He was scolding her. She was lying in a hospital bed hooked up to an IV and he had the nerve to reprimand her?

"I had my first appointment and was going to tell you. I

don't think that's unreasonable."

"Isn't it? You could be carrying my *heir*."

Never before had Natalie heard James use that tone. That pompous, patrician, aristocratic tone. "*My heir*." His statement turned her into a vessel.

"Your heir. I see. What if it's a girl?" Natalie knew full well a girl wouldn't inherit.

"That's irrelevant. It's still my child. I should have been told."

"James, I was going to tell you, but you were busy. Too busy to even step out of your office and see me. Your out-of-town guest had your full attention."

"Natalie…"

"You don't get to tell me what I should or shouldn't do. I was coming to see you with as much information as I had including a sonogram picture of our baby. And no, I don't know if it's a boy or a girl. I don't care. I just want that baby to be healthy. And I'm scared to death…"

Before she lit into him again, the door opened, and Doctor Dryer walked in the room. She was wearing scrubs instead of her street clothes and white coat, and she also looked grim. Like something was wrong.

"So," she said as she rolled a small stool to the side of the bed. "How are you feeling?"

"Better than I did last night. I felt like my head was going to explode."

"A combination of stress, dehydration, and high blood

pressure. That's why you have an IV. It's to rehydrate you. Did you drink anything yesterday?"

"Of course, I did. I had a cup of tea in the morning, some water before I came to see you..."

"Natalie, that's not enough. The high blood pressure coupled with dehydration is dangerous. The stress on its own isn't going to hurt the pregnancy, but you could put yourself and the baby in danger if you don't take care of yourself."

Her heart tightened, clenched hard. Hearing the words from her doctor hurt. Folding her arms across her chest protectively, there was no way to stop the tears this time. They spilled out of her eyes and down her cheeks. Hot, burning tears, that she couldn't stop.

She wanted James to hold her, but instead he leaned into the large windowsill, his hands propped behind him. He didn't look at her, didn't make eye contact. The only thing Natalie could feel in that moment was her heart cracking in half. It seemed she was on her own after all.

Chapter Twenty-One

H E MISHANDLED THAT situation like a bloody champ. Natalie barely spoke to him for the last hour they were together, obviously hurt by the distance he'd put between them. But what was he supposed to do? He arrived at the hospital and was told Nat was in an examination room because she'd fainted. And she hadn't fainted because of her grandmother, but because she was carrying his child.

His child. He was so happy he couldn't think straight. He had no idea how gravely ill she'd become, so all he could think about was the fact that he was going to be a father. And then the news started rolling in and there was a very real chance she could have lost her. Life without her would be unbearable.

When he entered his house, he was greeted by the smell of English breakfast tea and expensive French perfume. In the living room his mother, Evangeline, the Countess of Rutherford, was standing by the French doors gazing out at the sound.

"It's impressive, isn't it? In its own way it's sustained this land, while also wreaking havoc. It seems you can't have one without the other."

"It's all right," she sniffed. "Was it necessary to be gone all night?"

"Yes, when I arrived at hospital, I discovered Natalie had taken ill. I sat by her bedside all night."

His mother almost looked concerned. "She's recovered?"

"Mostly." Did he tell her? Did she deserve to know? He didn't think it would change her opinion of Natalie, Mum already had grandchildren, so it wasn't as if Natalie would fulfill that function. But if it was a boy...

"What do you mean mostly?"

"She's still a bit under the weather."

His mother rolled her eyes like a recalcitrant teenager. "No matter. I hope she recovers. I came here to talk some sense into you. I don't agree with what the earl did, but I don't see any reason to dwell on it. Water under the bridge and all that. Come home and put this sordid mess behind you."

"Sordid mess? I love Natalie. I intend to marry her if she'll have me."

"MARRY! Are you daft? You can't marry her. She's not one of us."

"No, Mum. She's better, and I will make her my wife. Now, you can either accept it, or not." James walked to the window where his mother was standing ramrod straight. She was doing her best to hold it together, but the countess wasn't used to being told no. "Come on. I want to show you something."

"What?"

"You'll see."

An hour later they were walking down Main Street in Compass Cove. His mother was wrapped in a bright red wool cape, and James in a parka he'd picked up at the local ski shop.

"What is it you wanted to show me? It's a small town. I've seen small towns before."

"Not like this one."

She looked in windows at the bookshop, picked up a treat at the café and stopped short when she came to the gallery. "Belgravia Gallery? Natalie?"

"She opened her own business. Her debut show was ten days ago and the reviews are smashing. She's staying."

His mother's face softened, relieved. "Oh, well. I am sorry for you, my dear. I know you care for her, but if she's staying…"

Wasn't she going to be disappointed? "I'm staying too, Mother."

"You're staying? But, James, your title, the family. You have a position to maintain."

"And do what? I'm a teacher, a professor, a writer. What do I do as a member of the peerage? My work is important. My title is window dressing. I'm not dismissing it, I wouldn't, but there's more for me to do with this life." He'd just scandalized her with that last statement. So be it.

"There's one more place I'd like to show you. Come on."

They walked one more block and then crossed the street where the compass was inlaid into the intersection. It was a gorgeous mosaic that even stopped the countess in her tracks.

"They certainly take their compasses seriously here."

The bell over the door of the compass shop signaled his entry, and Liam came out from the back room. James had called ahead letting his friend know he would be coming by with a visitor from home.

His mother, on the other hand was staring up at the large Christmas tree in the entry that was fully decorated with Liam's ornaments.

"This is breathtaking. Are these ornaments handmade?"

"Yes, ma'am. They are. I'm Liam Jennings, the artist."

His mother extended her hand, putting on the charm before James could even make an introduction. "Mr. Jennings, it's a pleasure. I'm Lady Rutherford, James's mother."

"The pleasure is all mine. Let me show you around." Offering his arm like a gentleman, Liam gave his mother a tour of the shop. He focused on his glasswork and custom jewelry, but like every newcomer eventually his mother stood in front of the case with Lucy's compass. Without any hesitation, Liam opened the top and allowed her to examine the contents.

There was a letter in an archival envelope that was dated Christmas, 1750. It was from Caleb to Lucy in which he invited her to accompany him to Christmas services. According to Liam, she accepted.

"The Jennings family, and the Velsors were both found-ing families in Compass Cove, but the Jenningses had more status than Lucy's family. That didn't stop Caleb—he loved her and nothing anyone said would change his mind. They found their way to each other; against all odds, they found each other."

"Is this a story for my benefit?" His mother was charmed by Liam, but she could easily see through his story.

"Just because it applies doesn't mean it's not true. Love always wins, Lady Rutherford. And hearts meant to love always find each other."

"You're a poet, too, Mr. Jennings?"

"No ma'am, just a believer."

James reached his hand toward the compass but stopped and looked at his friend for permission. "May I?"

"By all means. It's been waiting for you, I think."

James hesitated for a second before taking the antique instrument gently in his hand. It should have been cold, but the metal warmed in his palm. It was almost as if the com-pass itself had a heartbeat, a sense that the person holding it needed answers. James oriented himself to north, but the needle didn't swing that way; it spun twice, and then settled on east. Natalie's cottage was to the east. Her tiny cottage by the sea, decked out with lights and garland and full of love. The compass knew he belonged here. It was time he fully embraced the truth of it.

"I'll be flying home with you, Mother."

"You will? I thought you said you were staying."

He smiled. "Oh, I'll come back. But I need to get a few things in order. Also, I'm bringing great-grandmother's ring back with me. I'll be giving it to Natalie, if she will have me."

"But, you can't. James…" His mother had the stiffest of upper lips, but he thought he saw a hint of sadness in her eyes.

"On the contrary, Mother," he said before setting the compass back in the case, "I can, and I will. Liam," he said to his friend. "I need a compass."

HE'D BEEN GONE for seventeen days. James stopped at the hospital to see Natalie one last time before he left for England. He explained that he had to go home to take care of business, and to clear her name. He knew that wasn't what she wanted, but he had every intention of doing so anyway. His family had caused her a world of heartache, had cost her immeasurably, and in James's mind it was the least he could do. She'd heard from him from time to time, a quick phone call and a few text messages had been sent, but he didn't reach out often. Natalie wondered if the distance between them was more than just the miles; she wondered if their souls had grown apart too.

It hurt to think about, but she tried not to dwell, because it was too important for her to make sure she was doing the right thing for the baby in her belly. That was her focus. Her grandmother had come through surgery without complications. It was a true miracle, all considered, and Natalie believed it to be her greatest Christmas gift. That and her tiny baby. Their baby whom she'd found out was a little girl.

Currently, Gram was in rehab, running the place, and getting stronger every day. Christmas Eve was tomorrow and the plan was for her to be at home. Natalie had moved from the cottage into the big house so she could be there with her grandmother through the rest of her recovery. She was also planning a grand family Christmas. The halls had been decked, presents bought, and today she was going to bake.

She liked the big house. She liked the space, the grandeur, the age of the place, and she liked the stories. The house was full of tales, and Natalie swore she could learn about the place just by listening. The walls whispered.

She'd vowed to get more sleep, to eat properly, and not let herself get dehydrated again. There was too much at stake. She had no clue when James was coming back but she had to have faith that he would. His words, that he would *have her back*, echoed in her mind. Those words were her touchstone, and she'd just have to trust that it would all work out.

It was a very un-Natalie way of being. Just accepting that things were going to unfold the way they were supposed to was foreign to her. Stress and anxiety had been her constant companions since she was a child. She wondered if the hormones coursing through her system had changed her. She wondered if it's how she would be after the baby was born. The quiet in her mind was interesting, comforting, different.

She could get used to it.

It was cold for December, hovering in the low thirties during the day. There had been a light coating of snow the night before, making the ground glisten in the morning light. But even with the cold and snow, she still headed down to the beach at sunrise. She brought her yoga mat and while she wasn't going to do anything crazy on the rocks for fear of slipping, she did think a few minutes to center herself was the perfect way to start the day.

As she walked down the path, the leaves and sticks crunching under her feet, she came to the steps. Fifty-two steps. It was a long way down, and they were slippery. Deciding she could roll out her yoga mat in front of the bench her grandfather had put on the bluff, Natalie congratulated herself for making the grown-up decision.

When she turned, she sucked in a breath. James was sitting on the bench. He looked worn out, but he was smiling. "Good call. I almost broke my neck going to find you at the cottage."

"You're back," she said softly, so thankful she could barely breathe. It was incredibly quiet on the bluff that morning. The water was calm beneath them and there was scarcely a breeze. She swore she could hear their hearts beating. Hers and James's…together. "You didn't tell me."

"I wanted to surprise you. I'm sorry for the radio silence of the past couple of weeks. There was a lot of business to sort out."

"Like what?" Did she dare ask?

He rose and came to where she was standing. "I've taken a two-year leave from the university, and my brother is going to move into the family house. I fully intend on staying in New York. If Jennings will have me after the search for a permanent chair has concluded, I will happily accept a position."

"You're giving up your home? Leaving everything?" Her heart was about to burst out of her chest. This beautiful man was ready to give her the world, but was it too much?

"Natalie, I'm giving up nothing. My home is with you and our child. Wherever you are that is where I'll be. No piece of land is more important than what I feel for you, than the life I want to make with you, than the children I want to have with you. You are everything."

"James…I can't ask you to do that. Your family, and the title…"

"You aren't. I'm going to be a cultural liaison at the British Consulate in New York."

"You're what?" Had she heard him correctly?

"I know. In addition to my academic work, I'll be coordinating with museums and libraries in both countries to facilitate the exchange of documents and artifacts."

"That's…that's perfect for you." She couldn't imagine anyone better suited to the job. What he was telling her was that he was staying. It felt like too much to hope for.

"I know. It allows me to keep my life here, but still maintain a connection with my country. That's why I was gone for so long. There were some delicate negotiations."

"You made it work. For both of us."

"My mission in life is to make you happy, to be a good father. You're here, and that's where I need to be as well. You are my heart and soul."

"Well," she said on a shaky breath. "When you put it like that…" The tears she always tried to tamp down flowed freely, and Natalie didn't hold back. If he could bare his soul, she could do the same.

A small grove of evergreens behind them were coated with snow, and the lights her brothers had strung in the trees were still visible in the gray light of dawn. It was beautiful, like an enchanted forest.

Before her, James dropped to one knee. "I love you, Natalie. Marry me. Make a life with me. If you say yes, I promise every day will be like Christmas."

She kneeled before him, clasping his hands in hers. Natalie tilted her face to his and planted a soft kiss on his lips. "I love you," she whispered. "And my answer is yes. When you offer me a lifetime of Christmases the only answer is yes."

Epilogue

June

"WHAT DO YOU mean I can't have an epidural!"

"Natalie," the midwife, whose name was Kelsey, said calmly. "You're at eight centimeters. By the time the anesthesiologist gets here, you'll be ready to push. What kept you home so long?"

Natalie thought she was being a good patient, laboring at home. She'd had a lovely afternoon with her grandmother. They'd chuckled and chatted through her contractions, which were barely there, until her water broke. Once that happened her body went bananas.

Fortunately, Doug had been home to drive her to the hospital since James was stuck in the city. What surprised her most about that turn of events was that her brother was not the calm, steady presence she'd expected him to be. No, the big, tough Marine—the man with *three* daughters—was a wimp when it came to girl things.

"I thought I had time. My contractions were mild. I was waiting for my husband..." Nat, her heart racing like a scared rabbit's, knew she was probably babbling. No, she was babbling. James was making his way from the city where he'd had a meeting at the British Consulate. He'd worried about leaving town for the whole day, but there was no reason to think she'd go into labor today. She still had two weeks to go, so it didn't make sense for him to stay back.

"Is your husband on the way?" The midwife must have sensed Nat was on the edge, because she was using her calming voice. The one people reserved for hostage situations and unmedicated women in labor.

"He's—OOOOoooh…" Right as she started to answer another pain hit. While other contractions started out gradually and rose to a crest before dropping off, this one was anything but gentle. It was a freight train, and Natalie was speeding along stuck to the front of the locomotive. "AAHHHH. Holy crap."

Nat dug her hands into the bed sheets so hard, she was sure she'd pierced the mattress.

"Natalie, breathe," the midwife said. She was almost nose to nose, hissing out rapid breaths. Right, the breathing from her prenatal class. "Do you have someone who can help you? Who brought you in?"

"My brother, but he can't come in here. He might faint." That brought a laugh, but Natalie wasn't trying to be funny. She was serious. Based on how Doug handled her contractions, he'd be on the floor faster than she could say "Oorah." Right then, the door flew open and her mother, pulling on a paper gown, rushed into the room. Natalie had never been so glad to see anyone.

"There you are, my girl." Mom leaned in and kissed the top of her head. "I just saw your brother in the waiting room. He looks like he's going to pass out."

Natalie looked at Kelsey. "Told you."

She smirked in acknowledgment. "Got it. Well, I'm glad you're here, Linda. Let's do this."

Another pain hit, and Natalie heard herself howl. Just like a dog, she howled. "Mommy! Make her give me the medicine! Oh, my God! Mom. Mom. I'm sorry."

"Sorry for what?" Her mother dabbed at her forehead with a wet cloth. It felt so good.

"For everything." Another contraction. "Ohhhh. If I'd known what you'd gone through to have babies, I'd have been nicer."

Mom leaned in and pressed her cheek to Natalie's now-damp hair. "You were and still are the sweetest child."

"But what if I'm a terrible mother? What if I screw up?"

"Not possible. You love with your whole heart, and that is all your little girl will need. She's very lucky. Just as I am lucky to have you."

Natalie had been so distracted by her mother's words, she hadn't noticed the nurses who'd come in the room, quietly and efficiently getting it ready for her baby's arrival. She weathered more strong pains, focusing on her mother's azure-blue eyes. They were smiling eyes, and deep inside she could see the glimmer of pride. Her mama was proud of her.

Mom glanced at her phone, nodding as she patted Natalie's hand. "James is at the train station. He'll be here very soon."

"Not soon enough. The baby is coming. I can feel her."

Taking deep breaths, she readied for the next contraction. By this time, the midwife was gowned and had settled on the stool by Natalie's feet.

"Let me have a look." Kelsey leaned in to see how she was progressing, but Nat didn't feel what she was doing, because the only sensation in her girly bits was pressure. Pressure and the need to push.

JAMES STOPPED HIS car so abruptly at the valet parking stand at the hospital, he was sure he had whiplash. He didn't think to get a tag, he just tossed his keys to the young man and bolted through the sliding doors. He was met in the lobby by Mia, nine months pregnant herself, who started talking to him before he was even in earshot. Not that it mattered what she said. He only wanted to hear that Natalie was okay, and that he wasn't too late. He couldn't believe that of all the days he chosen to go into Manhattan, this would be the one that his baby came into the world.

And he might have missed it. "She's all right?"

"I haven't heard otherwise. Linda is with her, so you don't have to worry about her being alone."

"With this family, that's the last thing I'm worried about. I'm just upset I wasn't there when she went into labor."

"I know, but you're here now. And from what I understand it won't be long."

He came off the elevator into a waiting room that was filled with people he knew. He thought scenes like this only happened in films—a large contingent of people, family and friends, all waiting for the birth of a child. Natalie's brothers were there, with Doug looking a little bit pale, Jordan and Nick, Lilly, even Lina carried bags of food and drinks for anyone who might want to eat their feelings.

Mia gave him a shove toward a large door. "Ring the bell, the nurse will let you in." He didn't stop to talk, appreciative that no one stopped him. Doing as he was told, the moment James stepped into the corridor on the other side, he heard what sounded like a roar. An honest-to-God roar.

"I'm glad he's not here! He did this!"

James stopped in his tracks. That was Natalie, no doubt. A nurse came from behind him and handed him a blue gown.

"Natalie's husband, I presume?"

He loosened his tie, and nodded before slipping on the protective garb. "I'm a little afraid to face what's on the other side of that door." He was joking, but not.

"Don't be. She's been alternately cursing you and calling out for you. Better get in there, though. It's getting close."

James didn't hesitate any longer, and stepped into the room to see his wife holding the hand of her mother on one side, and gripping the bed rail on the other, while bearing down, looking fierce and red-faced. She was sweaty, her hair was pulled off her face with two rubber bands, and the wisps of hair stood straight up. She looked exhausted, brave and oh so beautiful.

Snapping out of his trance, he rushed to her side, grabbed her hand, and kissed it. "I'm here."

"Thank God," she said dropping back on her pillow. Within seconds tears flooded her eyes. "I'm so glad you're here. I didn't want to do this without you."

"I'm here. I'm here right beside you."

"She's stuck."

Her statement was so matter-of-fact, the words chilled him. "*Stuck?*"

"She's not stuck," Linda stated calmly.

"One more push, Nat, and you'll meet your little girl," said the woman in scrubs who sat confidently between his wife's legs.

"You're the doctor?" James asked, still trying to catch up. There were people buzzing around, a bassinet had been wheeled in. The reality of what was happening was starting to hit him. He was going to be a father.

"Midwife."

Midwife. Good, all right. Now that he knew who had what job, he could do his part. Whatever that was. For starters he kissed Natalie's brow. "I love you," he whispered.

"I know. Don't take anything I say personally. I'm not in my right mind. *She* wouldn't give me meds." Natalie waved an accusatory finger at the midwife.

"Kelsey is taking excellent care of you, Natalie. Focus on your baby."

"Okay, here comes the contraction. Bear down…"

James had watched athletes at the highest level, and he'd never seen anyone execute a more herculean task than his beautiful wife. Watching a woman—*this woman*—give birth was something that had no equal. It was humbling, life-affirming. All James could do was love her with all his heart.

She would be the mother of their children, his love, his best friend, his soul mate. He would protect his family with everything he had. Making Natalie happy was his life. He couldn't imagine anything more perfect.

When the midwife placed their daughter on Natalie's chest the tears he didn't know had been filling his eyes spilled over. Natalie cried too. Truthfully, the whole room was a mess.

"Oh, look at her. Our daughter. She's beautiful. So beautiful."

He leaned in, taking in the sight of the two most important women in his life. "She already takes after her mother, then."

"I love you. I'm so happy." Natalie snuggled into him, stealing his heart like she did on the very first day they met.

Linda Miller held a hand to her chest, marveling at her daughter and granddaughter. "I do believe, she is your best work. Have you decided on a name?"

Natalie looked up at him, her blue eyes shining. "We're agreed?" she asked him.

"We're going to name her Anna. After Granny. The Honorable Anna Lowell Phillips."

"Oh, your grandmother will be so pleased."

Just then a nurse poked her head in the room. "Linda, you're needed."

"Oh? A problem?" She rose, ever prepared to help a patient or family in need.

"Not exactly," the nurse said. "Your daughter-in-law?"

"Which one?" Linda asked considering Lilly a member of the family even though her wedding to Jack wasn't for another two months.

"Mia. Her water broke."

"Oh!" Natalie squealed. "Twin cousins!"

James stayed close to Nat, stroking her hair as the commotion ensued. Linda hustled out, the nurses helped Natalie clean up, while James snuggled their daughter. Once Kelsey had checked how Natalie was recovering from birth, she left them blissfully alone. It could very well be the last time they were alone for the next few months.

When he looked at his watch, he was amazed to see less than an hour had passed from the minute he'd walked into the hospital until now. Yet his life had utterly changed.

"I can't believe Mia is in labor. I hope she gets an epidural."

He laughed. Natalie was already getting back to being herself. She was thinking about others. "You seem to be doing all right. Feeling well?"

"I feel like I could move mountains. It was amazing. I'm so glad you made it in time."

"I am too."

"You need to call your mother." There was that kindness again. Even with all the problems his mother had caused, she would get a call. Deserved or not, Nat would make sure of it.

"I will, but I'd like to just sit with you for a while, if that's agreeable."

"You may sit with me for as long as you like, m'lord."

"Thank you, my lady. I do believe I'll take you up on that."

The End

Want more? Check out Lilly and Jack's story in *All of Me*!

Join Tule Publishing's newsletter for more great reads and weekly deals!

Acknowledgments

There's nothing simple about writing a book's acknowl-edgements. It's not just a list of "*thank yous*," but it's more a nod to the people who help turn a germ of an idea into a finished book. In the case of Compass Cove, and *My Christmas Wish*, there are more than a few of those people. I've said it before, I wish I had a whole book to tell you about them.

I am very lucky to have been blessed with wonderful writing friends who understand the bumps in the road and help me steer around them. Tracy Solheim, Regina Kyle, Lauren Rico, my fellow Tuligans and my Kiss and Tell author family, I am truly blessed to have you all in my orbit. Thank you for listening, consoling and talking me off the ledge, but most of all, thank you for not letting me give up.

My brilliant friends Amy, Joan, Laura, and Michelle— you keep me grounded and sane. I couldn't ask for better cheerleaders and confidants. Girlfriends are the best friends.

To the team at Tule Publishing, Meghan, Nikki and Cyndi, thank you for making Tule more than a publisher, but a home. It's a special place, and I don't know that I can pay a greater compliment. Lee Hyat is a genius with covers— that is all. And as always, many thanks, and much love, goes to Jane Porter. Your talent, your vision and your love know no bounds. I am grateful to know you and that you thought

I belonged in the Tule family is a gift I will never take for granted. Thank you.

I am so lucky to have an editor who gets me. Kelly Hunter, thank you for believing in the magic of Compass Cove, and in me. I would not have gotten through this book without your talent, patience and guidance. You are a pearl beyond price.

My agent Stephany Evans has the most amazing knack for keeping things in perspective and thank goodness I have you in my corner. An author couldn't ask for a better advocate or friend.

My assistant, Voule Walker, seems to know what I need before I need it. Thank you, my dear.

Readers, none of this matters without all of you. You keep the words flowing. I have met some amazing people in my author travels and I am thankful to those of you who have chosen to spend time with my imagination.

Finally, to my dear family, through the ups and downs, life with all of you is a gift and I wouldn't be able to write a word without you at my back.

With family, every day is Christmas.

xo,
Jeannie

If you enjoyed *My Christmas Wish,*
you'll love the other books in…

The Compass Cove series

Book 1: *Then Came You*

Book 2: *You Send Me*

Book 3: *All of Me*

Book 4: *My Christmas Wish*

Available now at your favorite online retailer!

More books by Jeannie Moon

Christmas in Angel Harbor

Daring the Pilot
Men of Marietta series

Weekend with Her Bachelor
Bachelor Auction Returns series

Finding Christmas

His Forbidden Princess
Royal Holiday series

Until You

This Christmas
Christmas in New York series

Available now at your favorite online retailer!

About the Author

USA Today bestselling author **Jeannie Moon** has always been a romantic. When she's not spinning tales of her own, Jeannie works as a school librarian, thankful she has a job that allows her to immerse herself in books and call it work. Married to her high school sweetheart, Jeannie has three kids, three lovable dogs and a mischievous cat and lives in her hometown on Long Island, NY. If she's more than ten miles away from salt water for any longer than a week, she gets twitchy.

Thank you for reading

My Christmas Wish

If you enjoyed this book, you can find more from all our great authors at TulePublishing.com, or from your favorite online retailer.

TULE
PUBLISHING